The Marriage Bed

The Marriage Bed

DIANA SAVILLE

LONDON NEW YORK SYDNEY TORONTO

This edition published 1995
by BCA
by arrangement with Hodder & Stoughton

First Reprint 1995

CN 1983

Printed and bound in Great Britain by
Mackays of Chatham PLC, Chatham, Kent

For Robert

Acknowledgements ∫

I should like to thank Michael Sissons and my editor Carolyn Mays; also Margy, Katie and Richard.

As usual on a sunny Friday morning, Laura Fenton left the kitchen and took toast, post and the new *Country Life* to the garden hammock overlooking the lawn. The three small spaniels, tracking the direction of her ankles, made their exit too, timing it immaculately to her abrupt opening and closing of the door.

It was already hot. The dogs jumped on to the hammock's seat where Eloise, the booted bantam, perched in readiness for breakfast. Doing a slow goose-step on the spot, she squeaked with excitement and puffed out her speckled chestnut fluff. 'Cluck-cluck to you too,' said Laura. 'Have you laid an egg for Mummy?' and she looked round guiltily, hoping Geoffrey couldn't overhear her.

She sat down, tilted the canopy forward to shade her face and began to open the small flurry of cards which had arrived a day too soon for her birthday. Oh hell, she thought, and gave a silent puff of protest. Sliding them under the chintz cushion, she began to rock gently to and fro whilst the littlest dog, tilted from side to side by the arc of the swing, gazed with furious intensity at an unclaimed crumb on the side of the plate. The other two Cavalier spaniels watched the white doves on the grass and wondered idly whether to stalk one in a pincer movement. They decided not. The last time they had tried this manoeuvre, the dove had made a vertical lift-off like a helicopter. The two dogs, unable to slam on their brakes in time, had crashed into each other at full tilt: bang.

Laura took in the view. It looked distinctly groomed. The lawn which Tom had mown yesterday was freshly striped. Its sappy smell and the scent of the old blush roses on the brick wall mingled to form a fragrance as warm and as fresh as peaches. Even the big border on the left was perfection, an artless toss of blue, purple and silver which she had invented to look like shot silk and this morning it actually did. If only it had a future longer than today. The garden of Lownden House was due for its annual opening the following weekend and visitors had grown increasingly hard to please. The years of dumb appreciation were over and everybody a connoisseur nowadays. What a relief when they just turned up for the food. Let them eat cake, she thought.

Anticipating the throng sweetened the peace and privacy of the moment. Nothing stirred the somnolence of the early hour except swallows and Geoffrey who was already lumbering about his first morning's task in the garden. Laura watched him stooping and rising, a large black flower-pot in one hand and a baton in the other.

'You have missed one,' she called out. 'Look, darling, over there.'

She raised her arm and the pale-blue sleeve of her cotton wrap fell back to her elbow. Geoffrey stood up to see where she was pointing. As always he managed his bulk with some difficulty. 'Where?' he demanded, trying to visualise a line between her finger and some destination beyond the clipped hornbeams. He scanned the gravel path and the lawn beside it. Both areas looked immaculate thanks to Tom the gardener who had combed them yesterday.

'Where?' he repeated, drawing the back of his hand

across his forehead. Even at this hour, standing in the sun had made him sweat.

Laura, her small burst of vivacity already spent, had begun to leaf through the magazine, savouring the agreeable smell of satiny virgin paper devoted to rich men's hobbies. Its soothing litany of treasures and grand houses reassured her. It underlined that life did indeed begin after fifty; *Country Life* was for grown-ups with grown-up tastes and grown-up purses.

'Where?' said Geoffrey again, tetchily, coming closer.

'Don't you dare come near me.'

He halted ten yards away where he brandished his pot of dog poohs at her. With his other hand he waved the stick he customarily used as a pooper-scooper.

'You are quite disgusting,' she said.

'*Your* dogs,' he replied. 'No dogs, no crap.'

'You should leave it to Tom,' said Laura, not for the first time.

'He only comes twice a week,' said Geoffrey. 'If I didn't do this, we'd be knee-deep in two days. They're like bloody fruit-machines, those dogs. Anyway, he has enough to do getting the garden ready.'

He looked round and located the final target that Laura had pointed out. As he potted it, he noticed she was frowning at his upper arms. For a second he was bewildered. Then he suddenly realised that her free-floating annoyance, which had rolled up like a haze over the hammock, was now focusing on his short-sleeved check shirt. Laura detested it. She was already cross with him because he had spent three full days on the golf course and had turned up at eight each night expecting a dinner. Actually Geoffrey felt justified rather than guilty. In the last few years he had grown aware that, whilst other men's wives were either working or charitably employed, Laura had enjoyed a life of uncommon comfort and style by courtesy of his own efforts. His business, an agricultural machine company, had provided a high income free of encumbrances, a fact that his wife still relished to the full. Geoffrey had always indulged Laura, whom he loved, sometimes painfully so, but he had recently wondered if this reduced rather than increased her flattering dependence on him.

He looked at her now. Other people said her beauty had become more substantial in middle age and he thought this was true: he took in her domed, palely-tanned forehead with its dark wings of hair, the large, glittering brown eyes, the curving solidity of her form which had altered little since the birth of their two daughters, Rosy and Allegra. There were moments – if she stretched slowly or brushed her hair so it went cloudy – when he would catch himself staring at her, bewitched. Even now, damn it, though she glared at his shirt and his big red arms, he felt amused rather than incensed.

However, Geoffrey could not fool himself. He did not doubt her ill-temper was a warning. They had not made love for ten days and would not do so, he knew, as long as he provoked her absurd irritations. For a week after sex, he could remain blandly indifferent to her moods but thereafter his own needs would force him to pander to them. That time had arrived now and he knew he must tread carefully. Madness though it was, it was this short-sleeved shirt in particular which had acquired a personality with the power to strike sex off the agenda for twenty-four hours. Tiny acts of barter, invisible to the outsider, would have to take place to reinstate it. If he changed his shirt, sacked his manager and walked the dogs today instead of playing a round, they would eventually make love. These silent concessions would bring sex in tow. Geoffrey assumed that most middle-aged marriages were built on these pragmatic ebbs and flows.

'Are the family coming for the garden opening?' he asked suddenly.

'Rosy and William, yes, plus the baby. Mother as always. Aunt Amy and Uncle James who are locked into one of their silent rows. Allegra? Well, you know Allegra.'

Some of this mixture sounded unpromising but Geoffrey was pleased at the thought of a fuller house. The girls, or Rosy anyway, saying, 'Daddy darling, doesn't it look wonderful?' Him sharing a brandy after dinner with William. The bedrooms busy. Rubber ducks in the family bathroom, plus the green frog that jumped across the kitchen table when you wound it. Him sweeping the baby Thomas away from these mere plastic aquatics and showing him the real black swans on the pond in the garden. Toddling round with him to the old brick barns and back to the cosy, prosperous Wealden house of the Kent countryside. All this belonged to him, Geoffrey Fenton, just as it had belonged to his own father in the past, and the years ahead would bring it to his new grandson. A destination gave bricks and mortar the value of a future. Somehow a grandson was more of a landmark than his daughters.

Laura had closed her eyes. Baba, the black and white spaniel, was chewing beatifically on a sodden piece of card on which a tasteful spray of roses was as yet uneaten.

I've forgotten, thought Geoffrey, no wonder she's cross. 'I'm sorry,' he said. 'I *hadn't* forgotten but I thought your birthday was tomorrow.'

She nodded, laughed suddenly and the little tensions melted.

'Those dogs can do anything,' he said. 'What would you say if it was me who ate one of your birthday cards?'

The spaniel, aware she was the subject of attention, decided her best chance of retaining the card was to grip it with lock-jaw, jump down and hide. She trotted to the foot of some shrub roses, lay down and demolished her trophy. Then with a post-prandial flourish squatted on the path, her back towards them.

'Geoffrey,' said Laura. 'Just one more, please. Your little task.'

He picked up his pot and baton with a sigh of resignation. 'You know the nursery rhyme, what are little girls made of? Sugar and spice and all things nice?'

Laura looked at him enquiringly.

'Well,' he muttered grumpily as he picked up the new turd, 'do you remember what little boys are made of? Slugs and snails and puppy dogs' tails, and all I can say is that it goes on all one's life. Men get the dirty jobs.'

He wandered away, but she heard him murmur: 'I must remember to warn Thomas.'

Later that day, Beth arrived back home after cleaning the Fentons' house. Her husband, Tom, looked after the garden, whilst Beth was 'the lady who does', according to Geoffrey, who would add 'more precious than rubies', hoping whoever heard him would pick up the quotation marks. Beth felt utterly exhausted. Laura had insisted on a mop-and-bucket day. Beth preferred those peaceful occasions when she could sit down and clean the jewellery and silver. She had developed a barrister's repertoire in arguing their case.

She now pushed open the front door of the old brick council house that they owned. She was proud of this mahogany-stained door with its semi-circular fanlight: it was new and it was called 'Georgian'. She thought it looked much more Georgian than anything in the Fentons' house, a wing of which Laura had told her actually was Georgian.

'Are you in?' she called out, uncertain whether to expect a response.

Her husband normally spent his Fridays helping out

in the vegetable garden of a hotel two miles away. He never grew any vegetables at home, nor anything else for that matter. Weeds like ox-eyed daisies and clover had colonised the concrete path with such vigour that it had cracked. Sometimes Laura gave Beth the flowers that were left over from the main batch that Tom planted in her garden. These extra flowers were the unlucky ones. In the wrong place at the wrong time, their number was definitely up, as Tom would never plant them in his own garden.

He now called out to his wife: 'In here. Just back.'

He was slumped in the kitchen, inhaling so hard on a cigarette that its smoke did not reappear. He rolled these himself, an activity that was arguably as addictive as the nicotine.

Beth plugged in the kettle, took a mug off the hook and dropped in a large spoonful of instant tea.

'All Laura can think of is her garden-do next week,' she said to Tom. 'She asked me to make two hundred fairy cakes and man the tea urns.' Beth was actually pleased. She was twelve stone, loved food and a convivial throng. Here was an annual occasion for a proper get-together. People came from miles. She filled up her mug with boiling water, splayed herself over the kitchen stool and scooped a doughnut and her magazine out of the Tesco carrier. It contained two really enthralling articles on chocolate cakes and wombs.

She was interrupted by the sound of swearing from next door. This was followed by the clatter of metal on metal. She looked at Tom enquiringly and he shrugged. Heaving herself up, she opened the door of the lounge and for a second stood there paralysed. Then she exploded. Gary, her only son, was mending his motor-bike on the floor.

'Out!' screeched Beth, her fat juddering with fury. 'Just out.'

'Mum,' he said, 'I wanted to watch the video.'

She looked with disbelief at the peach carpet, peach walls she had recently decorated and back to the bits and pieces defiling the floor. The carpet was a model called 'Diana'. She took a swipe at her son's head.

'Tom, come here, look, do something,' she yelled.

The worn and scrawny figure of her husband appeared and surveyed the scene. All he required when he got home was some peace. He hated noise especially. Even the clash of the gears on the ride-on mower pierced his head.

'You've never been able to control anyone,' he said. Mother and son faced each other, mirror images at frantic loggerheads over the most vital totems in their lives.

'I'll stamp on it,' she warned Gary, holding her twelve stones in reserve above the sunray of spokes she was threatening to crush.

Swearing furiously, Gary began to gather up the bits and pieces of his combustion engine. He couldn't understand his mother's dementia. His bike was far more precious than her bleeding carpet and had cost a packet more. It hadn't even stained its girly colour anyway. This was true, but the indentations and a few flakes of dried mud on its high synthetic pile enraged Beth. This peach room was a shrine.

'I paid for it,' she said to Tom, too hot with injury to be tearful.

'The Fentons, more like it,' he said, switching on the television. An eager face with fair hair swam on to the screen. Beth felt in a spoiling mood.

'You know he's a poofter,' she said to her husband.

'Bloody hell,' said Tom and switched over to *Neighbours*.

At the same time but thirty miles away, Laura's elder daughter, Rosy, was bathing the baby Thomas. Her name was Rosalind, which she had spelt with a 'y' during her A level course, then Ros when she worked on a magazine's desk, and was now, and for ever, she thought, Rosy.

Thomas banged the water with his hands, thrilled to find he could take effect on the world around him. That morning, suspended in his bouncer, he had discovered he was a biped. His legs, fumbling and rubbery flippers, were destined to be vertical after all. If he pointed his toes, they would actually reach the ground. He pointed and laughed and laughed, showing his newly emerged white tooth.

Rosy too was immersed in the process of her own as well as his discoveries. After his birth she had not found it boring, not once, to stay at home. It was this that made her the object of her own astonishment and her friends' envy. The latter – smart, overpaid and now newly disenchanted after witnessing Rosy's happiness – had become broody left in their London offices. One had even begun to show photos of herself as a baby to her boyfriend; he had taken the hint and melted away.

Rosy, who would not have believed it a year ago, was beginning to understand herself. She had recently experienced the happiest moment of her life with Thomas, much happier than his birth, violent and anxious; happier too than the moment she put her nipple in his mouth, the tender satisfaction of an animal urge. No, this moment, sweeter and more complicated than either of these, had occurred when she had put Thomas into his cot and gone to lie down for a brief rest on her own bed. As she dozed there, she listened to his happy gurgly noises and the sound began to mingle with the steady tread of William, her husband, climbing the staircase to her bedroom. They belong to each other and to me; we are all joined, she thought, even when we are separated. The thought of this unity filled her with light. It was a momentary cameo of total contentment, intense and unexpected, which she knew she could never forget.

Now she lifted Thomas out of his bath, patted him with the fluffy white towel and laid him on his back on the nursery table. The timeless and innocuous smell of baby powders and creams filled the air. Pink and as plump and soft as a puppy, he flailed his limbs in the air. How incredibly tender his skin was. Thomas looked back into the adoring eyes above him.

'Aaargh,' he said.

'What a clever boy, my philosopher, my Alexander,' crooned Rosy. 'Who's going to be Prime Minister, then?'

His parts, like a rosette pinned below his belly, looked too huge to belong to him. Their disproportions turned him into a Cupid. Rosy blew a kiss at his round tummy and, hearing William's car on the gravel drive, smiled, hugging her own utterly perfect happiness.

William ran up the stairs, embraced his wife and bent over Thomas.

'What are we going to be when we grow up, then?' He was reiterating his nightly routine.

'Ga, ga,' said his son, waving his tiny directionless hands in front of him.

'That's right: rich,' said William who worked in a City securities house as a broker. He grasped the infant fingers.

'Don't let Allegra hear you.'

'I thought she was still in India.'

'Back last week and already bored, it seems. Bored with having to wash, I imagine. Bored with having to dress. Cross that Mummy wants her to come home for the garden opening.'

'Oh God. I forgot. Do we have to go?'

'Not only go. Stay the night. It's a tradition.'

Rosy tucked the nappy deftly round Thomas and made a face.

'I enjoy it but could do without Allegra,' she said.

'We could all dump Allegra.'

'If you ask me,' said Rosy, feeding Thomas into an alphabetical pyjama suit which said *A is for Apple* and so forth, 'she shouldn't go next weekend. She is already working herself up by saying that Mummy is utterly selfish. Why don't I have a nice, well-adjusted and placid sister like me?'

'Quit complaining,' said William who was tired from having to exude a cheerful and pleasant personality all day in order to sell an overhang of stock. All he wanted at the moment was a happy baby, a soothing wife and no in-law problems.

They took Thomas to the nursery. Its pale-blue walls had been decorated to cater for a range of acceptable baby personalities that might emerge from the room. They were covered in Arthur Rackham prints and a picture of a furry dormouse on its back, Alice in Wonderland and the Knave of Hearts and, a manly touch so that Thomas would grow up dead straight, a run of illustrations from *Jane's Fighting Ships* and a cluster of Gulf War tanks.

Rosy gently laid Thomas in his cot and went to fetch a book of nursery rhymes.

'I know people will be people,' she said, 'but when Thomas has a sister, how can we thumbprint her to be right?' She had turned it into a question but was hopeful that an orderly approach to life would ensure its success.

'We would all like our ducklings to turn into swans,' said William, thinking gloomily of his stock which was set fair to do the opposite.

'But it mustn't turn out like Alleg—'

'Shut up, will you,' said William, bolting from the room. He knew she was capable of droning on endlessly.

Rosy loathed her sister Allegra, who was five years younger and had always caused trouble, borrowing her jumpers and sweating into them and saying fuck when she was twelve and inheriting her mother's ravishing looks which she had affected to despise. A Saturday to Sunday punk in the intervals between life as a weekly boarder, she had, after leaving school, channelled her unwashed attitudes into issues. This had been a relief to Laura who was terrified she would become a social statistic. 'She wouldn't be so silly as to take drugs?' she had once enquired of Rosy. Anything was better than the twin scourges of drugs and anorexia whose ghosts rather than their reality stalked their anxious imaginations. Rosy, who had always played prefect to her truant sister, recalled now how she had been dragooned into scouring Allegra's person and bedroom for signs. The police operation had not gone unnoticed by her sister and the occasion had marked a final breach.

'For Chrissake stop checking whether I'm throwing my food down the loo,' Allegra had yelled at her. 'And look, no puncture signs.' She held out her forearms. 'And here,' she lifted her head, flared her nostrils and stuck two fingers in them. 'See? Healthy.'

Rosy had found it revolting, and even now, although it was true that Allegra's social defiance had mellowed, she still felt nervous. On the rare occasions that they met, her sister would blast her with derision. It was six months since they had seen each other and Rosy would have been happy for this to extend for ever. So too, she imagined, would Allegra, who now lived in London.

Rosy turned the pages of the nursery rhyme book. It should have been soothing but somehow it reminded her of her sister. 'I've always liked this one,' she said loudly to Thomas although it was Allegra she challenged in her thoughts: 'What are little girls made of? Sugar and spice and all things nice.' She bent over the side of his cot. 'And what are little boys made of?' she asked him, drawing her finger tenderly over the plush of his cheek. 'That's right, darling. Slugs and snails and puppy dogs' tails. Let's make sure our politics are incorrect from the start.'

2 ∫

Laura always forgot how much work was required to prepare the garden for its annual outing. Tom did the mowing, the five hundred yards of hedge-clipping, and the last-minute replacement of failed plants. He mucked out the dovecote and clipped the pet sheep's toes in the paddock. Geoffrey walked round checking that the steps, staircase and banisters were in good order so that no one could sue him for falling. Laura thought her most useful action at this late stage was to go round and point. Look, the sidalcea needs more staking; can you shift that pot to this plinth; please could you just pop in this batch of *Hibiscus trionum*, it won't take a moment. That was now when she was too exhausted to bend or weed or dead-head or tie up any more.

Lord, how her back had ached last night. It really hurts, she had told Geoffrey, who had insisted on sex.

'It will make it better.'

'I don't feel like it.'

'Thirty years ago you stood at the altar and said with my body I thee worship.'

'That was just mumbo-jumbo.'

'It might have been a silly euphemism but we all know what it means.'

'My back is terrible,' she said again.

'I'll massage it.'

She had rolled over on her front in the big mahogany bed, her face buried in the white cotton pillows, their embroidery chafing her right cheek. He threw off the white duvet, straddled her with his heavy weight and made a token rub of the aching muscles between her shoulder-blades. It was very perfunctory.

'Over you go,' he said, feeling for her breasts as he tried to tip her on to her back.

'You didn't carry on long enough to make any difference.'

'It's the front of you that's interesting,' he muttered. 'Your back's got nothing going for it.'

'Oh God, breasts are so boring.' Laura groaned with exasperation, then looked round at him. She thought: I have another twenty years of this.

Both were briefly silent. Geoffrey recognised he was going nowhere. The feeling was familiar to him.

Must I, thought Laura, put up with this for the rest of my life? Every Sunday afternoon like clockwork except for the rare occasions, as recently, when she had been too busy to comply, so disrupted the schedule.

She stared at him, thinking.

'I've an idea,' she said slowly. 'It's never too late to change, but at your stage in life you need to be re-programmed.'

She wriggled herself to the side of the bed, stood up and crossed the room to the dressing-table with its dark auricula print. Geoffrey watched her, thinking to himself that she was still too beautiful for his own good. A bit more lined around the neck than when he had married her and her breasts swung lower than they used to, but they were still mesmeric. She was always reluctant to let him hold them for long. Maybe that was why she had slid out of bed, or perhaps this was just procrastination, postponing the awful moment. She was certainly taking ages. What the hell was she up to all this time?

Laura was ferreting around in her make-up tray, pushing aside mascara wands and an old silver scent cylinder, in search of the lip-pencil. Turning her back to the mirror, she looked over her shoulder to the reflection. Her back gleamed duskily in the light from the Edwardian candle lamps on the wall. There was a light dusting of freckles over her shoulders; more likely age-maculae, she thought. She also eyed with suspicion a mole she had not seen before.

Turning to the task in hand, with the lipstick she painted on two nipples and aureoles complete with dots, one in the centre of each shoulder-blade. Geoffrey sat bolt upright. He could see their reflection in the mirror and was scandalised. There were often times when he found her slightly alarming.

'There,' she said. 'Will this do, Geoffrey dear? Perhaps a bit bony but definitely focal points.'

She flexed her arms from side to side so that her blades stood out. She glanced back in the mirror. For all its surrealism, it did look quite convincing. She began to laugh at the ridiculousness of two old married people in search of a solution. She could never confess this to anyone. There was nothing more idiotic than middle-aged silliness. It was condoned when you were young and excused when you were old, but the in-between years were supposed to be the peak of propriety.

Laura glanced back at Geoffrey who looked as though he was in need of some cheer-leading.

'Doesn't it look good? Do admit it's a little bit sexy. You are the only man in the world to have a wife with four breasts. Now, why don't you massage the ones on the back.'

Geoffrey was not to be jollied along. He did not find this kind of caper terribly encouraging and had detumesced rapidly. The expression on his face was equally crestfallen. He had thought he had the equivalent of a good dinner in front of him and now it had been taken away.

'Laura, please, at your age. What is this Kama Sutra nonsense? I really need to.'

How quickly a little gaiety evaporates, she thought crossly. Now I'm going to get lipstick all over the bed.

'You've lost your sense of fun.' Laura looked at him accusingly.

Geoffrey felt quite desperate. Where would this end?

'Laura, please. Don't be selfish.' He held out his arms. 'Please.'

The word worked as always even though Laura often thought that you only accused others of selfishness in order to conceal your own. Still, there was nothing like saying please as an Open Sesame.

She came to the bed and lay down and put her arms around him. Ouch, she said, as he thrust into her quickly. He seemed to be penetrating to her lumbar region and she suppressed a spasm of pain. After all she did love him in her own way, she thought. In return, he gave her everything she might possibly want; and there was no doubt he needed her, was faithful to her, kept her, gave her love and every material comfort. There was nothing left to desire.

Yet as she lay there she found herself thinking that, in the last twelve hours, not only he but Allegra had called her selfish. In a sense she could discount both as each had a cause to promote, but still the accusation had rankled.

'I open the garden for charity,' she had protested to Allegra. 'The money goes to the nurses and a tiny bit to Tilly's pony club.'

'Honestly, you open it for vanity,' said her younger daughter and banged down the telephone.

Did she open it for vanity? In the early days perhaps it had been true. It had been nice to be thought worthy, comforting to have lots of flatterers. Two journalists had interviewed her and her picture had appeared in a Sunday supp. 'You must wear your Vita Sackville-West hat,' Rosy had advised, handing her the floppy straw sun-hat, though Laura had demurred, whereupon Rosy had suggested jodh-purs instead.

But there was no vanity in it now, of that she was sure, just hard grind. By the time Geoffrey had rolled off her, breathing as though he had suffered a by-pass operation, she had decided it was an act of positive selflessness to open the garden this year.

3

A week later Laura sat at the kitchen table with a dog on her lap and a shopping list before her. On it she wrote: watermelon, French beans, 2 apricot jams, *Clematis* 'Miss Bateman', pitta bread, new car – navy Jaguar? – raspberries, cheeses, Greek yoghurt, something for pudding. She paused. The butcher was delivering legs of lamb on Friday and the fishmonger a large salmon today. The vegetable garden could produce most of the salads, but the potatoes would have to be bought.

The list was brimful, so any extras must be vital. Necessities only, she thought, but added tapestry curtains and, with a defiant flourish, £10,000 of Cookson shares. Her suggestions were usually derided by Geoffrey who always dealt with his stockbroker, but she had often chosen well. She added an exclamation mark which she promptly deleted because it looked naïve. She finally scribbled, 'cheque for church fund', because it balanced the excesses above it. She had promised herself at fifty to give up feeling guilty but it had proved more addictive and lingering than expected.

She then started another list for the guests this weekend. Aunt Amy and Uncle James would go in the blue room. Although they weren't speaking – a periodic event – they would not be given a choice about sleeping together. As for her mother, Louisa, she would allot her the little green-and-white striped bedroom at the end of the corridor with its miniature bathroom. There would usually be no need for her to spend the night but she conceded that, since she was eighty, it would be wise to ensure that a strenuous day was made more relaxed.

Laura thought of the paraphernalia she would bring. Her unnecessary stick which she sometimes banged on the floor for effect. Her face-flannel and her fanny flannel, a pink one which everyone avoided like the plague, especially Beth who had a sixth sense about its purpose. Her ostentatious reading matter – always an 'approved' book which would be prominently displayed. At one stage in her life it would have been on the Bloomsburys; then Mary Wesley, though Louisa changed on whim; Alan Clark's diaries had been featured and anything of Mitfordian connection to indicate her vintage. Whatever the subject, Allegra would point and say, 'Look, Granny has learnt to read,' which Louisa would ignore.

Laura could see her mother enduring for ever, her heart strong, her manner ever more dominant whilst her less necessary organs and limbs weakened. And what do we do with Granny then? she thought. 'I am not missing out on 2000 AD,' her mother had said recently, 'nor am I seeing it in in a Home.' Yet Laura dreaded the idea of her living with them, which was another thing to feel guilty about, she supposed. Duty she could manage, though love was beyond reach; yet why must one love someone for historical reasons when there was no reason to like them now and probably less in the future?

The thought was disturbing. Indeed, thinking about the future in any form gave her mental vertigo. She pushed the dog off her lap, pulled open the drawer to take out another piece of paper and started a third list. The spaniel jumped back on to Laura's stomach. As always its greater persistence won and she let it remain there. Mixed corn, she wrote, dagging shears, wormer, four bales of oat straw, flea spray, poultry corn and rat poison.

Living things take so much looking after, she thought furiously. Human beings eat too much, dogs get fleas, sheep need their bottoms clipped, rats have to be killed. One day she would pull the plug on them all.

'I shall get rid of everyone but you,' she said to the spaniel, who had fallen into a deep dog sleep. Better still, she thought, I shall move into a nice bungalow on my own. There would be light sockets at eye level so there need be no bending down. A stucco exterior so no fresh pointing. Aluminium windows – lovely, no wood to flake. And a melamine kitchen.

She rose from the table, carrying Baba undisturbed in the crook of her arm. Happy as always to inconvenience herself rather than a dog, she struggled through the hurdles of making a cup of coffee with one hand, then settled back and looked round the kitchen. The view pleased her. Its walls were a smoky grey, and a huge amber Irish dresser stood in the corner, scented of beeswax. Beside it were the two white porcelain sinks, each deep enough to bath a baby in, with an arching brass tap that swung from one to the other. Medieval wooden settles with fat tapestried and tasselled cushions stood against the walls facing the long elm-wood refectory table in the middle. A big bungee sofa covered in a dusky-blue flower print lay at the end of the long high-ceilinged room. The white cat, Blossom, was curled in a perfect circle on one arm, glistening in a pool of sunlight beneath one of the sash windows.

Not half bad, thought Laura, in fact pretty perfect, yet free from any sense of striving. She congratulated herself and deleted the idea of a bungalow after all. Fortified with a sense of success, she drained her coffee and prepared for action. Shooting the dog from her lap for the second time, she fished out a cheque book and wrote, 'Pay Lownden Church Fund: £30 only,' then remembered the new vicar's black beard and probably – since she was disinclined to give him the benefit of the doubt – suspicious relations with a boy in the parish. She tore up the first cheque and substituted it with a £15 replacement.

All three dogs, peeping through half-open eyes, shook off their slumbers when they saw her go to the drawer to get the car keys. Baba flung herself repeatedly at her legs in an attempt to be selected for the trip. 'Stay!' said Laura in a commanding voice. '*Nobody* comes. You are all equally bottom of the heap today.'

She set the burglar alarm, slammed the door and walked briskly to the car, hurried along by the insistent beep-beep of the system setting itself behind her. Their nearest neighbours, a quarter of a mile away, had been burgled earlier that year. The old lady had been watching television in bed one afternoon when the alarm was not set. A balaclava-clad young man had erupted into the bedroom and taken all her jewellery. She had reacted philosophically. 'If I'd gone into a nursing home,' she had said to Laura, 'they'd have stripped me of my rings when I died anyway. One of the perks of the job.'

Laura had told her mother, who had promptly caught the 11.15 to London and sold her emerald-cut diamond ring in Burlington Arcade.

Laura drove her Volvo out through the gates and turned left into the winding lane that led to the main Tunbridge Wells road. She slowed down through the village, which had won a best kept accolade last summer. Weather-boarded and tile-hung, its picturesque qualities belied a street wrangling that was every equal of inner city life. Lately teenage pluckers from the chicken factory ten miles away had started to throw stones at the cottage windows. Mrs Bailey who ran the post office shop had taken to keeping a machete behind the till. 'I told the police it's for slicing the bacon,' she said to Laura. But Keith, the local bobby, had shaken his head: 'How to turn a lie into a whopper, Mrs B.'

As Laura drove through the village there were no locals to be seen except the vicar, wearing his usual defensive smile inside his beard. He was at the church gate, carrying a casket followed by four soberly dressed people. Someone's ashes, thought Laura, and probably not the right ones either. Who became who in a crematorium was best kept a trade secret.

The shopping took three hours by the time she had trailed from farmers' co-operative to confectioners, and from supermarket to the antique shop on the Pantiles. Here Oliver Simpson, an immaculate and plummy bachelor who never grew older than fifty, gave his best customers a coffee, amaretti and a plump discount.

'These tapestry curtains are château-bottled French,' he said to her authoritatively. 'A little nineteenth-century dust on them but otherwise perfect.'

'I am Geoffrey's despair,' said Laura, writing out another cheque, adding to it as an afterthought a mahogany sewing-box. She planned to give it to her friend Tessa Riley whom she would visit before returning home.

Tessa was younger than Laura. She was also broke, a state that had persisted for almost eight years. Her husband, Miles, a local society artist, had left her with a huge bill from the Inland Revenue when he disappeared to France with a girl of twenty. The nymphet, who was one of a succession, was less of a blow than the problem of paying the taxes and raising Polly, the daughter. In the event, Tessa had found the strength of character to do both. She now earned bits of money by doing a grocery round, painting cards and restoring chipped china for the rest of the week. Laura had once broken an Austrian teapot to provide her with work during a fallow period. These recurred frequently and the gesture could not be repeated.

Tessa now lived near the Forest in a clap-boarded semi where she referred to her ex as the Blown Gasket. Her tiny home, magpie-furnished from jumble sales, was composed with such skill that Laura was always astonished by its charms. A home-made quilt with an antique pattern of snowflakes covered the sofa. On the walls, paintings of paradise birds flanked a threadbare Persian rug, faded to buff and indigo. And, poised like a collection, the broken teapots, plates, cups and saucers – Sèvres, Imari, Staffordshire and early Woolworths – lined the shelves. Tessa had always loved clutter.

Laura found her hunched over the kitchen table, dividing her attention between a smashed Chinese vase and a sheet of scrap paper.

Tessa glanced up and passed her a note without comment.

Laura read: *Je vous prie d'excuser ma fille de manger le (la?) macaroni cheese.*

'She has a French exchange coming up,' Tessa added in explanation.

Laura put down her wicker basket and looked at her in amusement.

'Do they eat that gunge in France? Not a high-risk situation anyway.'

'That won't stop her getting nightmares.'

'Can't she just say no?'

'No.' Tessa sounded defensive. 'Anyway, is macaroni *le* or *la*?' Laura tried to recall her early-learning French class. Would Toto have met Monsieur Macaroni or Madame?

'Oh, male,' she said without explanation. Her friend was too young to remember Toto.

Tessa reapplied herself to her paper.

'Can I interrupt?' Laura, getting restless, handed her the

mahogany sewing-box. 'For you,' she said. 'Jolly useful too,' she added to prevent its classification as frippery.

Years of doing without had still not taught Tessa to accept presents gracefully. Gush was outside her range and gratitude unseemly. 'How kind,' she muttered, pushing back her fawn-coloured fringe and rubbing her forehead. It must have cost – what? Poverty was bearable, but not its embarrassments, the worst of which was feeling beholden.

'Look,' said Laura, 'you're helping me sell plants on Sunday. It's just a thank-you since you won't take cash. You can sell it back to Olly if you like.'

Tessa gave her a quick hug which Laura understood to mean that she probably would. She had better warn Oliver; she would have to buy it back if he insisted. It would all be much simpler if Tessa would take the payment instead. People's sensibilities did so confound the practicality of life.

Tessa placed the box with stage reverence to one side. It would stay there until she returned it to Oliver. 'How about a bite to eat by the stream?' she suggested. 'I'm starving.'

She tidied her pastes and paints on the kitchen table into a neat little group, putting a damp cloth over the Chinese vase she was patching. From the fridge she produced tomatoes and a month-old hunk of Cheddar. Laura added crusty bread from her basket, black olives, peaches and goat's cheese. Her food always looked nice. Tessa noticed the colouring: the dusky drupes, warm pink of the fruit and the ivory cheese.

The two women set off over the fields, which were filled with flocks of browsing, dark-faced sheep. It was a wonderfully blue day, the sun was warm and the light breeze had a soft, south-west feel to it. The stream was about half a mile away, just beyond a small copse. Laura eyed the grove doubtfully as they approached it.

'I'm not absolutely happy about this,' she said. 'A pair of lone women. There are such funny men about nowadays. It's awful how everything's changed.'

Recalling the self-defence classes she had attended two years ago, she took out her key-ring and arranged it so that the attached screwdriver poked up through her knuckles.

'What are you going to do with that?' said Tessa. 'Burst his testes?'

'No, I think I'll go for his eyeball first.' Laura jabbed her fist through an imaginary eye. 'Wham,' she explained. 'Did you hear it pop?'

'Look,' said Tessa in amazement, 'it's a lovely day. The sun is shining. There are orchids in the woodland. The birds are having a snooze. This is one of the few perfect places left in England. What's got into you?'

It's most peculiar, thought Tessa. Anyone looking at both of us would think she's the lucky one. Lovely face, safe country life, pots of dosh, daughters, grandchildren rolling off the line. Even Geoffrey in his own ineffectual way is a harmless sweetie. Yet me with my Blown Gasket and no central heating in winter, I'm fifty times happier. And it shows even on a wonderful day like this.

'It's tiredness, I suppose,' said Laura, hating to be caught moaning in public. 'I just have this feeling that it's the last time I open the garden. The last time all the family comes to stay.' She gestured helplessly. 'I used to love it and adore Rosy and Thomas spending the night, but the planning is awful and the work even worse.'

Tessa was silent. Reaching the bank of the stream, she concentrated on clearing a patch of grass where they might sit and eat. As she flicked rabbit droppings away, she noticed a bubble pop on the surface of the water and a fish like a tiny dragon dive back into the opaque depths. Polly had set up a water-watch here, declaring she had discovered an otter. Tessa was proud of the fact that her twelve-year-old daughter was a proper child, but it posed the problem of how to boot her to adulthood.

'You're not listening,' said Laura. 'Not that I blame you. It's awful drivelling on like this. You're the one with real problems, not whims like mine.'

Tessa shook her head. She handed her a chunky crust with goat's cheese. Both ignored the aged lump of cheddar. They rightly recognised it as a sociable offering rather than food.

'In a funny way,' said Tessa, 'real problems make it easier. For the last eight years I've known what I've got to do.' She bit into her bread. 'God, this cheese is heavenly.' She paused for a moment to savour the taste before she explained. 'I've had to raise poor old Poll. Terrifying but straightforward. Simple goals are so much easier to handle.' She made a vague gesture with her hand to emphasise the paradox that was forming in her mind. 'In some ways it isn't me but Miles, number one shit though he was, who ought to be pitied. Out of gear, all over the place, spraying here, there and everywhere like a frog. Pathetic. Even a child has been easy to handle because she knew what to avoid. The one person Poll didn't want to grow up like was her father.'

She lay back on the bank, adrift in the sun. Above to her right, she could see a vault of green leaves from a big oak. Flecks of emerald light swam through her half-closed eyes if she looked in that direction. The up-and-down voice of a chiff-chaff spoke from the dome of the tree.

'Did I ever tell you that when Polly reached seven, she wanted to dye her hair so that she wasn't blonde like Miles?'

'What did she think of the portrait he painted of her? She looked awfully like Miles in that.'

It had been a lovely one, the little girl wearing a cobalt-blue dress, bare brown arms and legs. She looked as though dusted by sun.

'We hid it under the bed for three years. Poll especially couldn't bear to see it. Now she's quite proud.'

Miles had also painted Laura, Geoffrey, Rosy and Allegra, their dogs and ducks in the garden. Louisa had wanted to be in it and was enraged when Laura said there was no room. To say yes would have entailed all that jostling for position that her mother always provoked. Nothing less than centre stage would have pacified her. In fact Miles had absconded before it was finished so there was an ectoplasmic quality to the portraits. Even Geoffrey's face, though wide and jowly, looked ghostly due to the fact that it had received one coat of paint too little. Laura had rather tentatively beefed up the lavender in the background with a fresh application of oils. She felt more purist about these than her own face which was as pale as muslin where the canvas showed through.

'The one I really couldn't bear to see,' continued Tessa, 'was the nude he did of me and Poll when she was first born. Little fair thing at the breast.'

She sat up and pulled at a daisy on the ground, narrowly missing a beetle at the foot of the grass blades. A nearby butterfly, startled by the vibration, flitted away. 'The trouble with nuclear families is that they atomise.'

'At least your Big Bang is behind you,' said Laura.

'And yours will never come.'

'Dependable Geoffrey, you mean.' I take him horribly for granted, Laura reflected.

What a fool you are to take him for granted, thought Tessa. That's what thirty years of marriage with no electric shocks does to you.

She was too fond of Laura to be truly jealous but there were often times when she felt just a tiny shudder to her sheltered life wouldn't go amiss. Nothing disruptive, thought Tessa. Just something that would make her appreciate it properly. A minor scare or a false alarm would be perfectly adequate.

Tessa's feelings surfaced in the need to jolt her.

'Quick, get your key-ring out,' she said. 'Screwdriver to the fore.'

'Where?' Laura grabbed the weapon, looked round and pressed her other hand over her heart which seemed to have bolted from her chest. 'God almighty. Who is it? I told you we shouldn't have come here.'

Tessa smiled and shook her head. Her face, always puckish, showed mischief.

'Just fire-drill,' she said. 'Here, have another peach.'

4 ∫

The family were not due to arrive until Saturday evening, but the day began early.

At dawn Laura had been woken by a distant crashing among bushes. There was an intermittent low groaning. It wasn't instantly recognisable, which made her panicky. Geoffrey was still deeply asleep, his eyelids twitching in time to some mental excitement. He must be catching rabbits like the dogs, thought Laura. She shook him.

'Geoffrey. Geoffrey. *Geoffrey*.'

He moaned slightly and reached out for her. His penis was stiff. It must have been twenty years since they had made love in the early morning, but the male body never seemed to give up hope.

'Get up,' she urged. 'Something dreadful's going on.'

He grunted and tried to burrow further into the bed but met an unyielding mass. She shook him again and used all her weight to push him to the edge of the mattress. Slowly Geoffrey surfaced.

'It's nothing,' he mumbled but resigned himself to abandoning sleep for the moment. He stumbled out of the house, so drowsy that he would have forgotten to release the burglar alarm without his wife's intervention. Seizing a besom broom from the porch, she thrust it into his hand. Thus armed, Geoffrey set forth.

As usual, the truth turned out to be more prosaic than her imaginings. Five heifers from their neighbouring farmer had broken into the garden and had trampled two lawns before fleeing from Geoffrey's avenging broom. A trail of hoofmarks and cowpats marked their passage. Laura plodded along the track of spoor.

Tom had mown the grass the previous evening. The newly-laid stripes, alternately dark green and light, glistening in the early dew, now had a scattershot of brown splodges across them.

'This as well as dog shit is too much,' she muttered in exasperation.

'Leave it,' said Geoffrey with some self-interest at heart, since he was the one who would have to cope. 'Garden visitors are too genteel to mention it. Rely on me, they will just tip-toe around it.'

He was privately more troubled that the cows might have eaten some clippings from the yew hedge. He would have been blameless but Dagwood the farmer would never have absolved him for five dead heifers. This might have motored for generations. He could see Thomas his grandson still bearing the torch in years to come.

None of this was worth losing a decent doze, however, so Geoffrey returned to bed for a couple more hours. Slow to rouse and quick to fall asleep, he would forget this disturbance by breakfast time.

Laura made herself a mug of tea, let the dogs out and walked back to the garden. It was the hour when everything looked at its most beautiful. A murmuring sound came from the dovecote. She opened their barn door to give the birds some grain and fresh water. Soft, white and dark-eyed, most were still clustered on their perches. A mother dove was feeding her two babies in the nest. They tore and struggled cruelly with her beak to take the pigeon's milk, as it was called. There was a fluttering of white wings about Laura's head as a group left the cote to swoop and circle round the garden. A few iridescent feathers drifted slowly down in the air to settle on the fresh green lawn.

The grounds had been laid out in the early years of the century on strong, simple Edwardian lines. Yew enclosures, after the fashion of the time, made several small, secluded gardens, opening like ante-rooms off the big central lawn, a calm green space, a lung, in front of the house. This was still partly in shadow from the tall pines but the terrace where Laura had gone to sit with her mug of tea was bathed in the blueish sunlight of early morning.

Here, bushes of glittering white cistus, their petals blotched with maroon, grew amongst the paving. The scent of cloves, heavy and sweet, drifted from the cushions of pinks. She liked their antique names. Queen of Sheba. Sops-in-wine. It was agony every year the garden opened to see people stepping on these paving plants. Most were immensely careful, but there was always someone who was a born plant-crusher. Last year a woman had jumped up and down on a flowering thyme: it likes it, she explained to a friend.

'Which of you is going to get spiked in the eye?' said Laura, addressing the pinks.

She got up, walked down the terrace steps and slowly through the rest of the garden, checking that all was in order. The old rose garden made her dizzy with its scent at this time of the year. It was almost too much. The French roses were bent to the ground with their weight of bloom. Their extravagance of smell, velvety texture, their crazy, intense purples, crimsons and greys, made her feel ill so early in the morning.

Such a relief to leave the hedged enclosures and reach the wilder part of the garden beyond. Here she sat beside the big pond with its banks of rushes and giant gunneras. The black swans, cob and pen, came paddling towards her. It was marvellous to hear their honking calls in the night. The cob now opened his lipstick-red beak and trumpeted. Though always aggressive in the breeding season, he trusted her. He recognised her to be female. He hated men.

The dogs who had accompanied Laura this far now stayed at a safe distance. As a puppy, the littlest spaniel had been cornered by the cob and rescued just in time from the flail of its wings. Now the swan arched its muscular neck to take the handful of grain Laura had brought him. As a reward he let her stroke the feathers, such soft down, on his breast. She moved the flat of her fingers in a gentle rhythm up and down as he pushed his breast against them. The smaller swan, his wife, waited pensively in the background. Like all their kind, they were mated for life so she showed no jealousy.

Once again, Laura thought: how I take Geoffrey for granted. After thirty years it was difficult not to, even though she knew she had been guilty of this before she had married him.

Geoffrey had been her mother's choice. It was Louisa who had sized up his future inheritance and capacity to look after her only daughter in the style which her beauty deserved. Laura suspected that her mother had also hoped he would have a sufficiency to look after her in her old age too. Louisa's husband, an accountant, had died young, but left her and the young Laura in a sheltered nest which his widow had been determined to perpetuate. In Geoffrey she had recognised the method. The only son of rich, elderly parents, Geoffrey had presented promising material which could only flower with age. Good-natured, lazy, geared to a quiet life, he had also been assessed by her mother as malleable. In this she had been right. Where she had been wrong was in reading her own daughter, or, rather, what she might become.

When younger it was true that Laura had been easy to dominate. Much of the confidence her beauty had given her was eroded by her mother's exercise of control. Even her few years of working in her early twenties – haphazard jobs in an art gallery, in two antique shops, once briefly as a secretary to an MP with sleek, brushed-down hair – all these had been insufficient to give her a rounded adult experience of the outside world. Standing on her own feet and the self-confidence it bestowed – so easily learned by a generation merely a few years younger – never became a habit. Only half-pushed from the nest, Laura had not learned to fly. The penalties of an easy life were considerable.

Her beauty had not gained her experience and the men in her life were few. The MP, who had taken out a succession of ballet dancers, decided she would be an adornment to his arm and ultimately in his rise to the Cabinet. But whilst Laura hesitated he married a model with thin, disdainful eyebrows, whose haughty face dispensed scorn from the pages of *Vogue*.

A City solicitor proved equally temporary. For a time there was no one, until, through the art gallery, she met Leo Ranson.

He was a solid, dark man, good-looking, watchful, who had once bought some little old master drawings which were cheap then. He didn't spend much but came in regularly, which she began to suspect had as much to do with her as his purchases. When he eventually asked her out, he proved conventional and generous and they went to Wheelers for its serenity, Rules for its old-fashioned ostentation and Pruniers for its food. He taught her about the recitative in Mozart, the modelling in Dürer and the principle of the flying buttress. She would watch his hands during his explanations. There was something foreign in the way he used them for expression. She liked his hands, strong but with sensitive fingers, brown and smooth: she could never bear the thought of hairy fingers groping between her legs.

He was the first man she slept with but she had been too shy to tell him that. Too hurt too that when he travelled abroad for his company, often absent for several months at a time, he would never ring her or write to her. Until then Laura had taken attentiveness for granted.

Her mother had not met him but sensed an attachment had formed, which she read as a threat. Ranson's peripatetic work for his family's engineering company would take her daughter to the other side of the world. 'A shade unreliable perhaps. He doesn't care for you,' she said when Ranson stayed in India for three months. Laura, fearing failure for the first time in her life, took fright.

Slowly and with manipulative skill, Laura's mother propelled her into the undemanding arms of Geoffrey. 'Domestic happiness, darling,' she said once at this time, 'babies, a loving husband, a proper provider, a beautiful house. That's what a woman really needs.'

Within a year Laura and Geoffrey were married in a lavish country ceremony with a platoon of page boys, four embarrassed bridesmaids and Laura in a voluminous ivory dress with her black hair piled up underneath the long veil. A photograph in a silver frame beside the chimney-piece commemorated it. Laura felt mortified whenever she saw it, remembering the tired hired marquee, her mother clad in orchids, and the unrepentant mink coats on her side of the church, hauled out of cold storage to defy the sunshine of mid-May. Staring at the picture the other day, she felt she was looking at a child. Inexperience retards you, she thought. I had a few years out of the nest and then clambered straight back.

Yet now, sitting beside the pool, stroking the swan which was drowsy with love, she felt she had few regrets. Hers had been an indulged and idyllic life. When Geoffrey's parents had died twenty years ago, he had inherited their large, mossy Elizabethan farmhouse with its Georgian wing. It was then that her passion for gardening had begun, her discovery of a hobby that provided the perfect balance between pleasure and toil. For the last decade they had opened the garden each June, an annual occasion which attracted a horde of visitors, a fact that never failed to amaze her. More came every year. Old regulars and first timers; country house groupies and Socialists with allotments; fern fanciers and phlox fanatics. She loved them all, even the nosy-parkers and the huge hard core of pensioners craving a good cheap tea. Six hundred had come last year. Eight hundred portions of food were planned this year. She hoped they would prove enough. She felt vulnerable awaiting the convergence of nearly a thousand people.

5

'Will you pass the cream, please?' Aunt Amy asked Rosy pointedly as they started on the raspberries which Laura had piled upon a base of almond pastry. The jug was much nearer to her husband, James, but Amy was stagily avoiding the direct approach. They had arrived that evening in the same car but had still not spoken to each other. A tight-lipped aura towards everyone hung about them.

Rosy, who couldn't see the point of this, asked James if he could hand the little silver jug to her. She then passed it to her great-aunt. Geoffrey was oblivious, but Laura and Rosy exchanged a smile at this pantomime. William seeking out his wife's gaze was annoyed to find her expressing her feelings to her mother instead.

'This is ridiculous,' said Louisa. Amy was her younger sister and therefore considered below her, in that pecking order so cast in stone that it was impervious to any of life's reversals. 'I don't know what it's about but you started it. You always do and always did.'

'It is very simple,' said Amy, trying to pierce her sister with her gaze. 'James said my novels were . . .' she paused. 'He said they were an acquired taste.'

'I said they were tosh,' said her husband. 'No disrespect, Amy, just fact.'

Amy became very pink. Her voice lost its conversational

note. 'I pay for the food out of them, the telephone, the car. You arrived here by courtesy of them this evening. If we weren't dining here, you would be eating their fruits. As it were.'

Amy had started to write one novel a year in her mid-sixties and had now published four. The family called her the Household Name, in which Amy sensed mockery. She had, she said, a devoted readership, but James said, for devoted read small. Amy loved the notion of being a novelist and had cast herself in the part. She had taken to dressing in the *vie bohème* style of the artist and now always wrapped a bandana around her head. Tonight she was wearing a Chinese-yellow one with black scrolls woven into the thread. Both her wrists supported a cluster of ethnic bangles. These clanked now with agitation.

James was also growing upset. He hated the reminder that he had failed to provide them with much of a pension from his two printing-shop franchises. Amy had no need to imply it in public, especially not here where they'd never heard of short rations.

In his distress his hand shook and some of the raspberries fell off the edge of his spoon on to the floor. The spaniels, who were fanned out under the table ready for any fortunate events of this nature, rushed forward. They sniffed at the morsel and drifted in disappointment back to their stations. Even the added savour of a steal couldn't turn raspberries into a success. The grown-ups, bickering above the table-top, were unaware of these surges of passion and dismay around their ankles.

Laura felt she was presiding over a children's party where at any moment fractiousness might spill into serious tears. Except that, at their age, a stroke or a heart-attack could be the sequel. Really, that would be all she needed: three stiffs in the house the evening before eight hundred visitors were due to arrive. She now regretted the fact that she had laid the table for dinner in the kitchen as they might have been on better behaviour in the sombre dining-room. Maybe not: by their age, disinhibition exerted a stronger force than even the most formal surroundings.

Amy was in full flood.

'Most men would be grateful their wives had come to the rescue. Most men would refrain from biting the hand that feeds them.'

'Amy, all I said was that . . .'

'I know what you said.' She did not want it repeated. 'It was neither wise nor true. No one agrees.'

'I am not aware,' said Louisa, 'that James is in a position to pass judgment.' She did not dare say it, but James knew she was referring to the fact that, after the army, he had spent his lifetime in trade.

'Me against my sister but my sister and me against my brother-in-law,' murmured William. 'There's an old Arab proverb like that.'

'Who would like some more pudding?' asked Laura plaintively. She found it infuriating to go to the bother of roasting a lamb and baking a tart when it was ignored in a sudden personality squall. However, there was no more attention to spare for Laura than for her food.

'I shall ring up your parents and ask them to collect you before the presents are handed out,' she announced, but this ultimate sanction failed to take effect. Rosy, the only one with whom it registered, gave a nervous giggle. Unruffled, Geoffrey was helping himself to the remainder of the tart on which he upended the jug of cream.

By now James, who knew that this episode would provoke indigestion anyway, felt he should be hanged for a sheep as for a lamb. The past week's silence with Amy had caused a log-jam of words to accumulate in the part of his brain that stored speech. He prepared himself to pour them out in torrential resentment. He felt the pressure of a lifetime's memories knock against his head to come out.

There was a second's silence during which he summoned up the irrevocable that might have caused a permanent breach of relations. In that tense stillness, there came a cry, staccato at first and then a joined-up wail of protest.

'It's Thomas,' said Rosy, leaping to her feet to see what had happened. 'Hush now. No more.'

Sleeping in his cot in the bedroom above the kitchen, Thomas must have been woken by the raised voices.

His great-great-uncle James sank into his chair, his memories routed and his cohorts of words dispersed. Unable to cope with the interruption, adrenalin coagulated in great lumps about his body; he could feel it lurching through his veins and wondered how many years it was taking off his life. Great-great-aunt Amy retied her yellow bandana in triumphal displacement activity. Privately she thought she had won and the flourish accompanying her action revealed it. Secretly James told himself that it had been an honourable draw, but at great cost to himself.

All in-laws are pretty frightful, thought William. He seemed to remember a row here last year though not as offensive. They were such an argumentative bunch, not like his own who thought polite control a cardinal virtue. In the background, he could hear Thomas's screams rising to a crescendo as Rosy descended the stairs and crossed the hall.

'The poor little darling,' said Laura as Rosy carried Thomas into the kitchen. He was bawling, his face crimson and streaked with trails of tears. She took him on to her lap, burying her face in the swansdown softness of his neck which was also wet with tears, and rocking him back and forward, an instinctive motion that seemed to soothe her rather than him. One of the dogs gave a frightened yap at the alien bundle of unhappiness.

'Look, Thomas, doggy,' said James, who, unlike Amy, had been made to feel thoroughly ashamed by his great-great-nephew's distress, but Thomas only cried the more loudly.

'Not doggy,' snapped Rosy. '*Dog*. They must learn proper words.' She was upset so spoke more crossly than appropriate. James felt humiliated.

'Give him to me,' said Geoffrey.

He shoved his chair back and leant over to take the child, the big golfing muscles standing out on his forearms. Rosy watched anxiously, hovering behind him. She pulled the green Victorian lamp lower over the table lest it should shine in Thomas's eyes. Geoffrey lifted him above his head and looked up at him. A few tears splashed on to his forehead. Geoffrey began to sing, softly at first:

> 'There was a tailor had a mouse,
> Hi diddle umkum feedle.
> They lived together in one house,
> Hi diddle umkum feedle.
> Hi diddle umkum tarum tantum
> Through the town of Ramsay,
> Hi diddle umkum over the lea,
> Hi diddle umkum feedle.'

Laura looked at the huge man with the tiny baby held high above his head. They were in that twilight just outside the circle of brilliance made by the dark-green lamp shining on to the table, with its raspberries, pale cheeses and empty bottle of burgundy.

She listened to Geoffrey's light baritone, a little off-pitch but still melodic, singing the wry old English song in its minor key. She had a slight smile, watching first Geoffrey's untroubled face, then Thomas's eyes. Slowly his cheeks began to uncrumple and the stiff corrugations around his mouth relaxed. Tears turned into hiccups. He put his thumb in his mouth and sucked it wonderingly; now and then he yielded a tiny smile.

The older members of the family sat still, wounds imagined and real, ancient and modern, forgotten in the timeless story that they had not heard since their own nursery days. Its familiarity lulled them back to an infancy that had been eclipsed for seventy or more years. Louisa and Amy recalled singing it at the upright walnut piano in their playroom. Amy remembered the dress she had been wearing, a flat cream pinafore with a swingy skirt, her hair in ringlets. She and Louisa exchanged a look that was filled with communal nostalgia. James was singing 'hi diddle umkum feedle' under his breath. Amy forgave him and put her hand over his.

'The song has a sad ending,' he said and Amy squeezed his fingers.

'Not sad. Life goes on is what it says.'

> 'The tailor found his mouse was dead,
>   Hi diddle umkum feedle.
> He bought another in his stead,
>   Hi diddle umkum feedle.
> Hi diddle umkum tarum tantum
>   Through the town of Ramsay,
> Hi diddle umkum over the lea,
>   Hi diddle umkum feedle.'

Suspended still in the air over Geoffrey's head, Thomas had fallen asleep.

6

The garden was due to open at two o'clock. An hour beforehand, Beth arrived with the tea-urns and two meals-on-wheels ladies to set up the stall in the former granary. Bored with her own fairy cakes, Beth was magnetised by a chocolate confection provided by Marjorie, one of her companions. She eyed it with the intense desire that borders on anxiety. By opening time, this had developed so urgently that she put a bag over the cake and hid it behind one of the tea-urns. Only now could her tunnel vision relax into a wider perspective on the afternoon.

Louisa had settled herself in a large wicker chair outside the conservatory. She had a cream parasol to hand in case the sun grew too warm but, like royalty, was reluctant to conceal her face. Meanwhile she contented herself with tilting the brim of her green straw hat. 'Amy,' she called out, wanting a companion, but Amy was parading beside a border with her latest novel in hand, front-face uppermost to advertise the household name.

Rosy had put two teddy bears in the drawing-room windows that overlooked the terrace. The house wasn't open, but Rosy explained it made the place look lovable. They had once stuck a teddy bear in the window at Hidcote and what was good enough for the National Trust should be OK for us, she told Laura who was head-down in a shady bed. Her mother murmured yes, but had to concentrate on Sellotaping the pink spray of a nomocharis back on to its stem. Her exquisite lily had taken four years of coaxing to its melting summer display when the spaniels had mistaken it for a rabbit.

'How could they?' groaned Laura, hoping that the head of the lily wouldn't know it was severed from its heart until the end of the afternoon.

Geoffrey thought: just five more hours of this and then it's over for another year. His place was at the entrance gate beside Tom who was wearing his gardener's badge of office with doubtful pride. It encouraged people to ask questions and the answers deserted him when faced with a predator after a plant name. The answers returned when he shut the gate at seven o'clock, but he did not know about *l'esprit de l'escalier*. Unable to diagnose himself he worried secretly about senile dementia. It had taken his father that way.

Beside him sat John Mason, the local Tory agent, who took the cash for the tickets. Not a courtier by nature but nervous about his job security for the last few years, he was keen to keep in with the local businessmen.

'Here they come,' he said as the trickle of early cars drew into the field. They would probably be the same people as in previous years. As at parties, there was a character-type who was a consistently early arriver.

Laura flew off to change. Geoffrey looked after her in puzzlement: already that morning she had switched from denims to a long black and white flower print. What now? She emerged wearing a plain white cotton shirt, fawn culottes and silver hoop ear-rings.

'Oh, Tessa,' she said, falling on the neck of her friend who turned out to be the driver of the first car. 'You're late.'

'Don't worry,' said Tessa, scurrying off to her position on the plant stall. 'No one ever buys plants anyway. They're too mean to do anything but pinch cuttings on the side.'

The first real arrivals, the churchwarden, Smethwick, and his wife, took this to be a personal assault on their probity and pinched in their mouths to show disapproval.

Mason winced: clunk, clunk, he thought, there are two more votes down the Lib-Dem gullet.

'Two down,' said Geoffrey, knowing what was in the mind of the Conservative agent, 'seven hundred and ninety-eight more of the buggers to go. Someone tell Tessa to shut up.'

As the churchwarden walked off, his wife hissed to him: 'They must have seen you snitch that cistus last year.'

'I doubt it,' he said. 'They didn't even twig that we walked in through the back entrance last year. We can be as stingy as them.'

The first real wave of the public came at three o'clock, as they scheduled their perambulation of the garden to fill in the hour before they took tea at four. There were hundreds by now, many new faces as well as familiar regulars who recognised each other annually with exclamations of delight:

'Caro.'

'Emma, darling.'

'Billy.'

'Simon.'

'How fantastic to see you.'

Apart from several coachloads of pensioners and an American tour, most of the animals, as Geoffrey put it, came in two by two. Some of the more serious wives carried notebooks in which they wrote the names of plant combinations.

'Bowles' mauve wallflower and violet alliums too. I could use that. How do you spell erysimum? Where do the i and the y go?' asked one quavering old lady.

'White on white,' said another woman to her friend.

'Rather overdoes the chic, doesn't it: really, *Clematis* "Miss Bateman" *and* "Marie Boisselot", what an over-egged pud.'

'Bog off,' thought Rosy who was standing just behind her.

'At Highgrove,' said her companion in a huge floppy hat, 'the Prince has an arbour at just such a junction. As Rosemary V. was saying to me the other day, junctions are so terribly important.'

A fastidious homosexual in a Panama hat and a light linen jacket leaned over a border and said to his partner of forty years: 'That's my combination – yellow alchemilla and violet hebe. They saw that in our garden first. They've stolen our idea.'

'We'll sue,' promised his companion, who was a lawyer.

A photographer was trying to balance the legs of his tripod in the shady bed to which he had been lured by the vision of the nomocharis. One photograph of a rarity like this would earn him four hundred quid in the right place and that was for starters. However, the money was proving elusive as that damned Sellotape kept intruding into his viewfinder. What kind of garden was this anyway where the plants were tied up in sticking plaster, he thought irritably.

Over on the main lawn, the spaniels were enchanted by the company and kept lying down to show off their tummies promiscuously. A pair of four-year-olds were rolling on the ground with them whilst their parents' attention was diverted by the geraniums in the border. 'She's very hot,' said one of the children about the eldest spaniel. 'Do you think she needs some water?' He and his sister rushed off to the row of watering-cans that Laura had lined up beside the conservatory. Struggling back with the can between them slurping liquid all over their shoes, they tipped it forward and proceeded to water the dog, which jumped up with a yelp.

On the plant stall Tessa was less out of the action than she had predicted. She had coped with floods of box-hedge junkies who had bought enough buxus cuttings to border the M25. She had seen off freeloaders like the churchwarden's wife who had begged a rose for a grave. And in between she had fallen in love with a delectable man who had two empty tubs in his garden. Plant angelica, she advised at random, praying that Laura wouldn't kill her for giving faulty advice. 'Your wife will like the surprise,' she added, probing further than the transaction required, but the man merely smiled and preserved his mystery.

In the granary Beth had just sold the last of the fairy cakes. A feeding frenzy was in progress. The scones were gone and the rock cakes too, and the coffee, walnut and iced lemon were all decimated by husbands returning for their third helpings. Thank the Lord, thought Beth, she had put that chocolate cake in a very safe place. How awful to think of it being pawed by these pigs. Through a foreground of cups and saucers she caught sight of Gary who had modified the spikes of his hair. What is he doing here, she wondered, but was distracted by Marjorie searching the stall. 'Where did my chocolate cake go?' she was muttering, suddenly aware of the missing member of her own flock of cakes. 'Isn't it eaten?' asked Beth, since a question was never a lie.

Amy was sitting at one of the tea-tables. Her self-advertisement had paid off and she was holding court to a small group of elderly disciples who had recognised her book. Her mind was scuttling as fast as a mouse over the new sales she might make. Was she on a rising royalty, she wondered. Was it ten per cent or twelve and a half per cent or more of the cover price? What would that make? Tick-tock, tick-tock, went her brain: £14.95 times twenty-five over two divided by a hundred times umpteen thousands equals the world is my oyster. She pondered whether she should exact a leather-bound copy from her publishers as Evelyn Waugh had once done. Poor old James, lying in bed after taking a BisoDol, was missing all this fun – enhanced, she decided, by the sight of Louisa glowering with jealousy from her bath-chair.

Like James, Laura had also escaped, though just for ten minutes. She had slipped into the vegetable garden, which was always a tranquil oasis on annual afternoons. It was Tom's province, a proper kitchen-garden rather than a 'trumped-up foreign do', by which he meant the more fashionable potager with flowers. As a result, only men visited it on open days, usually old men who liked calm straight rows of onions and lettuces and stick peas. Their wives would pop their heads round the hedge and, dismayed by the lack of exterior interior decoration, retire in search of more floral fol de rols elsewhere.

Tom was already in residence here, soothing himself amongst the parallel lines of vegetables. He had just escaped a bruising encounter with a woman who had asked him to identify a rose. For once he could remember the name with absolute clarity, but nothing would induce him to say *Cuisse de Nymphe Emue* since Laura had explained its meaning as 'Thigh of an Aroused Maiden'. He walked up and down the path, admiring the straightness of his brassica lines and pausing only to roll his cigarette. There was just one other visitor here, a dark man wearing an open-neck check shirt, corduroy trousers and boots. He looked round at Laura's voice and returned quickly to staring at the onions. He bent down and studied their label with considerable intensity as though it had just been invented.

'Your daughter was looking for you,' said Tom, hoping to flush Laura out of his kingdom before she flushed him.

The ploy failed as Laura had just found Rosy curled up with Thomas on the tree-seat.

'I wonder, dear Tom,' she said, 'do you think you could

possibly circulate a bit? People do like to know what everything's called. There's a woman rushing round the garden at the moment trying to name everything.'

The dark man, who must have re-read his onion label fifty times, looked up suddenly and laughed. Tom took one last loving puff at his cigarette, then, resigned to his fate, departed for the fray.

'Mrs Fenton,' said the man. He hesitated. 'Laura?'

She looked at him. He seemed slightly familiar but was impossible to place. She tried him for fit amongst Geoffrey's friends, her gardening acquaintances, local landowners, but he remained something of a rogue. It was baffling. He expected her to know him and indeed she knew that she did know him. She frowned and put her head to one side.

'Laura? Don't you recognise me? Don't tell me I've changed that much.' He looked amused and a little wary.

Who was it? she thought – she often failed to recognise old faces amongst the new at these gatherings – then thirty years rolled away and she knew it was Ranson.

'Leo,' she said. 'How amazing. How long is it?' She thought crossly that she sounded like the 'Caro, Emma, Billy, Simon, how fantastic' brigade that she had overheard.

'Christ, don't,' he said and pulled a face. He was thicker-set than she remembered, much more lined, but his hair was still dark with not much grey and his tilted eyes that wonderful deep-blue.

'You've worn very well,' said Ranson, obviously comparing and measuring, as she was. 'I'd have recognised you anywhere. That's not a rebuke,' he added swiftly as she made a moue of self-reproach at her own failure of response.

'What are you doing here?' she asked.

'Not sure, actually. I don't even have a garden, not at

the moment anyway. Well, two empty tubs waiting to be planted, will that pass?'

'Oh, Leo, it's wonderful to see you,' and she realised she meant it. 'Even among the onions.'

'I didn't read their label after all, even though I must have looked at it for five minutes. What are they, by the way?'

'Red Baron, a flavoursome maincrop, as they say,' and she pushed away the topic with her hand. 'Are you here alone?' she added cautiously. If his wife were here, she had better not sound quite so delighted to see him.

He nodded.

'But surely your wife wanted to come,' she persisted, probing.

'Not really. The most recent one is divorced.' He paused. 'It's a long story, not for now.'

Hmm, she thought, more than one wife. That never sounded like an accident.

'By the way, you can take that puritanical look off your face. I recognise it. Everyone who's marriage has stuck wears it when they meet a divorcé. It's not quite as you think.'

'Leo, I didn't.'

'You did, but it doesn't matter now. Take me round the garden instead.'

'You're in it.'

'Vegetable gardens don't count. I understand vegetables. I eat them. I meant guide me round the bits of the garden that are above my head.'

He was beginning to feel claustrophobic alone with her in this secret kitchen garden. It was like being stuck in a lift with someone you had not seen for half your lifetime. The problem was that you knew her intimately well yet not at all. It was difficult to handle.

'Shall I introduce you to my husband,' said Laura, also running for cover.

She was going through the same tussle of sensations as Ranson, exacerbated by the female fright that her enthusiasm might have run a little ahead of itself, saying it was wonderful to see him when he didn't even have a wife.

'Your husband is fully occupied, I think. He is being talked at very fast by a man in an executive suit.'

'That's Malcolm, his manager. I wish Geoffrey would sack him. The talk must be bullshit.'

'Didn't look like it. I recognise a manager delivering poor news to his boss.'

'Did Geoffrey look worried?'

'Not a bit. He seemed to be brushing things aside.'

'That's terribly like him.'

'That comment means it's terribly unlike you.'

She suddenly went red and looked down, absolutely furious with herself for having blushed at the personal remark. I am a middle-aged woman, she reminded herself, but it didn't help that she had only known him in the role of a girl. Unfortunately, as she talked to him fragments of dormant memory had stirred into life. New errant chunks kept breaking off and floating to the surface of her mind. Some were hard to fit with the reality in front of her, whilst others matched with disturbing exactitude.

She was saved from discomfiture by the sound of activity beyond the hedge, the scrunching of gravel and the boisterous sound of Rosy's voice.

'Mummy,' she said, putting her head round the hedge and coming to a halt. 'Sorry, am I interrupting? Everyone's asking for you.'

'I'm coming,' said Laura wondering why she wasn't introducing Ranson to her daughter, who was waiting expectantly.

Rosy looked at Ranson who returned her interest with a steady gaze.

'I'll be with you in a second,' said Laura. 'Hold their hands, will you?'

Rosy, radiating nosiness, gave her a curious look and disappeared.

'What a nice daughter,' said Ranson. 'Why didn't you introduce us?'

Laura, nonplussed, gave a slight shake of her head which Ranson read as an exclusion notice. I'd better back off, he thought.

'I'm in the way,' he said, 'and you're busy. I was just passing and wanted to say hello. You have a lovely garden and I'm really pleased things have worked out so well for you.'

Christ, he thought, I do sound pious. He slipped into the voice he used for neutral acquaintances.

'If you're ever in London, give me a ring. Here's my card,' he said and pencilled a number on the top.

She looked down at the business address and the private one he had scribbled above it.

'It's only a short ride from Peter Jones,' he said drily. 'I expect you take sanctuary there, don't you, when you come to town? My first wife always did.'

How many wives? thought Laura. Who, when, why and how ran in quick succession through her mind.

'Only two wives, if you're wondering,' and he began to laugh. 'Laura, you are as transparent as a sheet of glass. One very nice thing is that thirty more years of life haven't turned you into a sophisticate.'

He leant forward as if to kiss her on the cheek, changed his mind, said, 'I'm off,' and walked away.

Laura felt paralysed. She was tempted to haul him back, but lacked the polite vocabulary to achieve this. Probably the language didn't exist. I didn't deal with that at all well, she thought crossly. He is an old friend and I should have said to Rosy: here's Ranson, and to Ranson: here's Rosy,

7

On Sunday evening the post-mortem was conducted in high spirits by some. More people had attended than ever before and the heavens had bucketed down cash. Amy judged it the best open day yet, though she planned an improvement for next year with a signing session of her books. All the way home in the car she played with her calculator: she had progressed from hardback to paperback prices and was working out £5.95 times seven and a half per cent times fifty thousand and other more sparkling permutations. 'Pots and pots and pots of money,' she shouted at one point.

She is mad, thought James, stark, raving, bloody bonkers. He feared she would give him an ulcer since there was no chance she would inflict one on herself. In the see-saw of marriage, the higher Amy rose, the lower he was destined to fall. His old age loomed hideously before him as Amy's amanuensis and dustbin. It was a large price to pay for financial security.

Louisa too was furious. Out of eight hundred people that afternoon, she had eyes only for Amy. Such shameful parading of the household name triumphant. Oh, vanity, thy name is Amy, she thought. Until the last few years, everyone had said of Louisa, 'Isn't she wonderful? Such a reader, up to the minute with everything.' But what availed it to be a reader, when her sister was a writer? Oh, the fickleness of favour that her youngest sister, the only one alive, should overtake her on the final lap. She who was last now came first.

Beth too was a victor ludorum with a rather more tangible prize in the form of the chocolate cake. In previous years she had borne off the left-overs: this was the first occasion that fate, as she liked to think it, had bowled her a virgin trophy. 'Have a taste,' she urged Tom, but her husband was suffering the emotional effects of having to stand up and be noticed all afternoon.

Rosy was ecstatic after Thomas's first public presentation, dressed in his paisley dungarees. He had made heaps of new friends, most of whom were tiny tots staggering beneath the burden of huge names. A birthday party circuit was now lined up with Georgiana who was three in September, Augustus who was two, Glazebrook at eighteen months and Rory who undercut Thomas by five weeks. Rosy was steaming to plan the menu for her party: raisin and carrot teacake, apricot crunchies, banana mould, yoghurt and honey mousse and freshly squeezed orange juice, real food to scour out their baby arteries in time for the twenty-first century.

'At their age,' said Laura, 'they're not blocked anyway.'

'It starts in the womb,' replied Rosy firmly.

It was funny how this new puritanism had oozed all over the place, mused Laura: baby talk had been banned and now baby food was succumbing as well. It was only the grown-ups who craved rabbit-shaped jellies for their birthday parties.

However, she had other matters on her mind. She had expected Allegra to appear or to ring but there had been silence, which was both a relief and a cause for disquiet. More disconcerting still was the news on Geoffrey's business. Malcolm, his manager, had told him that sales of the agricultural machinery were declining; stock was out of date and prices undercut by rival firms. Nothing changes in this business, said Geoffrey, reiterating his father's first rule, which was steadiness under fire. He patted Malcolm on the arm and told him that discounting was the first sign of panic. These are the 'nervous nineties', he added, imitating a phrase he had picked up from the stockbroker with whom he played golf.

'My God,' said Laura when he repeated the conversation, 'aren't you on a small overdraft already?'

'I was at school with the manager's boss. No problems there, and as for Malcolm, he's fine unless he gets nervy. These salesmen are born neurotics.'

'Then sack him and get another. Better still, get involved yourself. You never look at the books.'

'We pay arms and legs for the accountants. Don't have a dog and bark yourself.'

'But there could be a disaster.'

'How like a woman,' said Geoffrey, picking up his golf clubs and moving to the door. 'Tomorrow catastrophe if not already today.'

Maddening, he thought as he clumped off, how she had got this little whiff into her bonnet. Usually things returned to blissful normality after the garden had shut for the next year. Rows diminished, food improved, the ratio of sex to days per calendar month increased, and Laura stopped fussing over the potential of visitors to fall into potholes in the garden.

This was not the only matter that was disturbing Laura at present. In a back drawer of her mind lay Ranson. He was ready to pop out at the least sign of attention but she kept her eyes steadily averted. She did not even intend to give him a look when she called on Tessa the following evening.

Polly said she would find Tessa in the kitchen. She was

playing chess with a friend on the table outside by the white picket fence. This boundary was only a few yards from the house but the space in between was a sea of orange and cream Californian poppies and blue phacelias. Lovely, thought Laura, nicer than anything I had on show yesterday.

'Pawn to king four,' muttered the youth sitting opposite Polly. He had kept his horn-rimmed spectacles glued to the board and was desperate to get started.

'So dreary,' said Polly, showing off. 'Can't you think of another opening move?'

'No. I know you're going to do something equally boring like pawn to queen three anyway.'

'You're asking for it. You know what happened last time. I slaughtered you.'

There was a long pause.

'Oh, do buck up,' he groaned with impatience. 'I have to wait for ever when I play with you.'

'OK. We'll time it. Ten seconds for every move.'

Laura left them to find Tessa who was about to boil the spaghetti.

'Want some?' she offered. 'I've got a few basil leaves and cheese to go on it.'

Laura shook her head in vigorous disgust. She couldn't understand this fashion for Italian stodge. Spaghetti, lasagne, tortellini, ravioli, macaroni – a million lyricisms for glop. The poetry of pasta was only in its names.

'I can't stay but just came to thank you for yesterday. You did wonders on the plant stall.'

'Went like a dream. I sold a million miles of box hedging.'

'So I heard. Were they aspiring gardeners or real ones?' Laura was always suspicious of people who bought box.

'Frightful aspirants. God knows where they're going to put it all. Edge their drawing-room carpets, perhaps.' Tessa gave the spaghetti a stir, then leaned pensively on her wooden spoon. 'There was one awfully nice man, however, with two empty tubs.'

'Why do you say it that way?'

'What way?'

'Oh, you know, heavy emphasis. Two empty tubs.'

'Well, he did seem rather lonely. I somehow sensed his life might be as empty as his tubs.'

Laura kept her face blank, but tried to seem inviting as she wished to hear more of this absurdity. The perfect pitch would be passive interest.

She raised her eyebrows into question-marks. 'What did you tell him to plant in his tubs?'

'Angelica.'

'Well, that's usually a biennial so it may die next year. I don't think Miss Lonelyheart's stall solved his problems.'

Tessa glanced at her curiously. 'Rosy said he asked you the same question – surely you got a whiff of what I said too?'

'He didn't really. Just mentioned it in passing.'

'Didn't you think he was nice?'

For a split second Laura hesitated on the brink. Did she admit an affair with Leo or not? She had suppressed the truth to Rosy, but surely she must own up to Tessa. I'll tell her everything, she decided, it's too trivial for silence. But there seemed to be a glass door between the words she wanted and those that arrived and she ended up with a compromise.

'He seemed quite nice, though all at sea in the garden. Funnily enough it turns out I was introduced to him once when I was young, but I don't remember anything about it.'

The contrariness of words was distinctly odd, she decided. They danced to a tune of their own.

'You sound as careful as Mary Archer,' said Tessa, as she dished up the spaghetti.

Laura thought suddenly, I'll tell her the lot, but as she opened her mouth to say 'Actually—' a howl of rage came from the garden.

'Checkmate!'

'You cheated. You fucking well cheated. You took fifteen seconds for each of your last moves.'

'Creep.'

'Crud.'

'God, I'm starving.' Polly erupted into the kitchen.

'Tell Simon not to swear,' said Tessa.

Laura pushed Ranson back in his drawer. Lie down, shut up and stay there for ever, she thought.

Although it was late, Ranson was still in his office. He was supposed to be preoccupied with a set of plans, but part of his mind kept breaking ranks to return to yesterday afternoon. He had thought it enjoyable at the time, but in retrospect it seemed rather less jolly. In fact he felt a tiny bit sorry for himself.

He pushed his large leather chair back and went to stand at the plate-glass window overlooking the Thames. Hulls and barges shifted gently on the swell of the wake from passing boats, the water now green, now grey as reflections dissolved and re-formed. Had it ever been that same ultramarine that glittered in Canaletto's pretty oil, a study of which hung on the office wall? It had been five years since he had indulged his tastes on the art market. Funded by the company, he had concentrated on eighteenth-century views of the Thames and its bridges. Even now, he loved to walk these views in real life, for the bridges had endured. There was a small Samuel Scott, his favourite, that was due to come up at Sotheby's. Perhaps he might buy it. Ranson felt in need of the odd consolation and this might prove more durable in the form of things rather than people. Right now artefacts held a stronger appeal than women.

Yesterday had been a mistake, he decided, a very small one but none the less depressing in its own minor way. An hour ago a ghost of a headache, no more than a frown at this stage, had forced him to take a brisk walk from Stamford Street to the South Bank and back. He knew he was tired, and relief at the company's prospects had yet to make an effect on his spirits. Four years of tense litigation against their Rio bridge had finally been settled in their favour; now the highway contracts had been signed with Saudi Arabia from where he had just returned following a two-month trip to India and Hong Kong.

He used to love these tours, gripped when he set out with a feeling almost akin to lust – their sense of purpose, achievement, the sheer satisfaction of useful, essential work with visible results in the bridges they built, the roads, the airports that would bring quantifiable human benefit. Recently, however, he had wondered if it was time to give up. The old energy had gone and he felt he exhaled spent effort. Beijing with its near certainty of a Chinese contract was scheduled for the autumn. At one time he would have lusted for the breakthrough: now he shrank from the fresh round of impenetrable foreign officials bringing new protocol to be mastered with every change of government and policy. He was beginning to feel this was a younger man's job.

A decade ago, his wife would have invariably ferried him to and from the airport, unflagging in her patience and support. Now, nothing. Her death, a sudden brain haemorrhage, had happened without warning in his absence. He had been told in his hotel room in Delhi and for years he had found himself unable to think of that moment. He would feel his brain making an almost muscular effort to push it away. The sensation that he had lost the ability to breathe, that his lungs were paralysed, would flood him with panic.

In an attempt to rid himself of the past, he had married Natalya who was then in her early thirties. A Russian interpreter at the Moscow Registration Chamber, her relative youth had seemed to hold the promise of a young family, perhaps. He had decided to marry her as they walked one November night across Red Square to his hotel. She wore her huge fox hat: and the falling snow had been caught in a sort of glistening halo on the tips of the fur. She was desperate to leave Moscow.

The first year of marriage had been relatively buoyant until the miscarriage. She had grown increasingly hysterical; the rows developed, insistent and entirely repetitive, every few months. The accusations of neglect, her loneliness, the miscarriage was his fault, she hated London, only Moscow had reality. She had started to drink, more off than on and selectively at first, though it promised to be indiscriminate. 'Excess is part of your nature,' he had once said to her lightly and she sank her teeth into the arm he had placed round her shoulders to hug her, and began to scream and scream, continuously, until he called Hallam to come and give her a sedative. Their divorce had gone through uncontested in January. She was as eager to be free as he and returned to Moscow.

Ranson was in his mid-fifties but had looked younger until recently. Of medium height, thickset and dark, he had a powerful physical presence belying his contained personality. His eyes, slightly Sephardic in their tilt, gave a hint of his father's ancestry, yet their very dark blue which Laura had remarked was inherited from his English mother. Completely free of conceit, Ranson knew nevertheless that he was attractive to many women. Yet he hadn't touched one for six months and felt some peace of mind in his celibacy.

His last woman had been his Lebanese hostess at a dinner party. He had never liked her, but had noticed a small dark mole, strategically placed above the wine-red *décolletage* that she wore. She recognised his attention and had looked back at him. In that splinter of a second the message had been sent and received. Why not, he had thought. Since that night, there had been no one. At my stage, he thought, a man needs tranquillity and a settled marriage. It was a popular myth that change was a stimulant. It was merely disruptive and exhausting.

It was in this mood of sombre reflection that he ruminated on his past. Meeting Laura yesterday had given him an uncomfortable sense of his own failures. Beforehand he had imagined she was leading a stable country life with children, dogs and plants, but to see such panoramic evidence of its success was rather depressing, to say the least. The landscape of her life looked so different from his.

In his twenties he had assumed without much direct thought they might marry one day. But his youth, his unreadiness at that stage to tie himself down, his constant absence abroad for his father's company – it was for all these reasons, he thought, that their affair had been halting and hesitant. He had returned one summer to hear she had married an Anglo-Saxon squire. An affair which had been started by him was now ended in the absence of his decision.

Ranson had been aware for some years where Laura lived and had noticed too the inclusion of their garden among the public listings in *The Times* in summer. He had never attended. Happily married, or in the frenetic throes of divorce, he had not toyed with the past. Even now that he was unencumbered a certain fastidiousness, and slightly superstitious reluctance to re-examine a closed area of his youth, had made him shrink from a visit which had much more to do with himself than their garden.

Yet a kind of curiosity persisted and this year he had been tempted to drive into the Wealden countryside. He hated London at weekends and he had sold the garden near Burford after his first wife's death. He wouldn't mind a second house in the country and told himself he could combine a recce of Kent with a visit to the garden. As for Laura, he doubted whether she was recognisable. He had been shocked yesterday to find her beauty still intact.

He pulled open the top drawer of his mahogany desk where his secretary hid his bowl of cherries. He had grown addicted to them this summer. Not much to drink, plain food, no sex, he thought to himself. Where have all the old pleasures gone? He fished out a forked pair of dark-red cherries, the kind that his only daughter would loop over her ears when little. Look, Daddy, Daddy, see my ear-rings, she would say. He ate first one, then the other, holding them well away from his navy striped banker's suit that he was wearing, despite the warmth, for his meeting this evening. One of the kernels fell on to the cream carpet. 'Shit,' he muttered.

His buzzer sounded and he leant forward to listen.

'Mr Johansson to see you, sir,' said his secretary, who was working overtime. She had been trained to address him with utmost formality before all foreign clients.

'Show him up, Jenny,' said Ranson, rubbing the stain on the carpet with his handkerchief. He groaned. Bending down had confirmed his headache.

At that moment Laura was bending forward to smell one of the Gallica roses, inhaling its deep smoky intensity. Baba, the littlest spaniel, jumped up against her skirt, jealous of so much attention expended on a flower. It was growing dark and the dog's white forehead glimmered between its long, silky-black ears. Laura lifted the animal and pushed her face into the short velvet fur that grew on the top of its head. Oh hell, she thought.

8

William clambered into the big brass and iron bed. Once upon a time, two years ago, he and Rosy would have raced each other there because the loser was left with the bedtime chores. Now Rosy was always the one who pulled the curtains and turned the lights out. Of late she seemed to spend an age writing lists and folding things into neat little heaps with rectangular corners. Tonight she had completed this stage and was now rummaging in the chest of drawers, trying to find a clean nightdress as Thomas had been sick on the current one.

'What about that silk and lace one?' William recalled that she had yet to wear his Christmas present.

'Not right now. I'm into the flannel phase.'

She pulled out an old red and white striped shirt that William had worn in his 1980s days in the office. Its cuffs hung down over her wrists and she folded them back to form a thick soft pleat over her forearms.

A full moon had risen and she walked to the window to admire the slaty light it shed over the grass and tree-tops. Two cats raced across the lawn and up the trunk of an old cherry tree.

'Hurry up,' said William, extending his right arm.

Rosy threw a last look over the landscape, left the window open so that the night noises could enter and pulled the cream calico curtains. She came to the bed and lay down beside him, fitting her head into the hollow of his right shoulder. 'I do think it most awfully odd that Allegra didn't put in a show. Not a word.'

'Par for the course.'

He felt down beneath her shirt and discovered she had slipped on a pair of knickers, which usually meant she would refuse him any sex. She needn't have worried, he thought. He felt bloated. Rosy had tried out some of the birthday-party menu for their supper and it had tasted distinctly remedial. Thank God he had decent lunches most days at work. Were it not for this week's red meat and cream puds he would waste away to nothing at all. He had suggested that Rosy should do a cookery course but she had said raw food was better for you, at which moment he had heard a bell toll. Judging by tonight's menu, that same bell was tolling dolefully for his poor little mite of a son, thought William. Unless Thomas evolved a gizzard, he was in for a tough future.

'The other thing we must decide,' yawned Rosy, 'is what Thomas is going to call Mummy.'

'Certainly not Granny,' said William bitterly. 'Oh no, nothing so bleeding obvious as that.' In any case, his own mother – who had no such pangs about normal behaviour – had already appropriated that for herself. Better, on second thoughts, that there shouldn't be a fight over it between grandparents.

'Nothing silly. No baby words,' said Rosy sternly.

'How about Gloria?'

She swivelled her head. She was so close she could see her eye reflected in his.

'Get it? G and Laura and add an i.'

'I got it all right. That's just the kind of thing I mean, stupid. Nothing silly.'

William sighed. He tasted again the hazelnut loaf she had

fed him for dinner.

'How about Grandma Muesli?' he suggested, thinking of his wife's and mother-in-law's larders.

Rosy sat up.

'That's marvellous,' she said.

Allegra was resting upside down against the wall, her head on the floor in a pool of long, straight hair. All the blood had collected in her face, which had turned scarlet.

'You won't do it any good,' said the man who was watching her with some impatience.

'I'm helping its circulation,' but she cartwheeled round all the same to emerge the right way up. Slowly the colour ebbed from her cheeks to be replaced by the normal pallor beneath her tan.

She now settled herself in the lotus position, her long limbs clothed in black leggings. She sat facing the wall to empty her mind of distractions and began the transit to the world beyond. With meditation, as with every other discipline, there were degrees of achievement and the final stage of inner tranquillity was levitation. One day she would fly.

The man waited for her to emerge from her trance. The air in the flat was warm and resinous from the essential oil of lavender on her wrists. The scent, the still air, the immobility of the girl induced torpor. The man closed his eyes, his anger diffusing into drowsiness. Sounds from outside the flat receded out of focus – the distant see-saw of a police alarm, the slam of a car door, an abrupt burst of reggae, were all absorbed into a hum of white noise.

After the allotted period of stillness, the vacant space that had been Allegra stirred, yawned and stretched its limbs. She smoothed down her stomach and looked at it reflectively. Mine will be a global child, she thought to herself, not a parochial affair like Rosy's. Absurd how one could plot the entirety of Thomas's life: its predictable pipeline from nursery to boarding school to banking which one day Thomas would repeat for his own Thomas and so on in a succession of closed circles. My child, thought Allegra, will have freedom, and I shall call it Ranee or Ranjit rather than Emma or Sophie or James or Charles or anything at all that stakes out its claim to that little England of my family.

Thank God she hadn't visited them this weekend. The prospect of the middle classes at prayer in their garden had been nauseating. The bourgeois of the south-east as seen in Ma showing off her possessions and Pa showing off Ma and Rosy showing off Thomas, all of them so dreadfully pleased with themselves. Rosy was the worst of all, so proud to have snaffled a prize pig for a husband. Well, she was welcome to William. My baby, thought Allegra, won't have a father, just me, because it's mine. She glanced across at Jonathan and anticipated trouble.

After she had discovered she was pregnant, she had vacillated between wanting and rejecting the child. At times it promised to be a liability, which was when she hated it. Equally often it was transformed into an asset when she desired it. But as soon as Jonathan had laid claim to the rights of fatherhood, Allegra had felt like a tigress about the child. All mine, she thought. Scorning the possessions that her family assumed and esteemed had left a void in her life which she had inflamed with ideas. Now she had a possession of her own which promised greater excitement than those issues which had once filled that empty space.

Her attitude towards Jonathan quivered according to the degree of convenience he might offer her: his flat in Victoria, financial support if necessary, and other fuzzier ministrations of daily life, which included the rag-bag of therapy. At present he was teaching her the rudiments of reflexology as Allegra was toying with the idea of starting a personal practice for clients. That it was only chiropody with miraculous aspirations would never occur to her.

In the meantime, thought Allegra, he might continue his tuition by massaging her soles. She went over to him and placed her long, bare foot on his knee.

'I take it you would prefer that to be on my neck,' he said.

'Shall we carry on with the lessons then?'

'You are just using me.'

'You let yourself be fucking well used.'

'Don't swear. It's out of date.'

'As an out-of-date copywriter, you'd know, I suppose.'

He flushed. He had lost his job in a Mayfair advertising agency and only recently replaced it with another which scarcely counted as it was in Croydon. He found it agonising in the mornings to catch a train that was running in the wrong direction. A row, however, was better avoided with Allegra.

'How yah-boo you can be sometimes,' he said instead, coolly. 'The mildest reproof tips you over the edge.'

Privately Allegra agreed, but she had never, not even as a child, known how to apologise. Immature as ever, she felt there was greater loss of face in letting slip a mode of bad behaviour than of good. Yet there were times when the war of contradictions within made her hate herself.

Though not far from London, the Kent countryside was quiet and still. Tessa let the tortoiseshell cat out for its bedtime pee and walked outside herself into the luminous silver and dark-grey moonscape. The little cat caught a shrew, bit it and tossed it up on her paws. 'Not a shrew,' protested Tessa, 'their lives are short enough anyway,' but the animal, excited by its kill in the moonlight, began to pounce on moving shadows.

Tessa inhaled the damp earth smell of night-time. Just

me and the cat, she thought. The lightning stab of loneliness was untypical but deep enough to make her turn back to the house where Polly was already in bed.

Tessa made herself a cup of camomile tea and shuddered at its bitter taste, reminding herself of its apparent charm when she had called it tisane in France – but then it had the pleasant flavour of its associations, as had indeed her marriage. She let the mewing cat in, turned off the lights and went upstairs to her bedroom thinking how marriage and divorce from Miles had deterred her from accepting the idea of another man and another marriage. I shall never marry again, she thought, as she peeled off her blue cotton T-shirt.

She looked at herself full-length in the mirror. Slim and small-breasted with long legs, her best feature, she might have passed for thirty-five. It seemed a waste that there was no one in the whole world available to take an interest in her body. Fifty-five million people in Britain, over one thousand million people in China, how many billions of human beings in the whole world, half of them locked in slavish appreciation of ugly people, and here she was, semi-youngish and demi-glowing, yet there was no one to appreciate her – no one she wanted.

She rarely thought in this way. She was so used to being alone that she had ceased to be introspective about her past or her future, but on Sunday her encounter with the first appealing man she had met for ages had proved disrupting. It had reminded her that she had nothing to replace Polly, who had fulfilled her life until now. But one day her daughter must leave her, and then there would be a vacuum which she lacked the resources to fill. Her work had been chosen deliberately for its calm, boring and bill-paying qualities, and even serious painting to which she had started to return – pictures of big Stanley Spencer figures picking fruit, spotted pigs and hens with red wattles – even painting was a hobby rather than a vocation or a livelihood.

I love life, thought Tessa, looking at her reflection, I'm not afraid of it like Laura, I have energy, I can't pass the rest of my life with my nose pressed up against the window-pane of other people's marriages. Do I spend my remaining time on the periphery, typecast as the woman on the plant stall, the equivalent of the governess, that loneliest of Victorian figures, the gooseberry, the wallflower? As long as I'm alone, I am cast in the role of the observer.

How absurd, she thought, that now was the first time she had been struck by that poetic cliché, the brevity of life. Her body was sagging infinitesimally all the while and there was no one to pay homage before its collapse. Once a woman who had been widowed young had told her the lack of sex was the worst aspect. It wasn't so much sex, thought Tessa, though she could have done with a man tonight. It was the mixture of moods in bed: the laughter at shared jokes before, the doubt and indifference when he was inside you about whether you came and then the shock of intense pleasure when you were surprised, and the release afterwards when all your bones were melted into your flesh, such a sweet mixture and so very far away tonight. Oh God, she thought, I'll have to do it, and she put her fingers down between her thighs, though she knew it was an act of angry despair rather than of pleasure.

9

It was a good summer. The roses loved the heat and the ramblers festooning the trees flowered with abandon, their froths of pink and white blossom emitting waves of banana-scented perfume. August was hotter still. It was dry and the level sank in the pond so that the black swans, upended in the water, could dip their long necks to its floor, emerging with their scarlet beaks stained with mud.

The dovecote was invaded by a succession of racing pigeons who, exhausted by their huge flights, were relieved to have discovered the shangri-la enjoyed by their snow-white relatives. Tom removed them one by one and then fanned out the delicate underside of their wings to check their home address which was concealed in the fold. When Geoffrey or Laura were driving far, they would pack the intruder into a box in the car-boot and release it some eighty miles away. The offending pigeon would fly around in circles for a few minutes until the old computer programme in his brain clicked into working order. Then, its racing muscles stiff with determination, it would soar off in the direction of its previous owner.

September was horribly equinoctial this year and the weather changed into a pattern of heavy gusts of rain which flattened the golden rod and even the short violet asters of the autumn border. The pink diascias which had been blooming like foam around the clipped evergreens in the tubs turned brown. For days the dogs hung around the house, rushing back to their baskets when anyone showed them a lead which would threaten a walk. Laura tied up the fallen clematis in pouring rain, wearing wellingtons and a soft-brimmed hat which dripped water down her neck as she leant forward.

Then suddenly the belt of noisy weather broke, to be replaced by a sequence of polar-cold, still grey days with a low ceiling to the sky. Autumn had come. Eloise, the booted bantam, stopped laying eggs, the ducks grew winter plumage and the garden changed colour. The birch trees yellowed and the five-fingered leaves of the maples went crimson before drifting down to form a ruby carpet on the ground beneath.

Tom and Laura picked the golden quinces and began their annual tussle over planting the spring bulbs in grass. Tom's taste for rectangles was incorrigible. Trained in the vegetable garden, he thought a man was judged by the straightness of his lines. Each year he assembled the bulbs like a squadron-leader with a platoon, and each year he was frustrated of his Utopia. It was a ritual he was doomed to lose. Spying him out of the window, Laura would pounce: 'Oh, Tom, but we agreed last year. Look, like this,' and he would wince to see her rearrange his meticulous parallels into a higgledy-piggledy mixture. He felt sick to see the uneven lagoons of bulbs with the odd outrider that gave her so much pleasure. 'That woman has no sense of order,' he told Beth.

As outdoor life began to close down, so indoor activities built up. With the dark evenings came a volley of invitations. Laura groaned at the list: gloomy cocktails in South Kensington, a masked charity ball at Polesden Lacey in Surrey and a handful of posh dinner parties in neighbouring villages.

Thomas's invitations sounded much more fun when Rosy explained he had been asked to his first fancy-dress party. She brought him over to her mother's for the day to show off his costume. He had just started to walk in the form of two steps forward before toppling down and shuffling around vigorously on his bottom.

'What a slippery little eel you are,' complained Rosy as he tried to resist being poured into his fancy-dress.

'What is it?' asked Laura.

'Can't you see?' Rosy felt a bit put out. It had taken ages to sew.

The costume was bright-orange fleece with some green streamers which Thomas intended to stuff into his mouth. Baba pulled at them and it developed into a tug of war.

'Stop that,' yelled Rosy, too late to prevent one of the ribbons splitting in two. Baba took her half to her basket at which Thomas went red and prepared to grizzle.

'For God's sake, Grandma Muesli, you might watch your dogs.'

Laura wondered what the costume might represent. Was orange significant? There were so many theories to child-rearing these days that it might be thought good practice to encourage an adventurous outlook on life.

'It's a carrot,' explained Rosy.

She held Thomas upright. She put his legs together to form a taper and pulled the orange hood over his head so that the tuft of green petersham ribbons sprouted from the roof like a pineapple top.

His nappy bulged in the middle, upsetting the proportions, but Laura clapped her hands in admiration.

'It's simply wonderful, but you don't need to hobble him to show it off. Better still if he went as a forked carrot. Then he could walk.'

Rosy laughed, then looked worried.

'I can't turn him into a deformed vegetable.' She was not sure whether this should be taken seriously.

Laura wished she could sally forth as a carrot herself. Her own wardrobe was distinctly dull in comparison. They dug through her clothes and unearthed last winter's selection in the form of a long, medieval, velvet dress and a glittering gold tunic. Rosy tried on both, pursing her lips and turning her right profile to her reflection as she always did when she looked in the mirror.

'Can I borrow them?'

'No.'

'Oh, Ma.' She put on a silly voice.

'Thomas will mess them up.'

'Just once. Your dog's already ruined one of his carrot tufts.'

'We'll see.' This was a recognised code of surrender.

In truth Laura thought her daughter looked better in the off-the-shoulder style. Her own neck had grown slightly stringy in the last year. She had heard that in the sixth decade the skin began to part from the muscles beneath and had feared her turn was drawing close.

'It needs ear-rings.' Rosy turned her head from side to side, pushing her dark curls away from her cheeks.

Laura went to her chest of drawers and opened the two serious jewel boxes containing the ruby ring, the garnet necklace and the long, faceted ear-drops to match. All three had belonged to Geoffrey's mother and, in turn, to her mother.

'I can't lend you these,' she said, smiling at Rosy as she opened the box. Rosy smiled back; implicit in her warning was the promise that she would lend the dress. Her mother, however, was staring down into the boxes. She was rigid.

'They're not here,' she said.

Laura tried to put a brake on the rising panic, but it was at once grimly evident that there was no easy or happy explanation for their absence. She had returned the jewellery to the boxes after Beth had cleaned them some months ago and had not worn them since then.

She looked up at Rosy and grimaced.

'They've been taken.'

Rosy pooh-poohed this with a shake of her head.

'Well, they haven't gone for a walk.'

'You can't have been burgled. The alarm would talk.'

'Not if it wasn't on.'

'It always is. This place is Fort Knox when you're out. Beady red eyes everywhere.'

Rosy started to unpeel Thomas from his carrot suit before he shuffled out of range. He was already getting its bottom dusty.

'What about when the garden was open?' she asked. 'It wouldn't have been on then.'

'No one strange is allowed to go in the house. I told you. The organisers warn you every year not to allow anyone in – not even for the loo. I felt simply dreadful turning away a man whose wife said he had prostate trouble.'

'What did he say?'

'He didn't, poor thing, terribly embarrassed, but his wife looked like poison. I knew what she was thinking. All this and no heart.'

Laura slammed the boxes shut and put her head in her hands.

'It's not the jewellery,' she said slowly. 'That's insured and anyway, it was never really mine. What's so awful is something else.'

She lifted her head and looked at but did not see Thomas who was eating a Bonio he had mysteriously found on the floor of the bedroom.

'The point is,' she continued, turning her head towards Rosy, 'it must have been an inside job, don't you see? Since only the jewellery's missing and nothing else is disturbed, they must have known where to look.'

There was a long silence in which they both digested the thought. Rosy folded the carrot suit back into its tissue paper. It had lost its ability to please. She looked back at her mother.

'Who?' she said.

'Who?' asked Geoffrey when Laura told him later.

'God knows. Only you, my mother, the girls and Beth knew where they were kept. None of us would have lifted them. We may never learn who did it. Even though they're photographed, and insured, the police don't have much hope of finding out.'

Geoffrey had been in a bad enough mood when he had entered the room. Now this put a match to the tinder.

'Fuck, fuck, fuck it all,' he said.

He left the kitchen and returned with a bottle of whisky. Wrenching its top off, he poured a tumblerful. His hand shook a little and Laura went to put her arms around him, surprised and concerned at the degree of his distress. Exasperation would have been more in character.

'I know they're your mother's and grandmother's, but really, be sensible, they're insured. Worse things happen and to everyone. Look at that old lady earlier this year.'

Geoffrey turned his head away, without looking at her. She was worried.

'Geoffrey, what is it? Is it something else?'

He drained his glass, switched the tumbler to his left hand. He put his right in his pocket and she heard the sound of rustling paper.

'The fact is,' he said slowly, 'we're having a spot of bother on another front too.'

'What?'

'With the bank.'

'What do you mean?' She was frightened. 'What have you got in your pocket?'

He pulled out a letter.

'You'd better read it.' He pushed it in front of her nose, shaking it in anger. 'Just look at this poxy little note from that fucker at the bank who's half my age.'

Laura took it, holding it at arm's length, having difficulty focusing at close range.

'Dear Mr Fenton,' she read, 'As a result of the business plan and forecasts which we discussed with you and your finance director . . .' she paused, looking at him over the top of the paper, 'What's this? I know nothing of this.' She turned back to the letter, '. . . the bank has taken the view that we should not extend the loan facilities we have negotiated with your company beyond the agreed term. The fixed amount and accrued interest are due for repayment by March 31. I trust that you will be making arrangements for funds to be made available by the due time and I confirm that the deeds we hold in safe keeping will be returned to you on repayment of this loan.'

She put the letter down on the kitchen table.

'What loan is this? I thought you had a small overdraft. I didn't know about a loan. You haven't told me anything about a loan.'

'I wasn't going to tell you. I thought you'd fuss. You get in a state and start nagging.'

'You thought I'd fuss. Perhaps I have a right to fuss. Don't I have a right to fuss that you haven't told me? What loan? How dare you take out a loan without telling me.' She had started to shout.

'There you are.' Geoffrey glared at her, but his fury actually eased as he saw her proving his point. He continued, lowering his voice and speaking slowly as though she were a tiresome child, 'The bank loaned the company money. We needed to upgrade our machinery and install a new computer system to control our stock and components supply.'

'How much?'

He half-turned away, rubbing his thigh as he always did when agitated.

'Geoffrey, how much?'

'You never wanted to know about these things. You thought machinery was boring. It was silly of me to bring you in. His letter upset me.'

'Geoffrey, how much?'

'Half a million or so,' he muttered.

She stopped breathing.

'Jesus Christ. Half a million. And you never told me.'

'Half a million means nothing in a business.'

She was finding it hard to inhale. She took little gulps of breath as though she were sipping the air.

To calm herself, she went to the window to look out and noticed for the first time that the putty had flaked off the bottom row of panes. Outside, the booted bantams were scratching at the path, their feathered shanks sending up small clouds of dust. She had forgotten to feed them.

'Half a million,' she repeated. It didn't seem to have much meaning. Everything trailed noughts these days. 'When?'

'A year ago.'

'A year? And you've never told me? All this time? How dare you?' A bolt of rage shot through her. She felt dizzy and put her hand on the window to steady the spin. The bantams saw her and started clucking hopefully.

'Nothing's changed,' muttered Geoffrey. 'The only difference is that you know about it now, whereas you didn't five minutes ago.'

He regretted terribly that he had blabbed. He had been caught off-guard by the theft of the jewellery and the way she had put her arms round him. He had thought she might have an excess of sympathy to spill over this as well. Better for him to have seen the bank on the quiet, he might be able to smooth it over. She was still looking out of the window. Eloise had jumped on to the sill and was trying to peck her way through the pane of glass.

'Stupid hen,' said Laura. She turned round and looked at Geoffrey.

'What deeds does he refer to?' She spoke quietly.

He didn't answer.

She repeated her question. 'What deeds secured the loan?'

'The silence was broken only by the tap-tapping of Eloise's beak upon the glass.

'What do you think?' he said.

'The office, I presume.'

He hesitated and she knew at once that the truth was far, far worse.

'Not the house. No, no, not the house.'

He closed his eyes.

'Dear God.'

He started to bluster but faltered before the piercing look in her eyes.

Laura scanned his red, Anglo-Saxon face, his pale-blue eyes, the fair hair pulled over the top of his head. The scar on his cheek was white as always when he was upset. She saw in his face the indolence which was the bad side of his good nature. She saw the trusting confidence that came from six centuries of rooted yeomanry behind him. The solid belief in continuity. It is his ability to trust, she thought, that makes him obsolescent. Me too, perhaps, I trusted him. I should have known better. It's my fault as well. I've lived in my own world, happy to be surrounded by trivialities, my garden.

'You gave me a sandpit, a bucket and a spade,' she said. He looked perplexed. He could not guess what she meant yet it seemed strangely of a piece with the madness of the moment.

'What?' he said.

'What I mean is that you just let me spend my time playing in my garden.'

'You loved it.'

It was undeniably true. She had grumbled but had loved it, she had adored her escapist, fantasy world. A sudden surge of hate for herself battled with her contempt for Geoffrey and both emotions evaporated as quickly as they had come, leaving her winded.

She went out to pour a whisky for herself. It was not yet five o'clock and she never drank at this hour, not even when it was growing dark as now. She felt the whisky burn her throat and slide down sourly to join the cup of tea in her stomach, and shuddered.

'Why,' she said thickly, 'why forfeit the deeds and the house? You had money to cushion the business.'

'Then, not now.'

'What happened?'

'It got used. Eighteen months ago. We had to give collateral.'

'Surely we have some money to pay them off.'

He said nothing and then rallied.

'I'll sort it out with him.'

'How?'

'I'll sell something.'

'What?'

He was silent. The air went out of his face again; even his cheeks seemed deflated.

'We can't sell the house.'

'No one's talking about selling the house.'

'It's half a million you've got to find.'

'I'll get another bank in. No problem about that.'

'You're crazy.'

'We've got till spring. Banks will be desperate to lend.'

'Not with their record of bad debt.'

Geoffrey banged his glass on the table.

'What do you want me to do?' he shouted. 'Give up? Is that it? Just give up trying? Because I fucking well won't. They carry me out of here in a box or no way.'

He had drunk three glasses of whisky.

'You're drunk,' she said coldly.

He lunged near her and for a moment she thought he might strike her but it was just unsteadiness and he turned and left the room. She heard his footsteps smacking on the flagstones of the hall and then the loose board creaked in the television room across the way. She detected the faint sounds of what seemed to be an old Western film from the intermittent bang of guns.

Laura poured out the last two inches from the whisky bottle and walked to the little sitting-room in which they spent their winter evenings. She didn't turn on the light but went straight over to one of the old velvet armchairs and sat down. In the dusk she could just discern the pattern on a huge wall-tapestry with a dog and some partridges amidst an Elysian eighteenth-century scene. The last rays of light made the top of the lowboy gleam under the window. She counted the cushions she had made over the years for the chairs. Five of them. She thought fiercely how much she loved the place. Now the bank seemed to own it – she had made those five cushions for the bank.

After a while she thought how quickly one adjusted to a changed universe. Geoffrey had told her only an hour or so ago, yet the news already seemed an old familiar to her, an old enemy. Then she stopped thinking and just sat on in the gloom. Alone in her room, she could hear sounds of fresh gunfire from where Geoffrey sat alone in his room. Then the clock chimed in the hall. It was seven. Laura jumped up suddenly, remembering she had forgotten to feed and lock up the bantams.

Putting on her old gardening jacket, she went out of the back door and walked over to the shed to fetch wheat. As she turned back past the trees at the edge of the lawn, she saw a small hump of material and some outlying fluff. She broke into a run, dreading what she would find on arrival. The head of the little bantam was missing and some of the downy chestnut feathers had been pulled from her body. Unfed and hungry, Eloise must have been having a last foolhardy peck in the ground after dark and had fallen to the fox.

Tears of remorse and guilt poured down Laura's face. She put her hands over the tiny lifeless body which was still warm and wept into her fur.

10

'Oh, damn you, go away,' muttered Tessa as she went to answer the phone. It was the third interruption this morning and she was striving to concentrate. At least the telephone hadn't been cut off, a likely threat if she failed to settle the latest bill.

She was rushing to complete her first commission in years: an oil painting of scarlet poppies and Queen Anne's lace in a sunlit orchard. Even without distractions, it was hard to remember in winter all those early summer colours – hard but necessary when the commission represented a thousand pounds. This was a round figure that she found dazzling to contemplate for she had never before earned three noughts in a row for one painting.

'Oh, it's you,' she said when she heard Laura's voice. Then, 'Oh no, poor Eloise, quite ghastly,' then, 'Oh, oh,' then, 'Things seem bad at the time but they do pass.' Finally she said, 'You must let me know if I can do anything to help,' but she made a face as she spoke the anodyne formula, which was meaningless when proffered by her.

After a brief farewell she replaced the receiver and returned to her canvas, seething with *schadenfreude*. Her genuine sympathy had spent itself on the bantam, leaving only its alloy for Laura. She was both sorry yet not entirely displeased that one of life's little injustices should be rectified. She, Tessa, had been served a larger dose than was right of the nastier facts of life and the time was overdue for them to be spread more widely and thinly around her. Better if Laura were spared, but on any impartial view, she was ripe for plucking.

Tessa was disgusted with herself. For years she had successfully suppressed her sense of unfairness which she saw as an unworthy reaction of little people to the adversities of life. Magnanimity was in her view far nobler than faith, hope or charity though it was sometimes confused with the latter. Yet here she was feeling a sneaky sense of appropriateness in a friend's distress. So much for the noble spirit and capacious heart, both of which seemed to have done a bunk when tested.

'You horrible old hypocrite,' she said to herself, but she picked up her brush with gusto. She had a discomforting feeling that her picture would be a success.

In contrast, Rosy identified with her mother absolutely and it was a while before William could sort out the facts from the lamentation. 'Poor Mummy, poor Daddy, God how awful,' she kept repeating.

'Can't you do something?' she said to William who was changing his City suit for a jumper and jeans. 'You know so many people. Can't you get one of your merchant banker friends to help?'

William looked at her pityingly. Women who didn't work were so painfully naïve.

'Merchant bankers? Who do you think they are? Comforters?'

'Well, somebody, something,' she wailed incoherently. 'Can't you get him a proper backer or help in some way? Even bits and pieces would do. They've got some time in hand.'

William was going to say no. Privately he thought it was likely his father-in-law was receiving his just deserts. He had taken no interest in the business and would convince nobody of his commitment to its future. However, at that moment the realisation took root in William that it was his wife's, indeed his son's inheritance that was at stake, perhaps even their own future home. More than once he had visualised himself and Rosy owning the large, pink-brick Elizabethan house. In this game of 'just suppose' Laura and Geoffrey were conveniently absent: nothing painful or nasty had befallen his in-laws, they hadn't died or been injured in a car crash or anything distasteful of that nature, they were merely etherised for the purposes of William's dream, turned into insubstantial beings who beamed down on him and Rosy and Thomas from heaven.

'Well,' he said, struggling with the zip of his jeans, 'I might have a think.'

It wouldn't be easy, he thought. Nothing too risky, no commodities deals, no dicey derivatives, no currency speculation, yet with only a few months to go before the bank's written deadline, the chances of taking a worthwhile surge on straightforward equities were distinctly limited, not to say non-existent from the viewpoint of safety. Insider dealing was out: though possible, it was illegal and too easily exposed if he were to invest heavily in thinly traded stock. From any rational viewpoint, it was madness to get involved, but, he argued to himself, but, but, but, he was already immersed to his neck given his own, his wife's and his son's future interest.

Breathing heavily, his fingers tense and his muscles pumping iron at the thought of substantial gain or loss, he pushed and pulled unawares at his zip.

'Damn,' he said as the metal tag shot across the room and his jeans suddenly collapsed around his ankles.

*   *   *

Ranson stood in his kitchen, stirring a glass of hot Lem-sip with a metal spoon. He had arrived back from Beijing only a short while ago and was longing to go to bed. He had sat for five hours awaiting his plane in the freezing airport, nursing a heavy cold, dreaming of the moment when he would be tucked in his own flat, with his own pillows, own mattress, reliable lights and thermostatically-controlled central heating. The radiators in his hotel had burnt him to parchment and the lighting had blacked him out of existence.

Even the tedious drive from Heathrow to his flat had been transformed into luxury, compared with his previous fortnight's travels in China where his road speed had averaged twenty miles per hour in the wake of trucks, bicycles, carts and animals. Commercially it was to his company's advantage that there were no trunk roads linking east to west or north to south but, personally, his body had borne the brunt of these effects.

It had proved a highly successful trip but the reward/discomfort ratio of these tours was tilting heavily towards the latter as far as Ranson was concerned. He pined for the comforts of domesticity.

Sitting in the airport, a sudden vision had materialised in his head of a good roasted leg of lamb, spiked with rosemary, mashed potatoes, slim French beans and a slice of sharp gooseberry tart with a little pouring cream. His nostrils had flared at the memory of the food's sweet, clean, spring smell, his mouth watered a little and he closed his eyes, suffering a pang of profound deprivation. Extraordinary that twenty hours ago his brain and stomach could so collude to present him with a vision of precise taste and scent – yet now he was back, all he could face was Lem-sip. The body was undeniably perverse.

He went round the flat, turning on all the lamps to savour his simple appreciation that they functioned to perfection. He altered a valve or two on the radiators, taking an engineer's pleasure in the fine-tuning of a good machine. Then he took off his day clothes and slipped on his maroon and fawn silk dressing-gown. He felt somewhat better, rejected the idea of bed and instead turned on the television and pulled up a footstool to one of the big rust armchairs, where he subsided with his legs up.

He sat back in the cushions, watching the early evening news with the extra satisfaction that came from relaxing in comfort whilst being a spectator of another man's work. Two politicians and an economist paraded their statistics but Ranson, drifting into a state of greater mental peace than he had known for months, merely wondered why they were always perched in front of an ultramarine backcloth. Was this the deep, deep blue of the televisual universe?

The telephone rang, punching a hole in his tranquil cocoon. He decided against answering it, but when it stopped and started again his resolve weakened.

'Hello,' he said coldly, intimating his right to reject the caller.

It was a woman's voice, low, uncertain, even faltering. 'Leo,' she said softly, 'is that you?'

He hesitated, searching for a face to fit the voice, but there was no one of his acquaintance who could possibly match. Had he met someone abroad this autumn?

'Who is it?' he said without compromising the original coldness of his tone.

Even when she announced herself, it was so unexpected, so remote from his immediate surroundings, that there was a split second before she clicked into place.

'Laura,' he said in surprise, 'I never expected to hear from you.'

She sounded so shy, so easily rebuffed, that he regretted the coolness of his initial reply.

For a moment he listened, concentrating on her voice but watching the Home Secretary mouthing soundlessly on the television.

'Of course,' he said, 'next Tuesday. Come to lunch.'

11

Baba lay curled in her basket, squashed between the two other spaniels, inhaling the scent of warm toast mixed with the fruitiness of damp fur on a wet day. If she opened one dark eye, she could see her mistress gesticulating at her, swinging her lead encouragingly, like a plumb-line in the air. The word 'walk' registered among the general blur of human exhortation. It was unwelcome. As she and the pack were aware, it was raining heavily again which meant that walks were out of favour as far as they were concerned.

The pack's instincts were selective, sporadic and immovable. Not one dog intended to shift from its basket. Baba shut her eyes tightly. Just in case of any further human attempt to prise them open, she decided a second line of defence was necessary. She eased her front right paw from where it was squashed below the other dog's flank and folded it in front of her eyes. It was not quite high enough to shield her from the threatening world. She dipped her nose down into its crook, then a little bit more, and again, so that, by a process of trial and error, inching and wriggling it into place, she could use her paw as a blinker.

Laura abandoned the effort to get the dogs moving. Some good intentions were useless. Although she had pulled herself together since the other night and decided on a purposeful regime for all, so far it was working only on herself.

Ashamed of her behaviour towards Geoffrey and shocked by its consequences on the pet hen, she had determined to check any slide towards a catastrophe syndrome. Disaster might yet be averted and she too would fight to find a solution. It was a pity she had telephoned Tessa before her new resolve was firm. There was nothing more tactless than parading a set-back before someone who had less than the level to which you would plunge. From now on, no squealing, she told herself.

She had sat for ten minutes beside the phone before she rang Ranson. Shyness was one reason; embarrassment was another; a greater deterrent still was the odour of disloyalty that must hang about her initiative. Any disclosure of financial problems would betray Geoffrey, yet weighed against this was the fact that Ranson might be able to help. Although she knew nothing about him now, she trusted his experience, honesty, capability, commonsense and, above all, silence. That Ranson was discreet and trustworthy she had no doubt.

Yet in all this, she recoiled from the fact that she was acting behind Geoffrey's back. Secrecy was inevitable. If she had told him, he would have read it as a transfer of faith from himself to another, more successful man. Wounded in one area, he would be especially vulnerable in another.

Aware of the tightrope she was treading, Laura had resolved on a short, formal business lunch with Ranson in which she outlined the problems and sought his solutions. It would be an isolated occasion in which the conversation must be confined to objectives and means. It was however one thing to plan and another to enact, as her telephone call had warned her. Nerves had swept aside her matter-of-fact persona and emotion threatened her neutrality. The lunch loomed alarmingly large.

Meanwhile she strove to block it from her mind. She tried yoga, deep breathing and self-hypnosis. She told her muscles to go slack, her bones to dissolve and the loops of her brain to uncoil. She lay on the bed of the ocean and floated on clouds in the sky. When none of that worked, she gave up aspiring to real relaxation and settled for its pretence. A bland ease of manner was the most that could be accomplished. This she bestowed on Beth and Tom especially, now 'poor Beth and Tom' as they were called. Their jobs were linked to the house and it was horrifying that the plight of one would spell the ruin of the other. It may never happen, became Laura's mental refrain.

Though ignorant of any future threat, Beth was already in a lather of anxiety about the loss of the jewellery. Laura had warned her that the police would have to make systematic inquiries, but nothing prepared her for the humiliation of their visit.

'Two of them,' she told Tom, 'one who asked questions and one who watched.'

'It's nothing to do with you.'

'We all know that but that watcher made me feel guilty.'

'Since you're not, you shouldn't.'

'It doesn't work like that, does it?'

Beth walked heavily round the kitchen. She thought she had put on another half-stone since their interview and knew who to blame. How she hated the law. It had made her so anxious, she had eaten a whole cake after they had left. When she had visited the doctor, he had said, 'You're too fat.' No one had ever called her fat before. Sturdy, strong, well-built, sometimes 'one of our larger ladies' or, best of all, a 'weight-watcher', which she liked a lot. And even those leaflets in the surgery referred to obesity, which sounded at least like a dignified condition, but fat – fat was an insult.

'A fat thief,' she said to Tom, 'that's what that watcher was thinking, wasn't he?'

'That's right,' he said, 'a fat thief is helping us with our inquiries. Read all about it in the local rag.'

Tom rolled one of his cigarettes. Through its smoke he watched Gary swagger past the window to the shed. He had recently got a huge, new, glittering bike, black, star-dusted and sprouting tubes. It was too good for the lounge so Gary kept it like a pet in the garage. He wasn't at home much now but spent his time burning up the roads. He had at last mastered the biker's gait: bowlegged, jaunty and rather menacing. Both Beth and Tom had become a little frightened of their son. They felt they had spawned a monster, not of their genes, when they saw him mount his 850cc Yamaha steed, wearing boots, gauntlets, baseball shoulders and sci-fi dome of a helmet. Was he threatening because they were meek? Or did it work the other way round? It was a puzzle.

Beth wondered if she should decorate another room in peach, with some frilly Austrian blinds too. She felt she needed something extra feminine in her life after all these aggressive men – her son, the law and the doctor. What a good thing Tom was a wimp.

12 ∫

William sat in the office, watching the blue and red pattern of rising and falling shares on his screen. Behind him he heard the rhythmic clicks and rustles of Sasha Rachel walking down the aisle. All his senses strained to the back of him, alert to the scissoring motion of her long legs as she passed to the rear of his chair. A chilly Canadian, she was known as the Baked Alaska because she was ice without and, by reputation, fiery within. Carswell, an elite futures fund manager in the securities house, claimed they had had each other in the lobby downstairs. This defied belief since Carswell spent more of his time extolling the thrill of complex computer models than of women. Still, it was sufficiently credible for William to feel jealous: Carswell was the financial equivalent of an SAS officer and power was sexy. William disguised his envy by patting him on the back in the avuncular manner that befitted a husband and father, but he felt himself stiffen at the thought of the grapple.

Now, from the corner of his eye, he saw Sasha returning up the aisle clad in her red jumper and short, tight plaid skirt. Her heels tapped on the polished floor, their needle-tips grinding down before they sprang up from the surface. William was tempted to extend a foot into the aisle just to watch her tread on his brogue, mustering sinews and tendons to pulp his toes. What a bitch, he thought admiringly: you Sasha, me masochist.

All this was a distraction, he thought, a sexual tea-break from his task in hand: to find a vehicle for Geoffrey's remaining money, which had dwindled to a bare £70,000. He had considered giving it to Carswell for margin trading, but passing his father-in-law's kernel of cash over to the hazards of high-leverage dealing was the choice of a lunatic. It would involve anticipating correctly the amount of future rise or fall on a chosen main share, a challenge when the stock market was, as now, in one of its indecisive phases. A much safer approach would involve hedging his purchase of a stock, using the option as an insurance policy, but, again, he would be confined to a limited range of main stocks. This carried little allure for William who increasingly favoured the idea that his prey should be a smaller company stock, not a large one.

He had in mind a specialist American stock which was also listed on the London Exchange. It was not actively traded but he had followed the pattern of its movements and prices for the previous six months. Its reports were announced at quarterly intervals, which helped to concentrate investors' interest on the share. In addition, the plan had been announced to allow American investors to buy bundles of this UK share in the early spring. In the light of previous examples, it was likely they would pile into the stock, appreciating the arbitrage potential between the cheapness of the British price compared with its American equivalent. William had also noted that, over the last few months, each of the four directors had, one by one, purchased substantial shareholdings, a highly likely indicator of the future good performance of the stock.

All this added up to a most tempting cluster of attractions. After checking with an analyst friend about the sector's improving performance in the States, William felt confident. If he bought the shares, now standing at 25p, he could sell in March. With luck he might get a four hundred per cent rise or more on Geoffrey's cash. There was little doubt that the bank would accept this as part-repayment of the debt and delay foreclosure.

Although he was used to dealing with far larger sums of money than this and would not normally falter at the brink, the personal nature of the responsibility on this occasion made him nervous. His forehead felt sweaty: he rubbed it with the back of his hand and pushed back a dark lock of hair that had fallen forward. His neighbour, Tim, looked at him sharply.

'OK?' he asked.

William nodded smoothly. He thought of Rosy and Thomas. What were they doing now? It was eleven thirty mid-morning. I can see you, Thomas, he thought: shuffling around the kitchen, now on your round soft nappy bottom, now levering yourself upright on the soles of those two very wobbly pink feet, hoovering up as systematically as a puppy any crumbs on the floor, engrossed in life at the level of Rosy's ankles – amoeba, dust mites and fungi, how yummy.

Picturing his son's chubby face made William feel calmer: his breathing eased and the knot in the centre of his waist began to unravel. Go for it, he said to himself.

It had been a hell of a relief, thought Geoffrey, to deal at last with a man who was on his side. Thank God for William. It was only now that he recognised the overwhelming oppression he had previously suffered: how odd that its presence should become apparent only in its absence. Everyone had set themselves against him. I was triple-burdened, he recalled, by my sales manager, by the bank and, most of all, by Laura. The cumulative pressure was immense, culminating in that row the other night when they had sat drinking in separate rooms.

As he had slumped in his chair, gazing resolutely at the old Western film, the amount of whisky he was sinking had befuddled him into an unearthly *déjà vu* sensation of watching a cowboy film in his childhood. J.J., his best friend, was sitting beside him in the room, wearing his feathered Indian head-dress, a most covetable birthday present which had been denied Geoffrey on account of some long-forgotten but apparently serious misdemeanour. He remembered the pair of them in their long, grey shorts, half-concealing their little bony legs and white knees, always grazed – in J.J.'s case, the whole surmounted by his disproportionately huge quilled crown. Geoffrey had been transported back into his eight-year-old mind and body, suffused with the shame that he had been foolish, unworthy and found irredeemably wanting.

Is it any wonder, he now thought indulgently, that I have escaped every day in recent months to the golf course? A little outdoor cosseting was vital to the spirits. At such times one needed to reduce one's horizons to getting a white ball into a green hole: there were few other simple satisfactions that could be so precisely realised. Whack the ball from a distance, tap it in close-up, bull's-eye, score and repeat the procedure eighteen times in a landscape tamed to emerald velvet. Such were the ingredients to translate turmoil into peace.

However, now finally that his problems had been transferred to William's control, it looked as though they would be postponed or even resolved. One needed young men for their energy, verve and experience of that new, mysterious world which was so inaccessible to the middle-aged. How his local stockbroker had squealed when instructed to withdraw the last portion of funds, but what could he expect? His portfolio – already bled white in aid of the company – had been sitting still for the last year, costive and immobile in his broker's hands, yielding niggardly returns to its desperate owner. Little wonder when the chap was ageing, hide-bound, unimaginative and, to which I am witness, thought Geoffrey, forever on the golf course or propping up some corporate entertainment tent.

There had been only one short moment of doubt during his discussion with William. Was he following a wise man's course, Geoffrey wondered, putting all his funds into his son-in-law's scheme, which seemed to be founded on the promise of plans that were predicated but not actually under way. He had grave doubts whether Laura would approve – no doubts at all, in fact: it would bring out the scourge and the termagant, she would wash him away in a positive cascade of gloom and doom, and would scorch him at five hundred paces.

'Better say nothing to the women,' he muttered to William, feeling sheepish.

'Quite so,' replied William, suppressing the fact that Rosy was already partially in the know.

The matter seemed agreed, but, unbidden, a postscript rose in his mind. 'Will it work?' he said suddenly. He was reminded of asking his father as a child, 'Will it be all right?' William had nodded, then modified his gesture by lifting his black eyebrows and saying, 'It should do.' However, the difference between will and should was lost on an optimist and, in any case, shades of the subjunctive mood rarely if ever entered Geoffrey's calculations.

As his last remaining doubt was soothed to rest, the final lines of some stoic Victorian poem came into his head, much quoted by his father (why, he wondered, must he be assailed by so many ghostly memories?). How did it go?

> And not by eastern windows only,
> When daylight comes, comes in the light;
> In front, the sun climbs slow, how slowly,
> But westward, look, the land is bright.

13 ∫

Tuesday was freezing but it was sunny and the light was clear, suffusing the drawn curtains with gold in the east-facing bedroom. Laura had been watching the glow light up the flowery pattern on the drapes for the last hour, since she had woken long before dawn. Lying supine for what had seemed a lifetime she could feel electric currents running through her muscles, inside her stomach and up and down her limbs. She tried to lift her right foot in bed but it seemed leaden and paralysed, too weak to move the weight of the duvet above it. I have flu, she said to herself, I am ill, far far too ill to see Ranson today. As soon as the clock reaches a civilised hour I shall telephone him to cancel the lunch.

Geoffrey emitted a ripe snore and turned over on his right side towards her. He extended an arm automatically and curved his sleeping hand over her lower thigh. Her leg jumped: it didn't seem to be paralysed after all. She pondered why his mood was so vastly improved since yesterday. 'Why ever so?' she had asked him, grudging the buoyancy that seemed to elude herself. 'What would you prefer? Sackcloth and ashes?' he replied. Then, peering more closely at her, 'Obviously, yes.'

She forestalled the alarm before it rang at eight o'clock and inched out of bed trying not to wake him. Though trembling with cold, she felt better once upright and on the move. She closed the door quietly behind her in the bathroom and turned on the taps. The bath, a white Victorian pastiche with a rolled lip and claw feet, crouched in the centre of the large room like a sphinx. Steam now rose in geranium-scented clouds and floated upwards and outwards into the arena of empty space, settling on the windows like a fog.

Laura let herself gingerly into the bath. Soaping her arms and stroking the suds away with a slimy Greek sponge, she mused on the day ahead. It seemed to be taking place, since it had become annoyingly apparent she was not ill nor paralysed but simply plain scared. She was aware of being poised to breach a code of conduct to which she had always adhered by instinct and by training. I am about to commit disloyalty, she thought, offending manners, custom, not to mention honesty and integrity. In four hours from now, I reveal my husband's errors of judgment to the scrutiny of a former lover, so making the latter privy to the secrets of the former. The truth is I would kill Geoffrey if he did this to me. Could he have reached out and touched the outside of my body in bed this morning if he had known what the inside was planning? And whatever my best intentions, does the end justify the means when betrayal is involved?

She heard the sound of Geoffrey stirring in the bedroom, then the whirr of the curtain-rings on the pole as he pushed back the drapes to let the sun in. The wooden floorboards creaked slightly under his weight and there was a muffled thump as he dropped something heavy – one of his size ten shoes which weighed a ton? It's not too late, she thought, to ask his permission. Then the door banged and she heard him leave the bedroom and start to whistle tunelessly as he went downstairs. Laura realised at that moment that she could not bring herself to break whatever degree of contentment he had managed to achieve. If 'thou shalt not commit disloyalty' was the eleventh commandment, then 'dishonesty is sometimes the best policy' was the twelfth rule in adult life when black and white dissolve into grey.

With a freshly confirmed sense of purpose, she prepared for the day ahead. Eating a bowl of Shredded Wheat, she navigated her way through the A–Z of London streets to find the restaurant where they had arranged to meet, then left the kitchen to prepare.

Battling against vanity, she dressed swiftly to project an efficient and sensible appearance. Chucking aside soft suedes and furry coats, she settled on a serviceable camel wrap over a loose cream jumper and fawn skirt. No jewellery, not even pearls, and she smiled to herself, remembering Mrs Thatcher's pronouncement that pearls should be worn near the face to flatter the skin. As edicts go, it might not make the history books, but how boring male politicians were in comparison.

She caught a train timed to allow her to arrive at the restaurant at one o'clock without rushing, but there were delays on the line, then the cab crawled to a halt in the heavy pre-Christmas traffic. What dinosaurs these taxis were, hurry, hurry, she groaned. She was in a panic that Ranson would be short of time and if she arrived late would show her the door after five minutes. Her armpits felt damp and she sniffed them surreptitiously to see if the deodorant was winning its war against her nerves. It was: its pong resembled the spray used on bitches to deter dogs, and her mind slewed away from the horrible parallel.

Ranson was seated at the restaurant table when she arrived with a shower of apologies, which he brushed aside.

'I've only just arrived myself. I phoned them to say take care of you in my absence and found you weren't here.' He added, 'I thought you weren't coming. Second thoughts, perhaps.'

'Plenty of second thoughts, but then third ones reversed them.'

She looked round the restaurant, absorbing its geography to help herself settle in. It was simple and spacious with dove-grey walls, white damask table-cloths and mitred napkins, old-fashioned even, its whole quiet ambiance a guarantee that no chef would hurl a saucepan to prove its reputation. It was patronised by a mixed bag of diners. Most were businessmen clustered at well-spaced intervals, but at a longer table sat a group of seventy-year-olds enjoying a decorous celebration. Two of them had instantly recognisable public faces, though it was obvious that no guest came here to see or be seen. Even the most famous would have their anonymity assured.

Laura turned back to Ranson. He looked older and more tired than in the summer but exuded the solidity of the quietly confident man. It acted on her like a balm, calmness being as infectious as hysteria. Some lucky people were fitted with stabilisers, she thought ruefully, but those of us without must make efficient use of theirs.

'This is good,' he said, pointing to a salmon croûte amongst the starters on the menu.

'Do you eat like this every day?' She was impressed by the apparent quality of the food, whilst lacking any appetite for it.

'A sandwich usually, but this is an unexpected treat for me. It was a surprise to hear from you.'

Is he offering me a chance to explain, she wondered, but veered away by instinct. Only an amateur would come to the point this soon. It would be wiser to conceal her intentions. She started on another tack, prepared to plod through a trail of well-trodden preliminaries.

'What have I interrupted you doing today?'

'Going over blueprints.'
'You still love the work?'
'Not always, but I built it up, it's mine, ours, the team.'
'It's your entire life?'
'Ninety per cent of it now.' Ninety-nine really, he thought.

How different from Geoffrey, went through her mind. Work seen as a ruling passion, an absorbing occupation rather than a ticket.

'I suppose you disapprove.'

He was eating his salmon croûte, she noticed, in the rapid, concentrated way of all Englishmen who had been sent to boarding school. Geoffrey also still gobbled his food.

'Actually I think it's enviable.'
'Not one-sided?'
'No: huge, global, makes me feel very parochial.'
'You've changed.' He pushed aside his plate and raised the napkin to his lips. 'When I knew you before, you were rather po-faced when I kept going away.'
'Oh, then.' She disposed of it with a wave of her hand. 'I didn't know anything then.'
'What is this hard-earned wisdom, Laura?'

She turned her head aside and drew the corners of her mouth down. 'Don't mock.'

He grinned. It was nice to patronise a good-looking woman. It had been a long time.

'The fact is,' she was groping her way by instinct towards concealed flattery, 'it's *your* wisdom that I'm after.'

This was the kind of approach that always worked with Geoffrey. Ranson, however, recognised it instantly for what it was.

'This is a pick-your-brains lunch, is it?'

She flushed. 'I'm in trouble. I need your advice. Please.'

He spread his hands to show he was open to listening.

'My husband's firm makes agricultural machinery. Bad trading conditions have been a body-blow. The bank is pulling the plug. The house secures their loan. It's quite simple. In a few months' time there will be neither business nor house.'

Ranson sat back silently in his chair. It was a familiar enough story, but never failed to shock: foreclosure and bankruptcy were always violent events. In this case it seemed incredible, but how appearances always deceived. He felt horror and sympathy.

'Oh, Laura. That June afternoon I visited you. Do you remember? It seemed like an idyll – the most enviable Arcady. You knew then and of course you said nothing. How could you say anything.'

'I knew nothing.'

He was astounded. 'And your husband?'

She fell silent. She would not and could not implicate him. Ranson suddenly remembered the scene he had witnessed between her husband and his manager that afternoon. She had stated at the time that her husband ignored problems. Here, in her entirely innocent and unintended condemnation, lay the key. Ranson could think of nothing to say.

'All I need to know is – can anything be done?'

Could anything be done? Not when the root of the trouble lay years back and embedded in a character.

'I can tell you what not to do. No desperate gambling. No idiotic last-minute excesses in a salvage attempt.'

'My husband would never do something like that.' She strained to preserve Geoffrey's dignity.

'Damage limitation is your only option.'

He wondered whether to show the extent of his pessimism. If the bank wouldn't support the fellow after knowing him for years, it was a vote of no confidence which would not be contradicted by anyone else. A younger man might have milked the assets, gone bankrupt and started all over again, but not this one.

Ranson felt no sympathy for him now he knew the origin of the trouble. Of all the biblical parables that his generation had absorbed in infancy, he remembered only one. The story of the servants with ten pieces of money. One man had wasted his portion, another improved his, but the third, the good and faithful servant, multiplied his tenfold. It was a biblical oddity, this one, endorsing the truths of the market-place whatever the intention of its metaphor. Geoffrey was the first man; he, Ranson, was the third. He had never felt sympathy for the weak servant, only contempt.

He looked across the table at this lovely, sheltered woman who was facing everyday realities for the first time in a life of ease. He thought, how different it could have been.

'You've eaten nothing.' He spoke reproachfully. 'I shan't bring you here again.'

It was true. She had just pushed the duck around the plate and nibbled a few broccoli flowers. Forty quid down the drain, not that it mattered. He was happy just to see her, though not in trouble.

He reached across the table-cloth, took one of her hands and gave it a brief stroke to counteract the harshness of his words. 'There is no easy answer. Some businesses could set up abroad but not yours. An export operation would cost too much.'

'Even with another backer? Can't we get another backer?'

Again, he thought to himself that there was not a chance. How to tell her that Geoffrey would have to lay out his failed stall before a group of unemotional predators. One could not expect him to be a street-fighter but his type was now ready for the mincing-machine.

'Sometimes one has to let go gently. Keep what one has and let the rest slip away.'

'It's almost everything we have.'

He felt desperately sorry for her and doubly saddened to have dashed her hopes. The white knight of Stamford Street, he thought dryly, becomes the messenger of bad news. All he had achieved was to turn expectation into despair. He could read in her face a pattern that he recognised from his own years of experience. How often as a younger man he had gone to a meeting expecting an optimistic outcome, an alchemist's solution, a stroke of luck, an opportunity for magic. How rarely it came.

He was sad for himself too, doubting whether she would want to see him again. He was surprised at the depth of his feeling, aroused no doubt by the fact that she had sought out his help. That act was in itself emotionally involving, bonding him to her troubles, fusing pity with his lingering affection.

'Laura,' he said, 'it's important that you let me know what's happening. I don't have a ready answer but I might be a helpful support.'

'That's very kind indeed.' She gave the most public of smiles.

'I don't deserve that.'

'What?'

'That hostessy manner.'

She said something that he lip-read as sorry but it was so quiet that it failed to reach across the small table.

Across the room, the group of ageing celebrants lifted their glasses and several rose to their feet. 'Happy ever after,' said a guest with cropped white hair to the man and woman in the centre of the table.

'They must have just got married,' said Laura. 'How long will happy ever after last at that age?'

'Don't even begin to think of that,' said Ranson. 'It's

wonderful. Be glad they have married in time. It's all about optimism.'

She stared at him and he stood accused of having drained her meagre supply.

As the restaurant began to stir and empty, he was reminded to look at his watch. He would have to leave for his next appointment but groaned at leaving her alone.

'I'll telephone you at home to see what's happened.'

She shook her head. 'Not a good idea.'

'Your husband does know you're here?'

'No.'

'Ah. Will you telephone me?'

'I'm not sure.'

She won't, he thought, and felt a violent surge of irritation.

'You can't just disappear,' he said. 'Not now that I've found you again.'

She looked uncompromising: there was a fixity about her jaw.

'You will phone, won't you?' he reiterated.

'In due course.'

He found her infuriating, fobbing him off with a formula. They walked out of the restaurant together and stood in the street, suddenly sobered by the clear, icy air. It reminded Laura of her manners and she began to thank him profusely, gushing the formalities of politeness.

'Don't,' he said, embarrassed.

He hailed a passing taxi for her and opened the door. He put his arms around her for a quick hug but it was like clasping a stone. His cheek rested briefly against her cold face.

'So chilly,' he said, then repeated, 'Ring me,' but he did not like his role as receiver of calls that would not come.

'You've been so kind,' she said again.

'Don't,' he repeated, wanting to shake her. He watched

the taxi putter down the street, wishing he could have warmed her back to life.

Laura slumped back in the taxi feeling like a train that had hit the buffers. Only this morning she had been frightened of being disloyal, yet now she had proved naïve as well. Watching one rock, she had ignored another and managed to hit both to no purpose. Ranson had been gentle, tender even, but it was manifest that there was no Elastoplast for a long history of mismanagement. What had she expected? An angel in daylight? The reality was that they must surrender everything, retaining only that last resort of failure which was an intact dignity.

The taxi drove briskly enough through the side streets of Victoria, making its way towards the station past the decayed stone façades which alternated with pockets of expensive gentrification. At the corner of Hugh Street she noticed but did not register a tall girl with long, dark hair who was having difficulty entering a car as she was heavily pregnant. Her profile was half-turned away and the taxi had sped a hundred yards up Warwick Way before Laura realised through the fog of her thoughts that it was Allegra. Shocked, she leant forward and told the driver to stop, but when she turned to peer through the rear window, the car carrying Allegra had moved off in the opposite direction. Ordering the cab-driver to continue, Laura felt stunned. Allegra with a baby, their grandchild, how could she have concealed it? Suppression of the truth was crueller than lying.

At the same time, she thought bitterly that the baby explained Allegra's silence. No wonder she had avoided them for months. Was it so surprising she had failed to return telephone calls? She would not relish the catechism that would follow when her family learned of the child. Are you married? Do you have a permanent home? A proper man? (What was that nowadays?) A proper job? (What right would Geoffrey have to ask that now?) How will you bring it up? (Do I have a right to ask that, seeing how Allegra has developed?)

What is happening? thought Laura. Without degrees of control, the very stuff of life went haywire, chaos became rampant and discord the norm. It was a lesson she should have learned from the garden where every movement was anticipated and each ingredient cut and subdued. It was a lesson that Ranson had evidently learned and this difference between them made her doubt whether she could see him again. It crushed her confidence that he knew how to live, whilst she had so signally failed. They could no longer meet on equal terms when his successful life was ill-matched by her weakness. The more he had pressed to speak to her again, the more vulnerable she had felt. When he had hugged her she had been close to tears, a poor recompense for an hour of his patient attention.

Ranson was striding to a meeting in a hotel with Mr Hatano. He had halted his taxi to walk the last half-mile through St James's Park, which was always soothing on a fine day. A cooling-down process had been called for. No getting involved, he told himself: there could be no question of living another adult's life. Besides, human problems were messy and he had learnt from his marriage to Natalya that the mess was ever ready to spread and extrication a challenge. He had been in danger over lunch of forgetting the rules of sensible conduct. It was simple to negotiate these when sober and easy to forget them when drunk. A lovely woman, in trouble, seeking help, combined with a shared past was the most inebriating of all cocktails. He must take care to avoid getting tipsy.

14

The following day Louisa suffered a small stroke, so tiny that its origin was disputed, not least by herself. It was a touch of flu, she told Laura when she went to visit her in hospital. 'It was a stroke, Mummy,' said her daughter but Louisa would have none of it. Strokes were a sign of age and infirmity; flu was more dashing, a high-octane illness which was here today and gone tomorrow, scything young and old in its path.

Regardless, however, of the cause of the trouble, Louisa recovered swiftly and by the end of the week she was suffering more from high dudgeon than ill-health.

'Do calm down,' Laura pleaded.

Louisa was sitting in a chair in the Wedgwood-blue painted hospital ward with ten women at various stages of convalescence. She grasped the *Daily Telegraph* and the change of clothes Laura had brought her: a sage-green twinset and a gun-check skirt.

She had ordered her string of pearls but her daughter, dismissing this as ridiculous, had substituted her fanny flannel. She handed it silently to Louisa in a plastic bag, but even this trophy failed to console her.

'Look at my hair,' Louisa said through her teeth.

'What's wrong?' It looked clean and white, obviously newly washed and set.

'Can't you see?' wailed Louisa.

'It was a tighter style than usual, but that couldn't be the trouble. 'Not nits, surely?' she whispered squeamishly.

'Nits? Nits? That at least would be gamey. No, nothing to do with nits. Don't be absurd. Have another look.'

Laura was nonplussed.

'Can't you see how she's set it?'

It was true it looked different. Her thick white hair was normally blow-dried in slight waves parting over her high forehead with the elegance of symmetry. By contrast it was now crimped into curls. Was this cause for a crisis?

'She's put it in tiny rollers.' Louisa felt close to tears. 'I'm covered in sausages just like a bingo addict.' Her voice cracked with despair. First the hospital misread her illness, then its hairdresser destroyed her style. The error of taste was almost harder to bear than the diagnosis.

'Mummy, how can you worry about trivialities like this? All that matters is that you come home well.'

'That's another point,' said Louisa grimly, raising her voice. She felt she had to shout to be heard against the television set which had been turned up to full volume for the sake of the deaf.

'Which home?' she emphasised. 'I think it's time I moved into my green-and-white bedroom in your house.'

'They say you're perfectly well. They've given you all the basic tests and confirm you're in good health, able to carry on in your flat as before.'

'That's as may be, but flu can strike again without warning.'

'It wasn't flu,' said Laura, for the umpteenth time. 'IT WAS A TINY STROKE.'

A young nurse appeared in her blue check uniform. It was amazing how its top managed to weld her two separate breasts into a single solid ledge. It contributed to her robust and bossy appearance.

'Have you opened your bowels today?' she asked briskly.

Louisa looked as though she had been impaled. 'What a question to ask in front of a visitor. Don't they teach you any manners these days?'

'I'm only your daughter,' murmured Laura.

'She doesn't know that.'

'Yes or no,' persisted the girl.

'Yes.'

'She's very difficult,' muttered the nurse in an aside to Laura. 'She threw her pills across the room.'

'I'm sorry.' Laura felt she was expected to apologise for her mother. Louisa was indeed difficult and now wasn't the moment to tell her that there would soon be no green-and-white bedroom at all.

'Look,' she told her mother, 'you must stay here till they're confident they can send you out. You can come to us for Christmas.'

'Christmas,' Louisa exclaimed. 'I can't stay here a moment longer. They've put me in with the morons. They're all gaga here.'

'For God's sake, keep your voice down.' Two of the nearest old ladies had started to peck and twitter around them. 'Can't you play a card game or something?'

'A card game? None of them has ever played bridge. Even if they did, they couldn't remember their own names, let alone a hand of cards.'

The lack of smart elderly people was clearly proving an intolerable burden. Glumness settled upon her like bad weather moving in.

'Well,' said Laura, 'we'll have to see.'

She knew the next thing Louisa would suggest was a nursing-home. She wasn't quite sure whether her mother's private health policy ran to a fortnight's continuing care. If not it would be impossible for Geoffrey to stand the cost.

'How is Amy?' she asked to change the subject. It was an impolitic move.

'Insufferable. Would you believe it? She sent me her latest novel this morning.' Louisa dived into her basket where it was concealed under a scarf. 'Look.' It was entitled *The Hair of the Dog*, the cover showing an Edwardian house with a woman in the foreground, wearing pre-war slacks, sun-glasses and a bandana.

Laura opened the front cover. Inside an inscription ran: 'Dear Louisa, what bad luck to have a stroke. This is to help you get over it. Love Amy.'

'What's she want to do?' asked Louisa plaintively. 'Give me another bout of flu?' She closed the cover with a snap and was about to return it under wraps when the young nurse returned.

'I gave that to my mother for her birthday,' she said. 'She loves them.'

Laura was about to explain the relationship when she saw Louisa's face.

'So do we, don't we?' she said, patting her mother's knee.

Driving home, Laura decided she had been wise to avoid mentioning Allegra's child. The knowledge that a new member of the family was on its way into the world might have reminded Louisa that she was on her way out, shunted further towards the exit by the advent of a baby. In any case, it might well be true, for the stroke must be seen as a warning. No one was immortal. We've all got to go, thought Laura: the pet sheep made a habit of it, so did the ducks, doves, the bantams (she winced and moved rapidly on through the list), then there's me and Geoffrey, it was only a question of timing.

This is morbid, she thought, negotiating a tricky bend on the Tunbridge Wells road in the afternoon rain – though it wasn't morbid at all, but actually quite cheering for a reason that didn't bear contemplation. Somewhere in the murky penumbra of her brain, thoughts of death were inextricable from expectations of money. If winter comes, can spring be far behind? Just suppose, one day, far into the future, and of course one didn't want it to happen, but just imagine if Louisa had a proper stroke, a real corker of a death-dealing stroke (let her not suffer, she wouldn't actually know anything about it), well, the question was, would there be much to inherit? Whatever it was, as an only child she, Laura, should have sole receipt.

But would she? The alarming thought struck Laura that there were other fish in the sea. One could not read the *Daily Telegraph* these days without being bombed by advertisements coaxing a portion of one's will. Indeed, she herself had nearly succumbed to the National Trust's invitation to make a legacy: 'I hasten to enclose the material that you asked for,' ran their reply to her request for information. What if Louisa responded? Worse still, what if *everyone* hastened to enclose wordings for bequests? Suppose Louisa was beguiled into leaving a chunk to these fortune-hunters on the assumption that her only child was too rich to be in need. Laura broke into a sweat at the very thought. The world was positively teeming with scavengers and she had actually given a copy of the *Telegraph* to Louisa. My God – bored, power-mad and pulling rank before the ward, she might *at this very moment* be signing away part of her daughter's future inheritance. The devil made work for idle hands. A veritable scattershot of legacies could be soaring out of reach.

Laura slammed on the brakes in reflex to the thought that she must return immediately to the hospital. A furious tooting behind brought her back to the reality that she was more likely to die than Louisa at this rate. Still, perhaps the time had arrived sooner rather than later to confess that they would be penniless. Any inheritance must be safely nursed until it was tucked up, warm, safe and sound in Laura's account with the blanket pulled over its head.

That evening Laura rang Allegra, once to no avail, then a second time but only to be offered a chilly welcome. Yes, she was pregnant, and in good health, no she had no need of help at the moment, and no, she couldn't come home for Christmas. At what point, wondered Laura, did commendable self-sufficiency become plain cold-fishiness? Still, a meeting was essential. It was the now-or-never moment for a fresh effort to entice her back within the family fold. Once upon a time I could have opened the door and said hurry up and come in, I shall count to ten, she thought wistfully; but the era of carrots and sticks was past. The one hope was that a child of Allegra's own would break down her intransigence. Surely the gush of calming hormones would turn hostility into love and, besides, it was Christmas, a psychologically opportune moment to melt anger into goo.

In any case, even if Allegra didn't need her, the infant did. It was an old principle that a child should be given roots and wings: the latter were not in doubt but the former would be vestigial. They would be weak little stunted roots without that cosy web of relationships, the warm clucking and nuzzling that kin alone could provide.

The more she brooded, the more anxious she became and the more frightened of failure. She telephoned Rosy.

'It won't work if I go and see her,' said Laura adamantly.

'I know what you're angling for,' replied her daughter. 'You want me to be the one to do the visiting.'

'You'd do it better than I would. Besides, you have Thomas.'

'You don't want me to take Thomas to see her?' Rosy was horrified.

'A baby might break the ice.'

'Hell,' said Rosy, 'we'll just be a pair of decoy ducks.'

'Have a little try. Just a teeny-weeny itsy-bitsy little try.'

'Don't baby-talk me,' said Rosy, incensed.

She was reluctant to agree. She had vague forebodings in the back of her mind that the situation would start to resemble that of the prodigal son. Was it possible that Allegra would be welcomed home as the prodigal daughter? Hell, there was no point in being a saint if sinners were so amply rewarded. Then a second point struck her with even worse implications. If Allegra did return to the family, she would be set fair to cause a dual eclipse, obliterating not only herself but, with her child-to-be, darling Thomas. What a double swipe to oust both from the spotlight of their family's affections. It was a position Rosy had taken for granted until now. How infuriating. Too awful used to be her schoolgirl verdict on things: too awful just about summed it all up.

'You're sure you want me to see her.'

'Rosy, she's your sister.'

But I don't like her, she wanted to say. I think she's horrible. She doesn't deserve this attention. I'm fed up with being Goody-two-shoes and mopping up the messes.

'All right,' she said instead.

15

How truly ridiculous, thought Rosy the following day. How do you arrange a meeting between two sisters who choose to avoid each other? It couldn't be planned (Allegra would never co-operate). It couldn't be accidental-on-purpose (she wouldn't loiter outside her door). All she could do was visit her at a time when she was likely to be there. Rosy made a grimace to Thomas who was spooning banana over his bib. Well, the sooner the better, she decided, tomorrow in fact: they would have a treat afterwards, medicine first and jam second in the way they had done things as children, which meant it felt right.

William had suggested a dawn raid and, in the darkness of the following early morning, it seemed an appropriate description for the visit to London.

'What the hell shall I say?' Rosy asked William, as she hurried to dress. Damn, all her underwear was in the wash. She would have to put on the previous night's lot. She picked up a pair of pants from the chair and sniffed their crotch delicately. Could she get another day's wear out of them? She decided she could.

'That's easy. You are passing her flat because you're taking Thomas to see Father Christmas at Harrods.'

She shook her head sadly. How could he be so psychologically inept?

'Harrods! She'll slam the door in my face.'

She pulled on her leggings and drew a long Jacob's wool jumper over her head. It smelt of winter damp. These ethnic materials felt as if they came straight off the animals in the fields. She wondered if she was dressing subconsciously for Allegra. Really, clothes as a peace-offering, whatever next?

She drove slowly to London, stopping only to buy a pot of white cyclamen which would serve as an apology for her visit. It was a tiring trip, spent trying to wheedle Thomas into a cheerful state of mind. He had slept badly and his right cheek was scarlet because he was teething. She kept glancing at him anxiously: a scratchy child would be worse than no infant at all. Desperate to forestall a build-up of grizzles, she kept up a running commentary on the journey with lots of vroom-vrooms when she accelerated, whees when she turned corners and woof-woofs at every passing dog. Despite all the energy she was expending, Thomas began to cry by the time they reached Streatham High Street.

'Oh no, not grizzles, please, please don't grizzle. Up into the cherry tree, Who should climb but little me, I held the trunk with both my hands, And looked abroad on foreign lands.' She gave a shudder at Robert Louis Stevenson's little jingle but it seemed to work as a bromide.

By the time they arrived at Victoria she felt utterly exhausted. The last drop of vitality had been squeezed, yet the main show had not even begun. She turned off the engine and gathered herself into being a coherent adult again, then unstrapped and lifted Thomas out of his seat. He smelt niffy, upset no doubt by a sleepless night and the journey. That goes for me too, she thought. She kissed his scarlet ear which felt hot to her touch and sat for a moment in the car, unwilling to leave the safety of their own little Volkswagen world.

She walked to the house, knocked on the door, then realised she would have to press the personalised buzzer. There was a long wait before Allegra opened it. Despite the anticipation, it was surprising to see her and even a slight relief. Rosy felt guilty of demonising her in her absence; her presence seemed a reassurance that she was human after all. The two sisters looked at each other. Allegra was wearing a long black and brown cotton gown and, although heavily pregnant, she held herself erect. Rosy felt a familiar pang at the unfairness of her physical beauty. There was a dark gloss to Allegra that had always made her own prettiness just ordinary.

'I was just passing.' It sounded like the idiotic lie it indeed was.

'Passing where?' Allegra showed no sign of pleasure or surprise but just raised her eyebrows.

'Oh, you know, chores for Ma.' I must be sucking up to say Ma, she thought, when I always call her Mummy.

'I was half-expecting one of you but what exactly do you want?'

'To see you. Hurry up and let us in. It's cold here.' It was: her teeth had begun to chatter but maybe that was just nervousness.

Rosy followed her into the ground-floor flat. She was ravenous with curiosity but felt inhibited from staring around overtly. She took in her impressions piecemeal, darting little furtive glances about the room. Though naturally demonstrative, she was silent: she had hit an atmosphere that stifled exclamation. There was an emptiness about the room that was chilling, a minimalism founded on bare boards, steel, metal, blinds not curtains, and not a shred of decorative clutter. In the corner lay *The Tibetan Book of the Great Liberation* with a picture of the great guru Padma-Sambhava on the jacket. It was the home of a stranger. What did one say to strangers?

'May I have a coffee?' That was surely right: one broke bread with strangers to turn them into friends.

'We don't have it. Not even Nicaraguan.'

Bloody hell, thought Rosy. As a broker's wife, she was prepared to see coffee as a commodity, but not as a political statement too.

'What else do you have? Tea would be fine. We'd like tea, wouldn't we?' She addressed Thomas as her best friend in an alien world.

Allegra moved off and Rosy followed her into the kitchen, which was much cleaner and neater than her own. It smelt of cumin and coriander. She saw Thomas's nose begin to wrinkle at the unfamiliarity of the smells and she began bouncing him rhythmically up and down on one arm. Her other was still holding the cyclamen. It seemed a bit late to offer her the potted plant but no earlier opportunity had presented itself. Rosy put it silently down on the surface. It would be the only living creature for miles around. She thought it would die soon. Allegra boiled the kettle and passed her a cup of some fawn herbal-looking brew. Ah good, thought Rosy wryly, just what I've always wanted but been afraid to ask for.

'It's hibiscus, in case you're wondering. Why are you actually here?'

Allegra led the way back into the living-room. Rosy had been on the brink of a volley of small talk. She scudded to a halt. Her sister waited. Her stillness was unnerving.

'Ma asked me to call on you. She's worried about your child.'

'But I've already told her – we're fine.'

'She needs reassurance. Can't you see that?'

Allegra said nothing.

'We don't even know the father.'

'I live with him.'

Read that as it's not your business, thought Rosy.

'Can't we meet him?'

We, we, always we, thought Allegra. 'He's not here.'

'Well, even if he's not around, Ma says please come home for Christmas.'

'Christmas?' Allegra indicated the picture of Padma-Sambhava. Rosy fell silent. The cross-legged great guru stared back at her from the book jacket. There didn't seem much point in banging on about Christmas to a Buddhist. Rosy sipped her tea, thinking about those sweet-faced Tibetan monks with their saffron robes and smiles filled with love and serenity. Only her sister could manage to be a nasty Buddhist.

'When is it due?' She was trying a new tack.

'In two months' time.'

'How lovely. You must be looking forward to it. Of course, the birth's awful. You feel as if your arms and legs are blowing off.'

'Rosy – sorry, are you back to being Ros these days – do, please, stop trying to make conversation. You do see there's no point, don't you?'

Rosy put down her cup of tea, stung by the suggestion that she assumed personalities with each change of name.

'You don't seem to understand. Even if you don't have a family, Mummy wants you to realise that your child does. It has an aunt, an uncle, a granny and a grandfather, a great-granny and here is its cousin.' She thought of lifting Thomas's hand as if he were present and correct, but instead she let him sit passively smelling on her lap. Unfortunately, as cousins go he was not at his most desirable. Still, Allegra ought to take some notice of him. She hadn't touched him, she hadn't smiled at him.

'You haven't even looked at Thomas,' said Rosy, bursting with indignation. 'Don't you think he's grown? He can say his first words now. Pony, Mama, Papa.'

Allegra moved away and turned her back to look out of the window. She reeked of disapproval which caused Rosy to feel as smelly as her son. What had made her so cold and strange? Most sisters would now be all girls together, sharing their baby clothes, laughing over old family photographs, tucking into scrambled eggs and saying over and over again 'do you remember'. Instead how different each was from the other. Two peas in a pod, the same gene pool, the same house, same education and upbringing but, so early on, the two parallel trajectories had started to diverge and were now committed to opposite directions. Once upon a time they had quarrelled, but by now their lives were too far apart for even that degree of engagement. Now they simply couldn't talk. Having children had not brought them together but confirmed they were thrust permanently apart.

Rosy picked up Thomas, burying her face in the soft pillow of his cheek. A flush of hate shot through her. Allegra had rejected her most precious offering; her dearest, darling baby son who hadn't even cried when he had every cause to bawl his head off. Teething, short of sleep, juddered by a car-ride at the crack of dawn, stuck in an empty flat stinking of garam masala with an aunt who rejected both him and Christmas. She loathed her. It was humiliating and she would leave.

'Don't worry, we'll see ourselves out,' she said. Then, as an afterthought, 'We're off to see Father Christmas at wonderful Harrods where we're going to buy millions of toys.'

She slammed the door. Allegra leant against it and closed her eyes. She felt a spasm of shame but knew it must be endured. Resistance was always hard and renunciation always contested. They would only believe in her separateness if she maintained it: and only if she maintained it could she keep separate. I must not be like them, Allegra thought, as so often, to herself. I have them within me and hate it and have always fought it. Poor Thomas, what chance did he stand? She could have hugged him had he not been the bait. So small, so vulnerable, so imprinted to say Mama and Papa, soon when his father asked him what he would be when he grew up, he would say a banker. Oh, the cloying tentacles of family life. Come into my parlour, says the mother to the girl. She put her hand over her bulge. I promise I shall never do this to you, she pledged.

An hour later Rosy stood in the queue for Santa's grotto. Happy for the first time that morning, she was jostled by over-excited children and their warier parents, praying that their offspring would not call Santa's bluff.

'And what shall we ask him to give you for Christmas?' she said to Thomas, adjusting the toggles on his green wool jacket. 'You can forget about getting a cousin, but a little brother instead? A baby sister? A rocking-horse would be easier still. I think he's got it in his sack.'

Behind her in the queue, the father of a small bespectacled boy leaned forward and touched her arm. 'Swap?' he suggested. 'Mine wants a slurry machine.'

16

It now looked as if this would be the last Christmas they would spend in the house. Laura expected it to feel like a mortal blow but, to her surprise, the threat of the death sentence made her rally. She found herself thinking that if this was truly the last Christmas, then she must make it a wonderful occasion. It was the season when you looked backward to a happy past, not forward to a bleak future. The New Year would be grim, but as long as she didn't have to turn the corner into January she could manage to be happy. Christmas was a bulwark against the coming year and, if the secret of enjoying yourself was a short-term outlook, Laura was determined to live solely in the present. This time they would have the quintessence of Christmas.

In recent years all the preparations had been a nuisance rather than a pleasure, but for once she threw herself into a frenzy of enthusiasm. She hung a wreath of pine cones and holly on the door; she veiled the fir tree in the hall with a scattering of silver stars; she bought huge crackers, which for years had been a banned substance; she pushed the dried apricots and muesli to the back of the larder and filled their place with two round Christmas puddings. She put sprays of pink scented viburnum in the bedrooms for Amy and James, for Louisa, and for Rosy, William and

Thomas, and she picked nosegays of garrya and winter jasmine for the rest of the house. She filled the big vases on the window-sills with the bushy tails of pine branches. Nothing was too much trouble; the rituals of preparation made her feel safe. As long as you repeated yourself year after year, everything would stay exactly the same.

It was normal on Christmas Eve for the whole family to arrive before dinner, a yearly tradition. It was also an annual custom for them to eat first, then host the church choir of carol singers before sending them on their way to midnight mass with a small cheque, mince pies and mulled wine. This was an obligation that Geoffrey had inherited from his father. An easy-going traditionalist in most respects, Geoffrey had been happy at first to shoulder his duties, even relishing his role as the owner of the big house. However, his acceptance had begun to wear thin at an early stage and, quite soon, this custom of *noblesse oblige* had started to irk him. It now infuriated him, but – lacking the social courage to change it – he had confined himself over the years to tinkering with its edges. Accordingly his treatment of the 'load of bloody beggars' as he called them became increasingly brusque as time went by. Some Christmases he relented, when he liked the vicar, thought him a man and approved of his Authorised Version. But since the advent of the cleric with the black beard, the pace of the annual war of attrition had been stepped up. In practice this meant that in recent years the ceremony had been pared down, or 'refined' as Laura preferred to see it. The three carols were reduced to one; the glass of mulled wine turned into instant coffee; the mince pies were replaced by biscuits; and the cheque began to suffer from melt-down. Last year Geoffrey had even demoted the carol singers from the drawing-room hearth to a perch in the hall. In all this, Laura had egged him on, happy to hand him the ammunition but afraid to discharge it herself.

This year Geoffrey had been nursing a further refinement. He planned to keep them in the porch: with any luck it would rain. Just suppose it really was the last Christmas he would spend in the house (and of course it wasn't, he corrected himself automatically, thanks to William), then he intended for once and all time to win his guerrilla war. I'm not *noblesse*, he thought to himself, and I'm buggered if I'm going to oblige.

When Christmas Eve arrived this time, plans went as usual. The family ate a late cold dinner in the kitchen, then progressed to the drawing-room. Waiting for the knock on the door at eleven o'clock was the only thing that kept Geoffrey awake all evening. It came dead on time, accompanied by the usual rendering of 'O come all ye faithful'. Geoffrey leapt up, primed for action. 'It's the porch this time. One carol, one biscuit, nothing to drink and a cheque invisible to the naked eye,' he said triumphantly to Laura.

'Please, no, don't do it. Not this year. Give them a decent time.' She felt tears start behind her eyes.

Geoffrey was horrified. The woman was awash with emotion. What a turncoat. He felt on the point of exploding. 'You don't understand. This has taken fifteen good years of my life. Fifteen years of tactical strategy. I reckon this is the last year. They won't inflict it on us next year.'

'That's just it. It may be the last time. Let's do it properly.' She was whispering in case the others overheard her.

He looked at her aghast. He might have expected this. She was a pastmaster at dashing the cup from his lips, whether it was in sex, food or – as here – battle.

'Gob-smacked,' he muttered. 'I've spent fifteen years inching myself to the point of victory, and now you stop me. Who's side are you on?'

Laura clasped his arm, walked by him and opened the door.

'Welcome,' she said, looking at the ring of freckle-faced angels, at least two of them social problems. 'It's lovely to see you. Come in, warm yourselves and have some mince pies.'

A glint of triumph flickered in the curranty eyes of Smethwick, the churchwarden, who was standing at the rear. It did not go unnoticed. From behind Laura there came a muffled explosion: it was Geoffrey sounding the retreat. The Fifteen Years War was lost.

Christmas Day promised to be perfect. Hoar frost, a rare occurrence, had fallen on the garden in the still air overnight, bordering each leaf and twig with a hard, glistening diamond edge. Such effects were usually fleeting, the strange glittering patterns melting as soon as the sun gathered strength. Laura peered out from the bedroom window and decided to go at once into the frozen garden. No one else was up, though she could hear chirrups from her grandchild and a grumbling undercurrent from Amy and James's bedroom, which was their normal manner of conversation.

Fortified with a mug of tea and a Swedish greatcoat pulled on over her nightdress, she walked out of the front door into the frozen silver and green world. There was no wind. The steam from the tea hung absolutely still. Nothing moved, not a leaf, not a bird, only the dogs trailing the scent of an overnight fox who had left his Indian file of tracks on the frosted grass. She followed his footprints into the sheep paddock to feed them their mangerful of hay, an everyday winter task which assumed a biblical flavour on Christmas Day. The smallest ewe, a woolly ball who disappeared within her coat in the cold months, butted her impatiently. Like the others at this time of the year, she looked more like a teddy bear than a sheep.

The pond had frozen over, though not quite, as the

warmth and paddling of the ducks and swans kept a small area near the edge at a liquid temperature. Seeing Laura, they honked and quacked, tumbling and skidding and sliding across the ice towards her. She scattered the bowl of grain she had brought for them over the frozen surface where they were joined by a robin who pecked beside the feet of the huge swans, like a pilot fish amongst whales. What will become of you all? she wondered, before banishing all thoughts of the future to where they belonged next year. Today was dedicated to pleasure.

She returned to the house, where she laid the table for Christmas lunch in the wood-panelled dining-room. A white damask cloth, napkins, all the King's pattern silver which was too boring and florid for her taste, plus Geoffrey's pair of George III candelabra which would bring in some cash if they had to sell. She also put out the emerald and yellow Coalport dinner service; she had never before wasted this on the family in case they broke it, but what the hell now. She stood back to admire the finished effects. It looked wonderful.

Amy, sticking her head around the door later that morning, was intrigued by the plates. 'Showing off, of course,' she said to James and reversed one of the Coalport pieces to memorise its marks. She would look up its price in *Miller's Antiques Guide* when they were back at home.

There was a big, rich, dark goose for their late lunch, which had been home-reared by one of the local farmers' wives. Laura had stuffed it with Bramley apples and cloves, and they ate it with crisp roast potatoes, crackling-hard outside and floury within, with onions roasted and caramelised in the Scandinavian way with demerara sugar, with spiced red cabbage and with broccoli. Then came the two round Christmas puddings, each topped with holly. Laura turned off the sconce lights on the walls, so that the room was in the twilight of a mid-winter afternoon with only the rays from the window sending a single shaft through the gloom. She put a flame to the candelabra, then set the brandy round the puddings on fire. It burnt quickly, sending blue volatile tongues around the spheres. The scent of sweet etherised alcohol floated in the air. There was a gasp of pleasure. From his high-chair beside the table, Thomas, bewitched, stretched his arms towards this new living toy. The old and middle-aged, seeing afresh through his eyes, shared his entrancement.

At last, replete with pudding and dozy with drink, they stumbled blinking into the firelight of the drawing-room where, one by one, they fell asleep. A vintage Christmas Day was in progress. The spaniels still decked with scarlet ribbons had followed suit, flinging themselves in heaps on to the hearth. Laura alone remained awake. She looked around her. James was still wearing a paper hat, tilted forward on to his forehead by the pressure of the armchair wing against which his head had lolled. Amy's mouth had fallen open a little in her slumber. Without the animation that egotism lent her face in waking hours, it had relaxed into the anonymity of old age when the skull starts to take over. Louisa too was diminished in sleep. She seemed smaller and more frail. Her scalp was visible beneath her white hair, now returned to its usual coiffure after its hospital excursion. Her hands, brown-speckled and papery, looked like two little claws. Inert, she lay on her chair, her feet propped up on a needlework stool. This is how she will look in death, thought Laura.

The annual ritual meandered on its sacred course of sleep, tea, television, then the opening of the presents. At six o'clock Laura went out to gather up the deep litter of parcels from under the Christmas tree in the hall. Beside it loomed their gift to Thomas, a dapple-grey rocking-horse, its outlines barely disguised by a wreathing of Christmas paper. Staggering back into the drawing-room, she poured armfuls of treats on to the floor. Everyone sat up and an air of expectancy braced the little group. 'Oh goody,' said Amy. Presents were always energising.

Nearly all, however, were for Thomas, who was soon head-deep with the dogs in a nest of shredded paper-wrappings. Laura had one parcel: an antique silver brooch from Rosy. Geoffrey had one, too: an inkstand, also from Rosy, for the desk he never used. Geoffrey sought out William on the quiet to thank him for the present. 'Money OK, you know?' he slipped in. 'Fine,' said William. In fact the stock in which he had invested Geoffrey's portfolio had dipped a little. William decided to say nothing: amateurs were notorious for being easily rattled.

Amy had two presents: a black and purple bandana from Laura and, from Rosy, a hardback thriller by a female author. Lightning crossed Amy's face at the thought of sales boosting the status of a rival. She had met her at a publicity stunt for authors over sixty. Recognising a new younger member breathing down the neck of her old-age group, she had resented her on sight. 'How thoughtful,' said Amy, scouring her great-niece's face for evidence of intent to damage. 'The poor woman needs all the support she can get.'

Louisa had three presents: a biography from Rosy, a jade and silver necklace from Laura and a pair of rope-soled velvet slippers from Amy with different motifs on the left and right foot. Louisa's mouth clenched. Amy had clearly economised by buying rejects in the January sale a year ago.

Amy leant forward to inject some necessary *savoir-faire*. 'It is extremely smart, Lou, to have unmatching slippers.'

A noise like a death rattle sounded, presumably from Louisa's throat. It was a reminder that the opening of presents always provoked the odd moment of tension.

There was a general chipping-in of 'how nice' and 'how novel' to fend off any crisis in manners.

Christ, thought William, remembering they were due to lunch at his parents' tomorrow, we've got to go through all this again with my own lot in twenty-four hours' time. He couldn't wait to get back to the office in the New Year.

Rosy nudged him. 'Look how he adores it.' She pointed to Thomas who, with great deliberation, was dismantling the more educational of his toys. Baba, the spaniel, was growling furiously at a pastel-coloured teddy bear.

'Go on, eat it,' urged Rosy, turning her nose up at the pale-blue plush toy. 'Oh God,' she said, noting that the label around its neck was signed 'With love from Beth', a discovery which caused a *volte-face* to positive discrimination.

'Isn't this sweet of her?' Rosy thrust the Taiwanese bear and its label at Laura.

She grabbed her mother by the arm and picked up Thomas. 'Come on, let's go and try the best present of all.'

'What do you have in mind?' Laura smiled.

'The you-know-what by the Christmas tree. Such a wonderful treat.'

Carrying Thomas the two of them set out for the hall with William in tow. They pulled the wrapping from the dapple-grey horse and sat Thomas firmly in the saddle, putting the reins in his hand. Gently Rosy pushed the pony into slow motion.

'We ought to have some coconut shells for sound effects.'

'Cloppity-clop,' said William, but his voice faded out. He felt silly. How like the women to trap him with soppy-ass talk. Thomas's eyes sparkled, his cheeks flushed with joy. 'Pony, pony,' he shouted.

'How does he know the word?'

'Actually we taught him weeks ago in preparation.' Rosy looked shame-faced because it sounded so calculating. She added hastily, 'We've taught him thank you, too. Say thank you, Thomas.'

'Tankyouplease,' said Thomas, to cover all eventualities. She put her arms around her mother and hugged her.

'Don't thank me. Thank the bank.'

'Don't say that. You mustn't worry. It'll be OK. William's sorting it out.'

William kicked her.

'What do you mean?'

'Nothing. Really.'

Laura turned to face her son-in-law. 'William? What are you doing?'

William wished again he was back in the office. No female hysterics, no in-law tensions, no human problems full stop. Just targets, screens, bids, offers and bonuses.

'Geoffrey asked for some help.' He strove to keep his answer vague. 'Cloppity-clop,' he added, concentrating on the rocking-horse.

'Like what?'

'Just some sorting out.'

The very woolliness of his response aroused her deepest suspicions. She walked away, put her head round the drawing-room door and called, 'Geoffrey.' Rosy and William exchanged glances. 'You fool,' he mouthed at her. Rosy made a nasty face. The temperature in the hall felt five degrees chillier. William made walking signs with his fingers to indicate the need for immediate departure.

Laura called again. Geoffrey was dozing with the inkstand, a five-second wonder, on the arm of his chair. She called again, more peremptorily this time. He heaved himself out of the seat, innocently anticipating he was about to witness the spectacle of a harmonious grouping around his grandchild in the hall.

'Shut that door behind you.' Laura whispered, but it sounded like a hiss.

He pushed it to, scanning the faces before him. There were unmistakable vibrations. So much for harmony. Another bloody crisis was in full swing.

'What did you ask William to do?'

Geoffrey did not need to enquire what she meant. William did not look at him. He was looking down at his shoes, raising his eyebrows and making a duck's mouth to indicate the end of his tether.

'He's maximising our assets.' Geoffrey had never been one to underestimate the positive.

'How?'

'He's helping to handle my portfolio.' He kept quiet the fact that he had transferred the whole amount.

'You withdrew it from Buckland-Weller?'

'You always wanted me to sack him.'

Laura turned to William but he was on the other side of the hall, terribly busy gathering up the coats, the high chair, the suitcases. Thomas began to wail at being lifted out of the saddle.

'We've got to go. It's been a wonderful day, wonderful presents. Thank you for everything.'

Rosy, too, was evaporating in a bustle of kisses. 'Don't worry,' she kept saying, 'it will all be OK.'

'Of course it will.' Laura smiled at them. 'Thank you both for trying to help.' She lingered over a loving goodbye. She hated to embarrass them, nor was there any point when she could blister the paint off Geoffrey instead. She noticed he was on the point of returning to the sanctuary of the drawing-room and moved to block his escape. She pinned him down at the entrance and ransacked him for an explanation. She listened in silence. As a counterpoint to Geoffrey's words, she could hear Ranson's warning. 'No desperate gambling . . . last-minute excesses.' She could hear it, like a deep insistent bell overhanging a heedless chorus.

'It was William's idea,' Geoffrey was saying.

'You put him under pressure.'

Geoffrey shook his head adamantly. He couldn't understand the timing of this explosion. How long would she persist? He ought to think himself lucky, he supposed, that this had blown up on Christmas Day, the traditional twenty-four hours of truce. He calculated rightly that Laura would be reluctant to flout it for long.

'Have a drink,' he said. 'Don't worry.'

'If anyone tells me that again I shall scream.'

She walked upstairs to the bedroom and stood over the telephone. She looked at it for a few minutes. I might just ring Leo and wish him happy Christmas, she thought. She picked up the receiver and dialled, remembering the number without needing to refer to his card. It rang repeatedly. She disconnected, then tried again. Of course, he wouldn't be there. He too had a life of his own.

She walked downstairs and met Amy and James in the hall. Geoffrey was nowhere to be seen. Laura returned to the drawing-room, where Louisa was alone. She looked perky.

'Good fire, isn't it?' Louisa smiled happily at her.

It was crackling and popping like a bonfire. Laura advanced and peered as closely as she dared at the blaze. The heat was scorching. The chimney didn't seem to be alight, but there were two mysterious shapes that were feeding the flames. Laura turned back to her mother, suddenly alerted by the fact that she was patently pleased with herself.

'Those rope soles burn like old rope.' For Louisa this was a Christmas to relish.

Ranson was enjoying a less contentious Christmas. He was

spending three days at his brother's pink-washed house in Suffolk. At the moment that Laura was telephoning him to no avail, he was on all fours on the floor giving a ride to his niece's twins. Following best practice, the twins had been raised to do everything separately. The doctrine only took spasmodic effect, and, at this moment, not at all, so the pair were both perched on Ranson's back as he roamed on his knees round the carpet. He noted that the Labrador, laid out in front of the fire, was having an easy time compared with him.

It was seven o'clock. His brother, a vintner, came into the room carrying a 1970 claret. Ranson eyed it longingly.

'Isn't it time you went to bed?' he asked the twins. He had borne his share for long enough and his lumbar region twinged.

'We'll go to bed if you play the backwards-words game with us,' Emma and Joscie lied in unison.

Ranson heaved himself up, shooting the pair without ceremony on to the carpet. One fell on the Labrador who opened an eye and closed it rapidly. A fourteen-stone man could step on the dog without causing a tremor.

'Just one then.' Ranson addressed the twins, but raised his eyes thankfully to his brother who passed him his claret.

'Right.' Ranson settled himself in a comfortable armchair. 'An easy one. Gods go wob-wow and on a hot day say, "ffuw-ffuw what a scorcher".'

Emma looked at Joscie. Had they been separated in age by several years there would have been much rivalry to find the answer first and no little contempt for the loser. As it was, they were solicitous that each should be equal first. They conferred in whispers, then chorused triumphantly.

'Dogs go bow-wow.'

'Ffuw-ffuw what a scorcher?'

Ranson's brother looked with pity at him. He was

certainly having to earn his Christmas break. The twins jumped up and down repeating 'wuff-wuff, easy, easy, it's too easy'. They pummelled him.

Ranson thought, not for the first time, how boisterous Anglo-Saxon children were. He compared them with the Chinese toddlers he had noticed last autumn. If only his niece had Chinese twins. They would spend all day mutely sitting exams.

'One more, please, please, Uncle Leo.' Joscie climbed on his lap in the chair. Em piled on top. The precious wine slurped in his glass and he extended his hand over the chair arm, holding it out of the orbit of their turbulence.

'This is the very last one then.' Ranson closed his eyes to think. He would have been relieved to be allowed to fall asleep. 'An allirog goes moob-moob on his chest.' He dropped his voice, which was already deep, an octave further.

The twins were foxed. Their mother, Ranson's niece Alison, came into the room. She noticed their puzzled expression.

'What are you doing to them?'

'The backwards-words game.'

'What's an allirog?' asked Joscie.

'Oh no,' said Ranson's niece, 'you will make them dyslexic.'

'It was the last one anyway,' replied Ranson, thinking how ungrateful she was for the fact that he had been absorbing their high spirits for the previous half an hour.

I bet Laura's having a more peaceful time, he thought, sipping his claret. It was difficult to reach it. He had to pass his glass through the narrow channel to his face between the Scylla and Charybdis on his lap. He wondered what had happened to her. He might get in touch in the New Year.

17

Tessa sat at the kitchen table – paints, turps and linseed oil pushed to one side. The new canvas was propped up on the other side of the room and waiting to be filled. Like all blank sheets it was both inviting and repressive. She looked down at the writing-paper in front of her. It too was blank though the rough page beside was covered with crossings-out and arrows.

She got up, boiled the kettle and made some tea. The kitchen was so cold that it lost heat rapidly. It was freezing outside. Reluctant to turn up the radiator, she went upstairs and rooted out a second jumper. She was already wearing three vests on the principle that trapped air between layers was as insulating as blubber. Like most principles, it was defective when tested in practice.

She sighed and looked at her watch. Eleven thirty on a bleak late January morning. She had wasted hours already on the letter. For the twentieth time she wrote *Dear Miles*, then looked out of the window. A little owl had landed on the telegraph wire. He was instantly recognisable even at a distance and against a leaden sky which failed to light up his mouse-grey and white feathers. Chunky head, the same size as his shoulders and no neck in between. Last week, in a light covering of late winter snow, she had seen him at close quarters. He had twisted his head round at

her approach, assessing her coolly and without apparent
fear. He wore a permanent scowl on his face due to the
furious angle of his brows. She had begun to laugh at his
crosspatch expression. Startled by her facial movements,
he had flown off.

Tessa turned back to the sheet of paper. It was the third
time Miles had written to her since Christmas. Neglect for
nearly eight years and now a barrage of attention – how
foreseeably characteristic. The first letter was apologetic:

*Dear Tessa, silence, I know, for so long. I hear about you from
friends. You have started painting again. Do you remember
we once worked together. I wonder about you and Poll. I am
terribly sorry about what happened. Yours – you know it has
never been otherwise – M.*

No mention, thought Tessa, of the Inland Revenue bill she
had paid on his account.

The second letter after a mere fortnight's interval: *Darling
Tessa, I wait for each post to hear from you. Why don't you
write? It is freezing here now but why don't you pay me a visit
in spring?*

It would seem, thought Tessa, that his latest girlfriend
had left him. It was clear she was no longer burning the
home fires in France.

The third letter: *I am coming to see you in March. With
my love.*

Perhaps, thought Tessa, he needs his dirty washing
laundered. A lot would have accumulated in nearly eight
years. You only went back to mother when the rest of the
world ran out of forgiveness.

She had come to dread these letters with their rustling
French envelopes postmarked *Tarn et Garonne*, and his
large, self-expressive handwriting that curdled her with
a sweet and sour mix of memories. They filled the room

with their presence. This was the more powerful for his absence, which gave the imagination the meat upon which it normally fed.

Tessa looked down at her crossings-out. There were numerous false starts. *Dear Miles, neither of us wants to see you.* Wrong. Polly might have hated him but she could soon be at the stage of adolescent curiosity. She might think it fun to visit her father in France, not that he'd bothered to include her in his invitation. *Dear Miles, leave us alone.* Absurd. That would just act as a spur. *Dear Miles. Dear Miles. Dear Miles.* Tessa drew a doodle of a vase which could morph into a facial profile. *Dear Miles.* She began to doodle the umpteenth letter: *Dear Miles, I shall have moved by the time you come to England. I am marrying again.* Oh, if only she could write that. It would be as garlic to the werewolf. The final proof to a former husband that he was no longer the shrine at which she was expected to worship for the rest of her life. She had replaced him, the ultimate insult to such a ferocious ego.

As she looked at her letter which had been written in jest, she thought suddenly, and why not? Shouldn't she see it as a swashbuckling defence rather than a wistful lie? For a moment she hesitated, then with a rush of confidence that she had found a solution, she picked up her biro and wrote swiftly on a clean piece of writing-paper:

Dear Miles, Forget about your visit. You will not be surprised to know that everything has changed in the last eight years. The past is completely dead. I shall be marrying this year. There is no point in contacting me. If Polly ever wants to see you at a later stage, I shan't stop her of course. That must be her decision. Yours sincerely, Tessa.

Fat chance of it all coming true, she thought as she slid the letter into the envelope. However, she felt relieved and quite cheerful. It was an invigorating way of disposing of an ex-husband's attentions. And as for the second husband? Well, he might be a ghost at the moment, but the written word did make him that bit more credible. And weren't owls meant to be omens? She glanced out of the window. He was still there. What a hoot, she said to herself wryly.

18

On the last day of January Geoffrey took Malcolm, his manager, on a sales trip to the Midlands. Its avowed purpose was a final bid to shift the machinery, but in truth he was simply relieved to escape from the house. Relations with Laura had been tricky ever since her discovery of the stockmarket plan. He acknowledged that she was less a scourge than he'd feared, but there was no question that a good deal of simmering was in progress. Every now and again a bubble would escape in the form of a wish that he had told her of his intentions. Occasionally the eruptions had been worse. 'Gambling at this time is insane' had been a first reaction. 'A bad situation made dreadful' was the latest pronouncement.

Geoffrey did not think there was any chance of an immediate improvement at home. Laura had even pleaded with him to withdraw the money from William, but the latter had been reluctant for a variety of reasons that Geoffrey did not entirely understand. When pressed further, William had said timing was important and now was not the right time. All in all, an uncomfortable week in distant hotels seemed preferable to a blistering atmosphere at home.

Laura too was pleased to see the back of him. January had been a trial. She had been horrified to discover the transfer of money for two reasons. On the one hand, she was alarmed by Geoffrey's recklessness; on the other, by his involvement of the rest of the family. She had tried to restrain her displeasure but the double dose of suppression was proving a dual strain. In Geoffrey's absence, at least she could now fulminate on her own. Her sulphur and brimstone, however, needed an object on which to focus. With that despatched to the Midlands, they soon gave way to depression.

By the second morning on her own, Laura decided it was much better being angry than low. To cheer herself up, she decided to go into the garden and see if any noses of the bulbs they had planted in the autumn were poking through the soil. Normally it was a sight to trigger optimism in even the dead, but this morning she feared it would arouse mixed emotions. Still, it was a brilliant day. She went into the lobby to scuffle through old coats, boots and dried mud when the phone rang. She scurried back into the hall wearing one boot and her coat half on and half off.

'Hello.' She tried to disguise her breathlessness in case the call was professional. Now the buffer of Christmas was over, it was hard not to get thrown into jitters by the telephone.

'I want to speak to Mr Fenton.'

'He's not here at the moment. Who's speaking?'

There was a pause. 'When will he be back?' The tone was impatient.

'Have you tried his secretary? Do you have his office number?'

'I have his office number all right. They're not exactly helpful.' He sounded more than testy though he was obviously holding himself in check.

'Give me your name. I'll make sure he gets your message.'

'Tell him it's Cranston. He knows what it's about.'

The dialling note sounded. He had rung off in a fury.

Oh God, she thought, who is Cranston? She felt menace in his voice. She looked round at the hall. The calm Dutch black and white tiled floor. The grey-green walls. Paintings of fat cattle and sheep, their breastbones enlarged by the artist to enhance their saleability. Till now the house had felt like a haven, however illusory. Already it was beginning to dissolve.

She pulled on her coat, put the other boot on and went out of the back door trying to think positive thoughts, but she was shaking. The phone rang again. She stood there in indecision. Then she took a deep breath. Face up to it, you mustn't let them scare you. She lifted the receiver, clutching it in a vice.

'Laura? You didn't ring me. It's—'

'I know who it is. I thought it would be someone else, someone horrible,' but she had recognised him instantly. Relief flooded her. It was a wonderful feeling to hear him, like touching earth again. Thank God he had ignored her warning not to contact her.

'I did try to wish you happy Christmas but you weren't there.'

'I spent Christmas Day crawling round the floor.'

'What?'

'Never mind. I'm looking at a house for sale about twenty miles from you and thought we might be able to meet up today. You could tell me what's happened.'

'It's awful.'

'I thought it might be. I'm really very sorry. Are you free?'

'They're all away on a sales trip.' She didn't like to say Geoffrey specifically, in case it gave the impression of sneakiness. The nuance was not lost on Ranson.

'That sounds free,' was all he said neutrally in reply.

'Where are you going to see the house?'

Ranson looked at the estate agent's brochure he was holding and read out the details of its location. She thought for a second, then made a quick calculation. She felt desperate to get out of the home and, besides, it was a shame to waste a wonderful late-winter's day. The sun would be coaxing the first stray camellias and rhododendrons to open in the gardens at Wakehurst Place. It was only half an hour's distance from each of them. She described it to Ranson.

'You wouldn't be bored, would you?' she enquired nervously. 'It's very beautiful. We could walk there.' It did occur to her that she would feel less wary in the open air with him. With Geoffrey away, she preferred to avoid being cooped up with Leo.

'I would love it.' His answer was genuine. He hated to waste the unseasonable sunshine and had spent every day since late December in the office. He had earned a complete escape. He arranged to meet Laura at noon. Then he rang his secretary and told her to say he was in Frankfurt for the day. It looks like I'm going AWOL, he thought to himself.

Laura arrived, parked the car, stepped out and looked round. She was alone apart from two other cars, one with a yappy terrier in the back window. She returned to the car, sat for a few minutes, looked at herself in the mirror for reassurance and then got out again. Though sunny, it was cold in the wind and she walked up and down to keep her feet warm. Fifteen minutes passed, half an hour, and she was starting to feel edgy when a navy Jaguar drove into the car park. She recognised the car she had put on to her shopping list in the middle of last year. What ages ago. How complacent she was then.

Ranson got out and waved at her, apologising for the

delay. He came over and gave her a brief hug in greeting. His navy coat hung open. He was wearing fawn corduroys, a check shirt, navy pullover and no tie. A scarf lay unfolded round his neck.

'I bought these for a picnic,' he indicated a plastic carrier, 'and then I got lost.'

'How lovely. What have you got?' He does look nice, she thought.

'Plastic knives and forks. Little jars of things from a delicatessen. I'm not sure what. I told them to put something together for the first picnic of the year. They thought I was mad, then decided the customer's always right.'

He really did feel in an AWOL mood. Surreptitiously he took in her appearance. She was wearing the same camel coat as for lunch, but this time with olive trousers and sweater. Her dark hair hung free round her jawbone.

They went through the ticket booth and started walking down the path leading to the big circular pond. As the land dipped, the wind dropped and the weather began to take on the softness of the first stolen day of spring.

'What is this about a house? You didn't tell me about buying a home in the country. You'll never have time to spend in it.'

'I can't go on staying at my brother's in Suffolk when I need a break from London.' He was walking too fast for her and slowed his pace for her to catch up. They began to match strides instinctively.

'So I need a home,' he went on. 'As I may have said, I was looking at the area when I called in on your garden last year.'

'A house just for you?'

'No, Laura.' He smiled. 'I only need a rabbit hutch. I want one large enough for my daughter when she brings her family over from California to England.' Though that seems to get rarer and rarer, he thought sadly.

He paused. Laura had stopped to admire a huge hamamelis; its branches were studded with sunbursts, spidery clusters of pale yellow flowers scenting the air faintly.

He looked at the hamamelis too. He had seen one in Onslow Square once: he hadn't known what it was but thought it an oddity.

'It was horrid this morning,' he went on. 'The house was quite nice. An old brick Wealden cottage with leaded windows. But the feeling was wrong. I think they were in the throes of divorce. The woman was on drugs, tranquillisers? The husband twitchy. It reminded me.'

She glanced at him. 'Of what?'

'Oh, you know. Just how my second marriage ended. I'll tell you some time.' The woman had even looked a bit like his wife. The same tilted eyes, though twenty years older. What was Natalya doing now? The question flicked across his mind. They walked round the pond. The ducks, mated in readiness for the spring nesting, were quacking. Several pairs, heads bobbing, were running through their perfunctory courtship rituals prior to coupling.

What rabid ducks, he thought. 'Enthusiasts, aren't they?' was all he actually said.

The sun glinting off the water was brilliant, light-yellow, blinding.

He turned to Laura. 'What's happened about the business?'

She hadn't commented on the ducks, which wasn't surprising, but she did indeed seem a little subdued.

She stopped walking, tilted her head sideways and looked away.

'Come on.'

Still she hesitated.

'You said it was awful, but they were away on a sales trip. Doesn't that make it any better?' It wouldn't, he knew. It was characteristic at the last stages of foreclosure to put on a spurt. An attempt to jump out of the hangman's noose. It rarely worked.

'It's not that. There's been a little stockmarket venture. Just as you warned against.'

'By whom?' He didn't need to ask.

She both told him and didn't tell him. He listened and in private he judged. He noted the care with which she avoided her husband's name. The fool is irresponsible to the point of negligence, he thought to himself. A house and a business are on the edge of a cliff: one may not stop them sliding over, but does one push them?

Laura saw his face harden. 'Don't judge,' she said warningly.

Ranson looked away to hide his expression. He wanted to say, I blame Geoffrey not you, but that would only make things worse. It wasn't fair anyway. Ranson knew he was guilty of judging his own gender more harshly than women. His generation usually did. It was a left-over from chivalry.

'I feel very much to blame without you judging me too.'

She had clearly misread his thoughts but he let it stand and only asked, 'How so?'

'I should have taken more interest.'

They were walking past the pond and along the path beside the grassy bank of slim, violet crocuses, though these went unnoticed. It was easier to talk when walking, harder face to face.

'You weren't the type to take an interest in that kind of operation.'

'Neither the type nor had the upbringing, but at some stage one pays the price.'

He thought of the women in his line of business. Younger usually, tough, capable and red in tooth and claw, though most lacked the stamina for the long run. No, she had never been the type. If you were unusually beautiful, there was no need to be anything else when she was growing up.

'Too late to change.' He turned his head to smile at her.

'Too late indeed. After fifty, one suffers from the three Fs: funk, fatigue and fossilisation.'

He began to laugh. 'Not you. You're very well preserved.'

She was standing under a huge tree rhododendron in early bloom. Its great icing-sugar clusters of flowers, ethereal and crystalline, hung down behind her dark head. It made an extraordinary portrait of which she was unaware.

He thought, not for the first time, she is a collector's piece. He went up to her and put down his plastic carrier bag. He took her face in his hands, looking at her with real affection. 'Remember,' he said, 'this is a stolen day. Outside real life. The three Fs are waiting for you tomorrow but not today.'

She lifted her arms and put them round his neck, the camel cuffs of her coat falling back from her wrists. As her fingers touched him, she noticed that his hair grew lower down his nape than Geoffrey's. They kissed, not opening their mouths but resting them lightly against each other's in camaraderie. They stayed in this position for a moment, the wind blowing strands of her hair across his cheek. She then withdrew slightly though kept her arms round his neck. Looking up, she could see a haze of blush trumpet flowers and black branches against the blue sky.

'See.' She indicated with her eyes. 'Bliss, isn't it. Ridiculous bliss. Not like real life.'

A flower detached itself from its cluster and drifted down. As though reminded, she took her arms from his neck and moved away.

'Real enough. I saw a whole hillside of them once.

Twenty years ago I was working in Delhi. I took a trip north to the Himalayas.'

'What was it like?'

'Unforgettable. Rhododendrons tall as houses. Blazing red like lava down the slopes.' He looked up at the tree. 'I haven't seen such big ones since then.' I was married to Jean then, he thought. She was with me on that trip. He smiled across at Laura. It was nice, comforting even, when experiences linked up. He remembered sitting down with his wife on the hillside covered in petals.

He looked down at his plastic bag. 'You know what?' he said. 'Why don't we eat under its branches?'

'What an old romantic. Earth is different from heaven.' She pointed at the sodden ground. Resolved not to be put off, he walked to fetch a bench some twenty yards away. Laura watched him. So much for romance: it would be concreted into the ground against vandals, but no, he was returning with his seat. She was amused at his determination to make things nice. They sat down with the plastic carrier between them and began to take out its bits and pieces.

'Oh God,' he said. 'This is going to be a disappointment. Tofuburger. Sorry.'

She gave him a look. 'Kidney beans and cashew salad.'

'One carton of miso soup.'

'Deary me. It looks like we're in for a doctrinaire lunch.'

'Save the world, at least.'

'Revolting certainly.'

They looked at each other and began to laugh.

'Honestly,' he said, 'I told them to put together a nice meal. You can't take your eye off the ball for a moment without things going wrong.'

'Never mind. The feta pastry rolls look edible.'

They were actually delicious. They sat in silence in the

sunshine savouring their curried mushroom flavour. A youthful gardener walked by trundling a wheelbarrow. He looked at them bitterly. Middle-aged adulterers, he thought. Married people didn't picnic in January.

'There's a litter bin at the entrance,' he called warningly.

'He doesn't approve,' said Laura. 'The young are awfully puritanical these days.'

'So were we in our own way.'

'Not true. Just rigid.'

'Certainly different from now.'

'Everyone changes. You're different.'

'Me? How?' Ranson blinked. He didn't like talking about himself: it was self-indulgent. But he was curious to know how she saw him now.

She thought: desirable. She said, 'Tougher, more confident.'

'I've made a mess of things.'

'You've been a success.'

'Two marriages? A success? The first wife dead, the second divorced.'

'Would just one marriage have made it any better?' Look at me for evidence, she thought grimly.

'Less debris.'

'The first was bad luck.'

'Not the second. That was misjudgment. I hate getting things wrong.'

'It takes guts to end a marriage.'

Ranson looked at her out of the corner of his eyes. She is dissatisfied, he thought, very beautiful and dissatisfied. It occurred to him that he could probably have her. People were like businesses and money. They went where they were best treated. But do I want her? he wondered.

Laura lifted her face to the winter sun and closed her eyes. 'When I was young, I thought that life changed very little. I thought that until a few months ago. I now see it as a process of constant adjustment.'

'I've had plenty of practice at that.'

'You, yes, but not me.'

'You must learn fast.'

He put an arm around her shoulders. She leant against him.

'You've been a good friend,' she said. 'Thank you.'

She turned her dark-brown eyes on him. Flecked with amber, they were opaque like most dark-coloured eyes. It was hard to know what she was thinking.

'Leo,' she said.

'What?'

'You think I'm after you, don't you.'

He was startled. 'It never crossed my mind.'

'You're a rotten liar,' but she was smiling at him as she spoke. 'Don't worry. I don't blame you. In that time-honoured phrase, a dozen middle-aged and younger women must be setting their caps at you all the while.'

He gave a puff of embarrassment, momentarily lost for words.

'Well, I'm not,' she continued gently. 'I've got enough on my plate at the moment without you too.'

'I haven't put my head on your plate,' Ranson protested. He was both amused yet very faintly insulted that his earlier assumption was so evidently wrong.

'I know. I'm being presumptuous.'

'You are. The fact is I'm as wary of involvement as you are.' Probably more so, he thought.

'Good,' she said. 'We're both in the same position. Just so long as we're equal.'

She looked at him steadily. Ranson began to feel vaguely uncomfortable. Control of this occasion seemed to have slipped from his grasp.

'Do you have anyone at this moment?'

'No.' He was surprised by her question.

'Why not?'

'It's been my choice. Of late.'

'Is that likely to change?'

'Who knows. Anything else you want to ask?'

He had forgotten how inquisitive women were. They had this terrible habit of wanting to get things cut and dried.

Laura recognised she had gone far enough. 'Sorry,' she said. 'Don't get cross.'

'I'm not cross. Just resistant.'

She leant over, opened his coat and folded back the flaps of his scarf. He caught hold of her hand in protest.

'What the hell are you doing? It's freezing.'

'I'm peeling off your resistant outer layer,' she said, laughing. 'One, two—' She looked suddenly young.

He had a memory of her thirty years ago and then the clouds joined up and he lost it again. It was disconcerting.

'Stop flirting,' he said.

The gardener returned, his wheelbarrow full of prunings. He had the self-righteous air of the worker. This time he kept his eyes averted as there was actual touching going on. It was disgusting when middle-aged people thought they were young. Ranson shrugged his coat back on and pulled his scarf around his neck again. He was aware his actions must look stuffy.

'Just cold,' he said. 'I'm not actually preparing to leave.'

'Don't leave, whatever you do. When you disappear, I've got to go home to an empty house, grow up and grit my teeth.'

I, too, am going back to an empty house, thought Ranson. What a waste. But what did she want? Her behaviour seemed ambiguous: intimate yet remote. He realised he found her more desirable since she said she wasn't after him. He thought of the ducks with their courtship rituals

on the pond. He considered he and Laura had done quite
enough head-bobbing of the human kind. He said quietly,
'Do you want to come back with me?'

She looked at him silently.

'No strings attached,' he added. 'On either side.'

He was strongly aware of her breasts underneath the
ribbed olive wool of her sweater. The nipples would be
larger, browner than those of the girl who was so elusive
in his memory.

It is thirty years since I went to bed with him, thought
Laura. What difference does one more time make? She
looked across the landscape. It would be easy with Geoffrey
away. She was going to say, 'What do I do with my car?'
but she stopped. To say that was to agree in principle whilst
arguing over the small print. Did she agree in principle?

'No,' she said. 'I can't. Not now.'

He nodded. 'Not now,' he repeated.

It was dusk by the time Laura returned to the empty house,
glittering with security lights popping on and off in her
absence. The dogs smothered her with love, believing as
always she had deserted them for perpetuity. No serious
messages on the answerphone – only Beth saying she
had flu, and a complaint from her mother that she had
not seen her for a week. In fact the whole mundane
world had stood still in her absence. Why come back just
for this?

She kicked off her shoes, lit a fire in the little sitting-room
and poured herself out a glass of wine. Curling up in a chair,
with her stockinged-feet tucked to her side, she dialled the
number of Geoffrey's hotel. She was put through to him
immediately. His voice, though perfectly normal, seemed
estranged to her.

'How's it going?'

'Snowing. Fucking freezing here.'

She remembered Ranson pulling his coat back on: 'it's freezing'.

'I meant the selling.'

'Oh, that. Too early to say.'

'Someone called Cranston rang. He sounded desperate to speak to you. I promised to tell you.'

'Cranston, hmm.'

'Who is he?'

'The chap's rather keen on getting paid. Wants to jump the queue.'

'You mean he's a creditor.'

'He is. Actually.'

Laura looked bleakly into the distance. She wished she had gone home with Ranson.

19

William glanced at his reflection in the glossy plate-glass window as he returned to the office. He was pleased to note that he looked as he felt: sleek, fit and predatory. For the first time in his life he knew he was on a roll. Things were moving with spectacular success. Sober fund managers, who had once treated him as a cur, now deferred to him with a degree of respect. Once just a salesman, he was now an achiever, a surfer, riding the pounding waves. About time, he thought with a sigh of relief.

He walked through the swing doors and rather than take the lift, leapt up the stairs. An athlete, he thought, in training, cleansed by the mineral water he had taken at lunch. He mused on the tour he had booked for the week ahead. Chicago, then Hong Kong. He stared with insolent confidence at Ailsa, a pretty secretary with a plait who was passing him on the stairs. Guess what I have in my bag for next week: first stop England, next the world. He went to the marble Gents and looked in the mirror as he soaped his hands. Blue eyes, high cheekbones, black lock of hair falling forward, one of us. I have made it, he thought. One of us. Join the club. His face looked back at him. Don't be cocky, he said to it.

He glanced at his watch as he went back to his desk: GMT −5 in New York, −6 in Chicago, +7 at this time of the year in Hong Kong. It was hot in the office compared with the keen, sleety edge of February outside. He took off his jacket and slung it over the back of his chair before scanning the screen on his desk. He loosened his tie, a navy silk one with umber and crimson reticulations. He leant forward, tapping his pen on the desk. All seemed well, mostly blues, not reds, which meant shares were on the rise rather than the fall, market greed in charge not market fear.

He checked his personal shares automatically, plus a couple of options he was calling with his own money. Options could be hell: like patients in an intensive care ward, there were times when they needed watching round the clock. All however were sleek and in the pink of health. He flicked over to Geoffrey's share and recoiled in surprise. It was red, wiped of a third of its worth since this morning. He lifted his head, thinking this was no rhythmic decline, but a bump, a hard-landing type bump. He scanned the share's sector for information: none there, prices were down but not to that extent. He leant his left elbow on the desk and rested his jaw in the cup of his hand. Was it serious? Maybe not. Small shares were often roller-coasters with a wide trading range, he would ride out the surf. However, his sense of high personal gloss felt somewhat abraded by the niggle of worry.

As he sat there thinking, he was interrupted by his telephone. He grinned: it was the friend with whom he would be staying in New York. He liked him: quiet, sharp and resilient with a wife who had long, floating hair.

'Sam,' he exclaimed. 'An early call for you. Is this about next week or are you interested in—'

'No. This is a quick call from your chum. You've got a problem.'

'Me?'

'You. They've pulled out.'

'Who? Where?' but he knew before he was told.

'From your stock. The four directors have pulled out of your stock. Have you seen the price? It's got further to go.'

'Jesus Christ. Why?'

'We don't know. But you're on a deadline with this one so as a friend I'm warning you.'

'Sam, why? What's behind it?'

'As I said, we don't know. Maybe they moved in to ramp the share.'

'Wait. What do I do?'

'Get out. Fast. It won't bounce.'

William felt his forehead break into a sweat. There seemed to be a tap under each armpit. He could feel water trickling from the taps down both sides of his body. He felt sick. If he sold he would realise a loss of half of Geoffrey's money. He put his head in his hands and groaned. He looked at the screen. Sam was right: the fucking price was still falling. Should he sell? Mesmerised, he watched the price drift down. Every quarter of a point represented a further loss of over three thousand pounds. Oh Jesus, he thought. He felt paralysed.

He looked round the familiar normality of the room: some laughing and talking, others staring with rigid intensity at their screens, brokers selling fantasies, dealers on the hype. Sell, he thought, I've got to sell.

'Sam,' he said again, 'suppose—' but the line had broken.

He was suddenly reminded of a cameo picture beside a column in the *Financial Times*. He saw it every week in the morning train, saw it but until now did not realise he had noticed it. It showed a tiny figure perched on the edge of a huge cliff top; it was reaching out towards a big carrot just beyond its grasp in the air. William shut his eyes. A little bit further, an inch more, almost there, but the carrot had been jerked away and he was that figure, stretching but stretching too late and now hurtling down the face of the cliff. As he fell he remembered Geoffrey asking him: 'Will it work?'

'You'll have to tell him.' William sat slumped in the kitchen. The smell of casseroled chicken and green peppers filled the air but he was not hungry. His appetite, normally bomb-proof, had failed him.

'He's away.' Rosy looked plaintively at him, her face streaked with tears. She had not stopped crying since he had told her. She felt both desperate and helpless.

'Then tell Laura. Or wait until he comes back. I'm away then. I won't be here to tell him.'

'You leave me to do your dirty work.'

'It's not my dirty work,' shouted William. 'And stop crying. Your only answer is tears. You just sit on the sidelines and weep.'

Thomas, frightened by the red faces and loud noises, began his hiccuping prelude to crying. He tottered over to his mother, fell, stood up again and clasped her shins.

'Christ, both of you.' William walked out of the kitchen. One second later he walked back again.

'In any case, you're as much to blame as I am. It was you who was desperate for me to do something. Help, you said, can't you help.'

There was no answer. Rosy cried the more because it was true.

Thomas began to bawl at floor level.

'Don't kid yourself,' William went on relentlessly. 'You know the score as well as I do. So did Geoffrey. There's a risk. Always. You do your best. If you can't take the rap, get out of the kitchen.'

'You could have pulled out earlier,' sobbed Rosy.

'Hindsight is a wonderful thing. How clever of you to suggest it.'

'You should have known.'

'Things go wrong.'

'You said the share had dipped at Christmas. You had a warning.'

'Jesus Christ.' William picked up an orange from the blue bowl and hurled it across the room. He had just enough control to throw in the opposite direction from his son. He looked at Rosy and felt a lava of loathing for his wife erupt from him. 'If this is how you react when things go wrong, you shouldn't have married me.'

Rosy stared at him. She stopped crying in shock. She felt suddenly vulnerable. He was dark, rich, nice, handsome and hers. What if he left her for an office secretary? There was a very pretty one with a plait.

Rosy decided to switch from her parents' side back to William's.

'Mummy? How are you?'

'Everything's fine,' Laura replied automatically. 'A bit lonely. Daddy's still away. How's Thomas?'

'Difficult. He refuses to sleep.'

'Poor little chap.'

'Poor me, you mean. I've checked my Hugh Jolly book – hunger, wind, boredom, cow's milk allergy – but those don't seem the problem.' Those weren't the problem at all, thought Rosy.

'How about tension?'

Rosy was silent. Tension was indeed on Hugh Jolly's list of suspects, but she had decided to omit it as tension was undoubtedly the answer.

'Rosy, are you there?'

'Yes. Sorry, just yawning,' she lied.

'Why don't you come over?'

'It's a bit difficult at the moment.'

'You sound odd. Is there something wrong?'

'Not really, just tired. How's Daddy's trip going?' Rosy wondered how long she must circle before landing. She could feel herself running out of fuel.

'I don't think it's a great success. He sounded glum. No one's buying.'

Oh God, thought Rosy, how can I hit him when he's down. 'When's he back?'

'In two days' time.' Laura began to feel fretful. Rosy wasn't usually so terse. 'Look, why don't you come over? Bring Thomas. Or better still, I'll come to you. What about today?' I must get out of the house, she thought.

There was no reply. Laura scanned this ensuing silence for clues. It was clear that Rosy didn't want her. What had happened? She hadn't, she couldn't have seen her with Ranson in the garden of Wakehurst Place?

'Rosy,' she said urgently, 'please tell me. Something's up, isn't it?' A mixture of anxiety and guilt was squeezing her insides. There was probably a Greek myth about a daughter seeing her mother *in flagrante*. But what *flagrante*, when nothing had happened but a measly kiss?

It is now, thought Rosy, I must say it now. Don't think but open your mouth. She was aware that an irreversible shift would take place.

'The fact is that things have been a tiny bit disappointing with Daddy's funds.'

In that moment and at that mealy-mouthed choice of words, Laura felt the anxiety of the unknown replaced by the dread of a total certainty that she didn't want confirmed. She found herself staring very hard at the black telephone dial. Ring 100 for the operator, it read helpfully, 999 for an ambulance, my number is 01732 005049. A tiny spider was crawling over the numbered buttons. She was between 2 and 5 at the moment. It is imperative, thought Laura, that she reaches 5. When she does, I shall answer. Why do I call her a she? Because, I suppose, there are only female spiders in the world as they eat up all the males when they mate. Or is that a praying mantis? The first of the spider's eight gossamer legs reached the number 5.

'How bad is it?' she asked harshly, though she already knew the answer. As a child, Rosy used 'a tiny bit disappointing' for anything dreadful. It was a legacy from her boarding school which had trained her not to catastrophise. Laura's head shook slightly from the tension of holding it upright.

Rosy closed her eyes. Dear God, let me get through this, I promise I will take Thomas to church every other Sunday. I shall teach him the creed, whatever it is nowadays. Dear God, please.

'Actually, quite a lot of money is lost. The stock suddenly pitched.' Her words were tumbling out at staccato speed. 'William has been wonderful. He saved the remainder through quick action.'

She felt as though she had been holding a pneumatic drill. She could feel a tide of blood rising up her neck into her cheeks, flooding her forehead. She caught sight of the blotches of colour in the mirror.

'How much, Rosy?'

'Only about half remains.'

She avoided mentioning the figure. There was no need. Her mother could add up, or rather subtract.

'I'm so sorry.' Having delivered, Rosy now relaxed sufficiently to cry. 'William said Daddy knew the risk.'

Laura listened to her daughter sobbing. She has probably done quite a lot of crying in the past day or so, she thought.

'Don't,' she said, looking at the beam running along the ceiling. It had some woodworm at one end. Well, that was someone else's problem now. 'I know Geoffrey knew the risk.' Or he did and he didn't; in short, he ignored it like everything else.

A chill flatness descended upon her, wiping away the upheaval of emotion. Very soon, she knew, perhaps by tomorrow even, the news would have become just one more item to digest.

After the telephone call, Laura went outside. She wandered unseeingly for a moment, then stood at the door of the potting-shed. It was normally Tom's province but she could still rearrange trays and sift a little earth mechanically through her fingers, mindless objective tasks that stopped one from thinking. She looked around her. There were plant labels hanging on the wall, this season's seeds newly arrived in foil wraps, bags of blood, fish and bone to fertilise plants earmarked for resurrection in the borders. All signs of optimism which she considered soberly. She realised there was a drawback to the shed: it was the engine-room of the future but it didn't seem to have a future.

It was raw and foggy in the garden and cold standing still. The fingers of her right hand were numb. Her brain felt numb too, well aware of the arithmetic of the occasion but slow to absorb its feeling. Maybe it didn't merit a lot of feeling. People's lives got shaken up all the time. Ranson's, Tessa's, others had been here first, they had warmed the bed for her. One must accept events. 'Well,' she said aloud, 'that's that.' And she repeated it, practising acceptance before an audience of herself alone. Baba looked up sharply, her long, silken ears flipping inside-out at the tilt of her head. She recognised 'well', as in 'well, I think we'll go for a walk', but the body language looked wrong.

Laura was eating a boiled egg and bread and butter when Geoffrey rang at eight o'clock in the evening. He sounded hopeful.

'I think we've got some sales.'

'Jolly good,' she said flatly, swallowing the last mouthful of bread. She had resolved to say nothing.

'I've been thinking,' he said. 'It'll all be OK.'

'You think?'

'There's this, then there's William. In a year's time we'll look back on a storm in a teacup.'

Laura hesitated. 'I'm not sure you can count on William.' One by one, she was carefully plucking the cat's white hairs from her navy jumper. A few seemed to have threaded themselves like pins into the wool. It was an engrossing task.

'I think we can. In fact I'm sure. Actually, I gave him the whole portfolio, I was so sure.'

Laura froze. 'You did what?'

On the other end, in Lincoln, Geoffrey also froze. His optimism had advanced ahead of his caution.

'Did I hear correctly? You gave him the whole portfolio?'

Not quite the moment to say yes, thought Geoffrey. There were sounds on the line. He hoped it was long-distance interference.

'And shall I tell you what has happened to your whole portfolio?'

Geoffrey was sitting on his hotel bed. With his left hand he smoothed down its sprigged cotton cover. His wife's voice, quiet and controlled, was cordite.

'It's halved. There's probably less than half. The stock plunged.'

'How do you know?'

'Rosy told me today.'

Geoffrey pressed in his mouth and rocked forwards and backwards briefly in irritation. 'Don't be silly. It'll go up again.'

'No, it won't. William's withdrawn it.'

He felt slightly breathless. Will it work? he had asked William.

'You've got this wrong. I'll speak to William.'

'He's leaving for America shortly. In any case, why believe him rather than me?'

'Because he's a man.'

Laura closed her eyes. Stick by stick a store of dynamite had assembled within her. Controlled and undetonated till now, it at last found its fuse. She felt it explode. The noise fell on Lincoln.

'You bloody fool,' Geoffrey heard his wife saying. 'Blinkered, ignorant. Do you know what normal human beings do? Shall I tell you what they do? They reason. They anticipate. They learn from experience. Have you ever—'

Suddenly Geoffrey could take no more. A wave of blind anger and resentment washed over him.

'Shut up. Shut up, you bitch. What support have you ever been?'

'What support could I be if you never told me what—'

Geoffrey banged the phone down on her. He could not listen. The ruthlessness of women was disabling. He sat with his head in his hands on the hotel bed.

The sound of the receiver smacking the base crashed through Laura's eardrum. He had in effect walked out of the room but her anger, unabated, was rising on its own dynamic. She could not believe his idiocy, his lack of caution and, most of all, his deceit. Not even malicious deceit, but the secrecy of a child shielding his game from the judgment of adults.

She sat still for a quarter of an hour in the kitchen. Then she picked up her dinner plate and took it to the sink. She scraped off the bits of boiled egg which had already hardened on the spoon, washed it carefully and emptied the bowl. She gave the spaniels fresh water and let the cat out of the window, which she shut and re-bolted. A gust of early February, made up of wet earth and rotting leaves, rushed into the kitchen. She then went to the telephone again and dialled.

20

'Will you be back?' Beth asked Gary. She was coughing so much it was hard to get the words out. She wondered if this was nervous rather than flu. She hated asking Gary questions.

'I'm off for a few days. Gotta lotta stuff to deliver,' he muttered in the glottal-stopping speech of his generation. 'The job's in Southampton.'

It was unusual for him to announce a location. As a brickie he went all over the place, and the places were rarely divulged. He only occasionally swooped back home where his parents sat like barnacles in the house.

Now he blitzed through the room in a blaze of bulging muscles, one ear-ring and jackboots. They heard his motor bike starting up outside. The monster cleared the phlegm from its throat, roared, gathered power and then plunged off into the darkness of the wintry night.

Beth looked at Tom. She felt old, work-drained and son-drained. She was fifty-four, Tom was two years older. Like everyone else, they had married when they were twenty, but unlike everyone else they had not had a baby. All her younger sisters had produced them like rabbits, but Beth had seemed fated to be barren. She had been nearly thirty-seven when she had given birth to Gary. They had been overwhelmed when after years of wanting a child they were blessed with a son. But in the last few years the son had turned into a stranger. The transition was mysterious, nor was it even possible to say when it had taken place, just a graduation from a child into a different man.

Reminded, Beth took out the photograph album. Gary at three with his white-blond hair and blue eyes peeping at the camera; at eight in his football kit; at ten with mumps; at twelve when his voice had broken early; at fourteen, arms akimbo listening to a blast of heavy metal with his pelvis stuck out.

'Maudlin,' said Tom.

'What is?'

'Your flu's making you maudlin. Looking at old photographs.'

Tom had written Gary off years ago. It was hard enough keeping the garden in check without a son too. He felt worn out by things running wild and his Gary was more rampant than any of them. He wished he could dunk him in a good dose of garden chemical. A bottle of dwarfing hormone would do the trick nicely. This stuff was wasted on plants rather than people. He lit a cigarette. Beth started coughing again. He knew she was more anxious about the smoke getting into her peach curtains than her lungs.

'All right,' he said, getting up and going into the kitchen to smoke it. Poor old girl, wearing herself out cleaning Laura's house all day long. He had felt very solicitous since she'd said she might have to have a hysterectomy. Fancy using your womb up on a Gary, he thought to himself and was instantly shocked.

The phone rang and he answered it. It was Laura. Tom listened, perplexed.

'Right. I'll come in to check on the dogs at seven o'clock tomorrow morning,' he said, puzzled.

What's up, he wondered. She was paying him extra.

21 ∫

Ranson opened the door, shut it silently after her and hung up her coat. He had not anticipated her telephone call and felt ill-prepared for a visit at ten o'clock at night. These reversals of expectation were neither here nor there when you were young – the more the fizzier, in fact. But in middle age when degrees of routine and self-organisation had become habits, they were disrupting.

Laura followed him through the hall into the drawing-room. It was masculine, with lots of good dark-brown furniture, yet the blend of cinnamon, rust and gold revealed the intervention of an interior designer. So too did the lamps: several slim brass standards and some bronze candlesticks with dull gold coolie hats. Here was a job-lot of taste fit for the chairman. She looked round, dazed by the light and by the new-fangled strangeness of the occasion. She had driven here with the blind purpose and speed of a rocket but found it disorientating to arrive.

'Do you want a drink?' Ranson asked.

She nodded, glad to go on to automatic pilot.

'Whisky? Horlicks? Hot toddy? It's cold out.'

She smiled, amused by the range on offer. How these divorcés learned to look after themselves. Categorised as rogue elephants, they were actually quite house-trained. She chose a hot toddy and followed him into the small kitchen, watching him boil the kettle and cut up the lemon for the whisky. Yet for all this seeming domesticity, the flat looked little used. Visited rather than lived in, it was designed for a night's perch instead of a day's leisure. It made her feel edgy.

He handed the glass to her unsmilingly and they went back to the drawing-room. He sat down and waited, deciding he would not help her to begin. As an unsolicited visitor, she would have to make her own way tonight.

'Nice pictures,' she said, indicating the walls.

'Nicer ones still in the office.'

'I like that one over there. Do I recognise it?'

She got up, less to study it than for the relief of movement and turning her back to him. It was a Dutch-looking oil of a group of men playing cards. Ranson looked at her back: or rather, at a long navy jumper at the top and a loose fawn skirt underneath. He saw little point in telling her about the picture, which was a ropey pastiche hauled in by his decorator. He wondered how long she would maintain this pretence of interest. When it seemed it could continue for ever, he decided to come to the point.

'Where's Geoffrey?'

'Still away.'

'He's coming back when?'

'Tomorrow.'

His dogged refusal to help her talk began to dissolve. The hot whisky was melting it away.

'Well,' he said with some impatience, 'what's up?'

He half-regretted the visit imposed on him by this self-absorbed woman. He had hoped for an early night. There was a large tender to get in by the end of the month. Besides he had already used up a day's holiday on her earlier this week and his readiness to play was subject to limits to which he alone had the key. He glanced briefly at his watch.

As Laura turned round, she caught sight of his gesture, so eloquent to the insecure.

'I'm sorry,' she said, putting her glass down unfinished on a neighbouring table, 'I can see it's a bad time.' She went to fetch her coat.

He got up to stop her, ashamed that his sense of charity was shown up to be wanting. As he put his hand out to catch her arm, he saw that tears were running down her cheeks.

'Don't, please don't,' he groaned. He had always been impervious to hysterical sobbing, but silent tears uprooted him. He put his arms round her and began kissing the side of her face, pushing the hair back from her forehead, stroking her like a furry animal. Her eyes were closed though she put her face up, her nose resting beside his and he was aware that they were breathing at the same pace. She smelt real and ordinary and human, unperfumed or only with the scent of warm flesh and cold tears. He buried his mouth in the crook of her neck. Moving his hands under her jumper, he began to undo her catch. As it sprang open, he spread his fingers over her back: her skin felt smooth like a slightly oily satin. They stood there swaying for a moment and then he turned, drawing her to follow him.

'Come and lie down,' he murmured. 'We can't stay here.'

The bedroom was warm, stuffy even, the bed a large walnut antiquity which had obviously belonged to an earlier stage of his existence, which must mean his first marriage. Laura detached herself from him, lay back on its immaculate maroon cover and watched him as he sat on the edge of its surface and slowly loosened his shirt and unstrapped his watch. She noticed with relief that he was not wearing a vest and said so, adding, 'I hate men in vests.'

He looked at her in amusement. 'No taste for rough trade, it would seem.'

'No taste for anyone, to be honest. Normally. Except for you and except now.'

He felt a flood of relief at her total lack of coquetry. Women, even of a certain age, so often attempted to play hide and seek. Others seemed to have dabbled in self-assertion courses. How tired he was of both extremes. No wonder he had cherished his celibacy.

He leant over her and, pushing up her jumper and underwear, began to kiss her breasts. She arched herself upwards, lifting her nipples into his mouth.

'Oh Christ,' he muttered as he put his hand down to the wet warmth between her legs. An agonising spasm of pleasure pierced him at the old, old feeling of a woman wanting him whom he actually wanted too, a feeling so long mislaid and now rediscovered.

He pulled off their clothes and as he pushed himself gently into her, he felt the sweetness of her parting to receive him and the sudden surge deeper as she tented her knees to draw him in fully. She came almost immediately and he followed her.

'Christ,' he said again, groaning at the sudden violence of sensation.

He lay for a moment beached upon her and in her, exhausted by the rush of feeling and melted by its satisfaction.

She pushed him off her breast. 'I can't breathe,' he heard her say and as he pulled himself up and out of her, she whispered, 'Don't go,' and drew him back to her side. Lying on one elbow he bent to kiss her on the mouth in gratitude.

'That's the first time you have done that tonight,' she said with reproach.

'It should come last. It's the most intimate of all acts.'

Laura sat up and looked at him. For the first time she took in the small patch of fur on his chest, partly grey now, the loose skin around his waist, the endearing signs of middle age. He lay there unflinching under her scrutiny.

'Do you mind if I spend the night with you?' she asked. 'I don't want to go home to an empty house.'

For an answer he kissed her again, drew off the bed-cover and folded down the sheet. 'Make yourself at home,' he said, showing her the small masculine bathroom. She looked at herself in the mirror after he left her. What have I done? she wondered.

For Ranson too, waiting in the bedroom, thought was beginning to replace feeling. Until now he had been dazed by the speed with which events had run ahead.

'Did you plan this?' he asked when she returned. He put both hands on her naked shoulders and looked into her eyes searchingly.

She returned his gaze with horror. 'Never. It was flight. And you had something to do with it too.' She paused and added, 'You don't regret it, do you?'

'No,' he said, 'no, certainly not.'

He opened the window for the night air to come in, kissed her and turned the light out. Neither spoke. They lay on their right sides, curving into each other. As she did with Geoffrey, thought Laura, and presumably how Ranson had done with his wives. He fell asleep at once, Laura listened to the deepening of his breath and the unfamiliar sounds of a London night. The slap of feet on the pavement, the urgent siren of an ambulance, the chatter of South American accents from the street. For a long time the lights outside the window kept her awake. Then she slept.

She woke up once in the night. It was cold: the central heating had gone off, she had no nightdress and this unfamiliar body beside her was not a furnace in bed like Geoffrey. She felt a moment's panic at the strangeness of lying here with another man against her. The line of an old ballad about love and adultery came into her mind: 'Lie still, lie still, thou little Musgrave, And huggle me from the cold.' She whispered it and pulled his arm around her and slept again.

When she woke in the morning, the space was empty beside her. She got up, checked the time, which was seven o'clock, and stretched. She put on the striped dressing-gown discarded on the bed and, following the sounds from the kitchen, found Ranson washed, shaved and fully dressed in a navy suit and an apron, running his dishes from last night under the tap. She went up to him and put her arms around him.

'I know,' he said. 'Men at the sink are irresistible, aren't they?'

She hugged him. 'Do you want a coffee?'

'I'm afraid I've had one but I'll do one for you.'

'Are you in a hurry?'

'Yes, but stay as long as you like.'

It occurred to him that the agency cleaner – an out-of-work actress – was due to arrive at nine but it seemed petty to point it out.

'Sit down and have something to eat.'

He put a loaf of wholemeal bread in front of her and a pot of quince jelly, which his sister-in-law had pressed upon him at Christmas. She had thought he needed looking after. It was with difficulty that he had fended off a bachelor-sized Christmas pudding to take back to London.

'This is rather earlier than I usually get up,' said Laura, spreading her bread with butter and the jelly. It was a good set and the colour of cornelians.

'I wouldn't have woken you. I was going to steal out and leave a note.'

'You were? What would it have said?'

'I started but gave up.'

He pushed a scrap of paper across the table. *Darling Laura*, she read, *I didn't want to wake you.*

'Looks fine so far.'

'I couldn't think how to go on. It was hard to strike the right note and there's no time to refine it.'

'In short you're glad I've woken.'

He nodded, taking off his apron. He had stacked the dishes on the draining board. Laura wondered whether to offer to dry them. Better not be too helpful. He would think she was ready to nest.

'I must go,' he said. 'I'm really sorry to leave you like this, but I've got a lot to get through today. Will you be all right?'

She put out her hand. 'I haven't thanked you. I land up on you with the briefest of warnings. In a state. You house me. Give comfort.' She stood up.

'My comfort too.'

They touched mouths briefly. He sighed, resting his head against hers.

'Bang the door firmly behind you when you go. Be sure it shuts. OK?'

He picked up a pile of coins from the kitchen surface and his black leather wallet which he slid into his breast pocket. He blew her another kiss as he walked out of the door, then stuck his head round it again.

'Maybe it would be better if you just pulled the cover neatly over the bed. The cleaner comes at nine.' He hated himself for saying it.

Then he was gone.

Silence. She sat still in the tiny room, feeling very much on her own, automatically feeding the remainder of the bread and jelly into her mouth. She drained her coffee, then neatly tidied everything away and washed the crockery. She made the bed, quietly erasing every sign of her existence here. Smoothed out the pillows and the dent in the centre of the bed where they had huddled together in the night. 'Lie still, lie still, thou little Musgrave, And huggle me from the cold.' Already the event was beginning to slip from her mental grasp. As she drew the maroon cover over the bed, she felt she was closing the box.

She remembered she had left the note on the kitchen table and returned to pick it up, then let herself out of the flat, banging the door firmly behind her as instructed. Now she was outside, leaving him inaccessibly within.

I did not need to leave so early, thought Ranson on his way to the office. Yet he had felt unable to sit, knees touching in the tiny kitchen, in proximity to the previous night's love-making. He realised now he was still not sure why she had suddenly arrived nor what had driven her. He had not wanted to ask for an explanation. Better not know. He knew too much already and had been catapulted into an intimacy from which he felt compelled to distance himself. It was the morning after.

He thought to himself that thirty years ago it should have worked and would have. If so, he would not be alone now with an empty future. He would still be married to her, would have children, different ones of course from his daughter in California, with different genes, and with different grandchildren. The archetypally perfect couple stumbling through the full span of life together. Instead of one wife dead, one divorced, and a single existence. But that was thirty years ago, a fantasy hotchpotch ago. Not now, not real time. It won't work, he said to himself. Geoffrey's business had gone, his house was on the way out, not his wife too.

He remembered a Russian friend who was having an affair with a married woman. 'How is it going?' Ranson had asked. In reply his friend had quoted the words of Turgenev. 'I am on the edge of another man's nest.' Another man's nest, repeated Ranson to himself, except that the nest was shredding apart.

The journey home took Laura some time, prolonged by the crawl through the congested roads of a south London morning. A robot at the wheel, she felt suspended in a timeless limbo between two unrelated worlds. At the end she turned abruptly into her drive, scattering the wet gravel, switched off the engine and sat for a moment. Her mind was dislocated, on a fork, then and now, there and here. Ten o'clock. Twelve hours after she had arrived at his flat last night. Ten o'clock. The cleaner would be tidying his kitchen, dusting his bedroom. Who's been sleeping in *his* bed then? – but good little Goldilocks had wiped her fingerprints away.

She got out of the car and shut its door, smelling the familiar wet decay of the winter country again. Tom was near by, watching her. He had been clearing some ivy from under the hedge where the white hoods of massed snowdrops were unfurling. She walked in a spritely way towards him, swinging her arms. Look. Aren't I normal?

'Thank you so much for coming in early.' She spoke with unusual vivacity. 'It was an emergency, I'm afraid.'

'All right, I hope,' he mumbled.

'Absolutely fine now. Gracious, what a wonderful job you're doing. It's so nice to have it cleared. See, even the crocuses are showing now.'

They both stared at the first lilac candleflames emerging from a carpet of *Crocus tommasinianus*.

'Yes,' she said, 'really nice,' and she turned round to escape him, to go into the house because talking and doing would smother last night with the brash layers of today. It was the past that she wanted, already receding, fragments erased. If she could stay silent, alone, immobile, she might recapture and bathe in it for another day. *Darling Laura, I didn't want to wake you—* Written a million years ago, it was the only tangible fragment she retained.

The dogs were barking a frantic welcome, hearing her footsteps, pressing their noses to the crack of the kitchen door – she could hear their loud sniffs. But she went instead to the bedroom with the intention of lying down and remembering. It was the sight of the large mahogany bed that stopped her. It was another bed she wanted to remember, but this one replaced and obliterated it. It had belonged to Geoffrey's father; they had called it the marriage bed. She stared at it now, at its mass, solid, her bed, his bed, their bed together, their children's bed. Here was her world – the real one, remorseless, the chosen one, long ago indeed, but the one which had formed her. She said aloud: 'As I make my bed, so I must lie on it.' Then she thought of the more famous rider. But please God let me unmake my bed.

22

'Steady on,' said Geoffrey, jolted from his thoughts. He was sitting in the car beside Malcolm, who was a maniac driver. Heading south on the M11, they were spending most of their journey in the outside lane.

Geoffrey had not spoken for an hour. He had sunk a fair deal of whisky last night and his head throbbed violently in consequence. One spot in particular was excruciating. He had no doubt it was the place which his wife had assaulted during the telephone call. An X-ray would probably show it to be fractured. He gave a quiet moan of self-pity.

Malcolm glanced at him. 'You're not going to throw up, are you?'

'No. Keep your eyes on the road.'

Geoffrey stared at the huge wheels of an articulated lorry they were passing on his left. Their diameter exceeded the height of their car. Mesmerised by the pounding machinery, he suddenly panicked that his door was not tight shut. He shuddered and then calmed himself. There was no doubt that he had become risk-averse since last night. Hold firm, he thought. He could feel his confidence oozing down and out.

For the first time in his life, Geoffrey found himself confronting a blank. Trained as consistently as an astronaut to travel in his capsule, he was now facing expulsion. The world he had known was cracking open. The loss of the business was in itself of no consequence, it was only ever a meal-ticket – but the loss of the house and the grounds was different, they were him. He remembered carrying Thomas round the barns that hot morning last summer. 'When you grow up, you must take care of this,' he had told him. The infant had stretched out his arms to the doves. Geoffrey grimaced in pain at the recollection. Thank God that Thomas would not grow up to remember it. It was a good thing that babies had noodles for brains.

Yet, for all his new anxiety, he still could not truly credit the possible loss of the house. It would be like a loss of faith. Not that he believed in anything numinous; his belief in God was, rather, part of faith in his capsule, that universe which was his house, his handful of acres, his father and his forefathers, all that past which gave him his insulated place here and now. He had a dark, varnished portrait of his great-great-great-grandfather. A good big nose, pale-blue eyes, red face, sandy hair. He was dressed in black with a couple of pointers and a spaniel at his feet and was recognisably Geoffrey. It was extraordinary how hair and eyes and even the bags beneath them could get passed down intact over a period of several hundred years. What's that portrait going to look like in a house which has a number in a road? thought Geoffrey with bitterness.

His mind, normally a slow means of locomotion, restlessly revolved one subject after another, or rather different facets of the same. It was not just the house; there was Laura too to consider. 'Do you know what normal human beings do?' she had asked on the telephone last night. 'They reason. They anticipate. They learn from experience.' She had called him a bloody fool. Normally impervious to abuse, he could remember every word she had said. He hated her suddenly. How he had adored her when they had married, worshipped her, couldn't believe his luck. Yet what had she done? She had spent his money and now reviled him. She had consumed first and blamed after.

He wondered whether she had ever really appreciated him. After she had given birth to Allegra, she had referred to him and the two girls as the meat and two veg. It had been a joke, of course, and he, poor mutt, had even quite liked his superior status as the meat. But it now occurred to him that it had summed up only too precisely his basic position as the mere provider of fuel. Wasn't it all she had ever wanted from him? He remembered that palaver when she had painted nipples on her shoulder-blades. He recalled her amusement and his distress. Deep down – not that he had a subconscious, which was for wendys – deep down, he had known that it wasn't just sex she was rejecting, but him.

He looked out unseeingly at the pasteurised landscape which had rushed monotonously by for the last hour or so. The meat and two veg, he said to himself. She had rejected him. No doubt she had turned vegetarian.

Malcolm glanced at him again and turned back to the road. It was obvious his passenger was in the pits. He hadn't wanted to tell Geoffrey before their sales trip that he was going to accept the offer of another job, one in Tonbridge. He liked his boss and shrank from puncturing his confidence. He had hoped to make some sales for Geoffrey and then tell him the news on the way home. But now didn't feel like the best moment.

23

Spring came in its usual erratic style of retreating every so often in order to advance. As always the alternating spells of frost and thaw managed to deceive the plants. Year after year the same ones were fooled into thrusting out green shoots in balmy weather only to suffer their death in the freezing days that followed. The tips of the hydrangeas were blighted and the rhododendron leaves curled up like hedgehogs.

It was in one of the cold snaps that Louisa died, quite suddenly. Laura had taken her to Marks & Spencer the previous day to buy a blue lambswool jumper and Louisa was wearing it the day of her death. She was a little tired and had a touch of indigestion from yesterday's outing which had ended with eating a rum baba on the Pantiles of Tunbridge Wells. She had not slept that night, though whether the insomnia was caused by her stomach or Laura's warning that they might have to move house was not easy to say – Louisa had staked her future on the green-and-white bedroom. At any rate, today she had found herself unable to eat her Meals on Wheels at lunchtime. A slice of pale-brown lamb, peas, potatoes and the usual wet tinned fruit.

However, at her age she had a short memory span. As a benefit, she had temporarily mislaid her problems and was enjoying a contented enough afternoon working the video machine in her flat. She had put her legs up on the small velvet footstool, with the remote control to hand. She was watching a romantic drama but it had too many sex scenes for her taste. 'Disgusting,' she said loudly. She used her remote button to fast-forward during any offending action but the scenes were so numerous that she had reached the end of the film within half an hour.

She then put on a film of her youth with the lissom Eleanor Powell swaying in a raffia skirt. It transported Louisa back to the thirties. She remembered wearing a long, black velvet dress with a bias-cut skirt to a ball. A scattering of silver beads around the neck and long black gloves, her hand on Dick's lapel, her hair smoothed on top and flounced at the sides, her face racé, her mouth lipsticked. She was skinny then and full of chatter, they all were, like sparrows – not striding and taciturn as women were nowadays.

Why did Dick have to go and die so soon after the war? At least he had left them in comfort. That was all she could remember about him now. God knows it was easy to forget a husband – women forgot living ones – and forty years ago was a long time. One forgot the face, the voice, the only thing she could recall was her long, black-gloved hand resting on his lapel as they danced. Strange, he would have been a veteran now if he had lived, wrinkled, reminiscent at the drop of a hat, and probably leaking – men always had trouble with their prostate. Instead he had died and left her and her daughter in comfort. Perhaps that was why she had married him, so he could leave her in comfort. That was what marriage was for and what she had wanted for Laura.

This reminded her that Laura's comfort was proving finite. The pot was running dry. I must change the will yet again, thought Louisa. The will was becoming as complicated as a Fair Isle jumper. A nightmare of codicils, it was running very hard to stay on the same spot. People kept springing out of position, now married, now single, now rich, now poor, dying, dispersed, out of favour, in vogue. No wonder she had left some money to the National Trust. Above the flux of human chaos, it would surely outlast the monarchy. It might one day inherit the throne.

Louisa sighed. Thinking hurt when you were very old. It was tempting to switch on the video again. She tried to remember the latest redistribution in the will, which was only a month ago: was it a half to Laura and the remainder between Rosy and Allegra, or was that the previous version of the will? She would have to switch it all back to Laura, who had probed yesterday about her bequests. Perhaps – Louisa perked up at the thought – perhaps on condition that she lived with her in the new house.

A flush of pleasure rushed through her. There would be no wardens, no old people's home, no mess-mates, none of the levelling processes of old age. She pushed herself up from the green velvet chair in a state of keen excitement at the very thought. As she looked down at her brown-spotted hands trembling faintly with strain, they turned slim and gloved, the left one poised lightly on Dick's lapel. A long glove, black, wrinkled around the wrist and snaking up her forearm. But as she watched, it began changing slowly to a vice which gripped her arm and squeezed upwards, moving fast now to fathom the pit of her chest. Unable to breathe, gasping with pain, her mouth working frantically, she threw up her arms and died.

She was found the following morning by the daily help, in a huddle on the floor. Laura arrived at the same time as the ambulance. She was steeling herself for the fact that her mother's tongue might be protruding, but thank God it was tastefully shut in her mouth and her eyelids were closed. Only her little white head and neck were visible above the blanket. Laura stared at the collar of her blue lambswool jumper. Something borrowed, something blue came into her mind. How poignant that it had been worn only once, like a wedding dress, except this ordinary thing had been chosen to mark an end, not a beginning. She bent down to her dead mother to touch her cold hard face. The mould that had borne her was gone.

The next few days were filled with the industry of death. The post-mortem, the undertaker with his practised condolence, coffins, woods, linings and prices, the funeral celebrations and the hymns all jostled for attention. There were jonquils for the church, wreaths for the corpse and food for the living to be arranged.

'A March funeral,' said Amy. 'Louisa did well. They usually die in February.' She spoke bravely, saying 'they', but was frightened inside. With her elder sister dead, she was next in the firing-line. Perhaps not: there was always James who was only a year younger – but on second thoughts, she would prefer to go first.

Laura telephoned Allegra. She had rung her at regular intervals since Christmas in case the baby suddenly arrived but had found her as reluctant as ever to talk. It was always hard going, yet today was even worse.

'You *must* come. It's Granny, Allegra.' She corrected herself, 'Was.'

'Please don't call me Allegra.'

Laura was lost. The name had been Louisa's idea. Was this why?

'What do you mean?'

'My name is Darleen.'

'Darleen?' It sounded like the new equivalent of Sharon or Darren.

'I have an Indian name now.'

'Darleen.' Unseen, Laura raised her eyes to the ceiling.

'That's right. I'm a Buddhist, remember?'

'Allegra, I mean Darleen, come anyway.'

'But I'm a Buddhist.' She seemed bent on not coming.

Laura lost her temper. 'So what? You're not going to turn into a pumpkin.'

Maybe I could manage it, thought Allegra, if I levitate through the service.

Rosy too raised problems. 'What do I do with Thomas?' she said when Laura telephoned her. It sounded as though another refusal was on the cards.

'What's the trouble?' She strove to keep the edge out of her voice.

'There's no one to leave him with.'

'Oh, darling, do bring him.' She could hear Thomas in the background, half singing and talking to himself, very busy with new words. There was the noise of splashing too. He must be in the bath.

Rosy hesitated. It didn't feel right.

'But isn't he a bit young for a funeral? He's only just been born.' She meant herself too. It would be her first occasion. Really, thought Laura, they have an excuse for everything.

'Look, Rosy, it could be me in that coffin.'

'You're different.'

'I'm not. Just come. No buts.' Then she added 'please' since Rosy was too old to boss.

She replaced the phone. It was scarcely surprising they found it unnatural to pay their respects. The old rituals were petering out. Infrequent weddings now, not many christenings, fewer funerals as the old were living longer. By the time her generation was due to fall off the perch, they would be lucky to be noticed at all. No wonder they were all swarming like bees to Catholicism.

*   *   *

The sun came out on the day of the funeral, though fierce gusts of wind flustered the violet pansies in the formal bedding outside the crematorium. Amy and James arrived early, Amy's face looking pale, framed in a big black fox collar. She pressed her cold cheek against Laura's and avoided looking at the chimneys which were a reminder of the real reason they were gathered here. Rosy and Thomas stood with Geoffrey; Beth and Tom a little further off; and Tessa alone. Grouped in their separate silent huddles, they waited in the wind outside the crematorium until its present occupants had seen the current coffin off. The early arrivals for the funeral after Louisa's, clearly a large contingent, were already forming their own cluster in the wings. The different packs eyed each other covertly. The unbroken succession of the dead did not lift the spirits.

The only gaiety came from a pair of eighty-year-olds, dressed to defy mourning. In bright red and amber wool coats respectively, they hovered on the edge of the two funeral groups, unsure which coffin they belonged to.

'Are they them or us?' Laura asked Amy. She frowned and put on her tortoiseshell spectacles. As she peered at them, she recognised they were the remaining members of Louisa's old bridge foursome. They had not played for several years now, nor would again, death stripping them of hearts, clubs, trumps and partners, but not of their zest for life. Amy cheered up. She was no longer the oldest member of the funeral party, nor the next in line to succeed.

No sign of Allegra, thought Laura. Summoned for their turn, the small group filed into the little wood-panelled chapel. Everyone looked for the coffin. So tiny, thought Laura, the pathos of its size making tears sting in her eyes. Geoffrey shuffled sideways and put an arm round her. She didn't deserve it, but he loved her more than he hated her at the moment.

I can't watch, Amy said to herself, I can't bear the moment when it slides out of sight. She could not count the number of coffins she had seen gliding down the chute. Each time was worse than the last and brought her nearer my God to Thee, or to nothing, which was more likely. She kept her eyes resolutely on the red wool coat of Louisa's old friend. Lulu? No. Ella? Estelle, that was it.

Rosy turned Thomas back to front so he couldn't see what was happening. He clasped her tightly round the neck and tried to pull her long silver ear-ring out of its pierced hole. 'Mama,' he said loudly, jogging on her arm to indicate he wanted a ride on the rocking-horse. As though in response, there came a cry from the back of the chapel. Thomas tried to peer over Rosy's shoulder and the heads of the bridge players in the row behind him. The sound came again. It was a cry like a new lamb, certainly the call of very new life. Rosy began to turn round but stopped, realising that Thomas would be facing the coffin if she did so. She nudged her mother instead.

'You have a look,' she whispered. 'It sounds like a baby to me.'

The cry came again, penetrating the canned background music of the service. Laura twisted round. She was wearing a low-brimmed black hat and its swoop blocked her view. She tilted it up, looked again and drew in her breath. Allegra was sitting in the back row, holding a child wrapped in a dark-paisley shawl. Newly dropped from its mother, it could only have been a few weeks old.

The sight of the child gave Laura the strangest feeling. A miraculous transubstantiation seemed to have taken place. A magic bid for survival. As though the spirit of Louisa had wrestled from its coffin and shaped itself into the baby at the other end of the chapel. Then the queer moment passed, the shock leaving joy.

'Look,' she whispered to Rosy.

'Good God,' she exclaimed. She was cross that Allegra looked stunning.

'What's up?' whispered Geoffrey.

'Shhhsh,' said Amy, then turned round herself.

Allegra noticed nothing. She sat perfectly still, her face lifted towards a dusty shaft of sunlight from a window, her dark eyes closed, her expression rapt, her glamour dazzling.

'Let us pray,' said the cleric who was conducting the service. He felt like rapping for attention. Distress he was used to, mechanical indifference at the other extreme, but never this passionate deflection of interest from the corpse to the living at the back of the hall.

Louisa would shift in her coffin that she wasn't the star of her own funeral, Amy thought dryly. Then she too was struck by the oddness of one dead and one new-born. Was Louisa indeed on the move? Amy raised her eyebrows to express cynicism to herself, but the fancy, as yet marginal, allured her. I wonder, she thought, a Buddhist novelist, how would that sound? She found she was watching the coffin slip out of view without fear. At a previous funeral she had imagined its progress, down the shaft, along the moving road, gliding, floating with terrible electric precision to the magnet of the incinerator. But what if the coffin were vacant? She looked round again at the child in Allegra's arms. Is this my new sister? I'm barmy, she thought, but the fancy was irresistible.

They all knelt, rose, and knelt briefly again, before being expelled to make room for the next occupants. Laura stood at the entrance, breathing lungfuls of air after the stale, spicy smell of mourning. The others broke into a chatter of relief at being let out of prison. No longer in inhibited huddles, they stood grouped together, united by experience. James unloaded his tension and abandoned all tact.

'You know,' he said waving towards the thirty-foot chimneys, 'they've all been ordered to burn at higher temperatures. The gas bill of these places could rise from £4,000 to £20,000 a year.'

'Everything costs a bloody fortune nowadays,' agreed Geoffrey dolefully.

Amy turned her back on them.

'Estelle,' she said, seizing at a change of focus.

'Amy, how wonderful. Do you remember Alice?'

Amy grasped her hand. 'I love your red coat.'

Allegra alone stood in isolation. She exchanged nods with Rosy, both clasping their children like shields.

'Pony,' said Thomas, stretching his arms to the baby.

Their mothers eyed each other warily. Rosy was surprised her sister had not whipped out a breast during the service; she was the type to feed on demand.

Laura went up to Allegra. 'Let me hold him,' she said quietly.

'Her.'

'Her.' She picked up the baby, recognising herself in its face, her dark eyes, her brown hair, her imprint though as yet unfurled. The child looked back, unfocused.

'Allegra,' she began.

Allegra looked anxious. 'Darleen.'

'Darleen. Why didn't you tell me when I rang?' Allegra looked aside, then down at the child in her mother's arms. Did they still not understand?

'Why? Why not?'

She sighed and put out her arms to gather the child back. Her mother was rocking her too fast. She would upset her peace of mind.

'You would all swamp me. Don't you see? Smother me. You think that having a child makes me your property again. One of you. Part of the clan.'

'We don't.'

'You do.' Allegra took a step backwards.

'Most daughters—'

'There, you see?'

'All I was going to say was that most daughters would find it useful to have grannies and grandfathers and aunts and uncles and—'

Allegra took another step back at the family litany.

'You wouldn't say this if I were a son.'

Laura was about to say 'I would' but, 'No, I wouldn't,' came out instead. She recalled Louisa clinging to her like a barnacle on a rock, a lifetime's adhesion. I mustn't do it to Allegra, she thought. What daughters did for their mothers was always exacted from the next generation of girls. The ticket kept getting passed on.

Laura looked at Allegra. She wished she wouldn't keep stepping backwards.

'Darleen.' She smiled. 'You're free.'

Allegra looked suspicious.

'What's your lovely child called?'

'Ranee.'

'Ranee.'

The bridge player in the red coat appeared at her elbow.

'Estelle Selwood,' she said, holding out her hand. 'It's been a wonderful funeral. Such a loss.'

'A great sorrow,' agreed Laura, tucking the shawl around Ranee's cheek.

'I hope I'm not speaking out of turn but—'

'Please do go on,' said Laura helpfully. She felt brimful of tenderness. The old lady must be feeling both frightened and sad.

'A truly lovely funeral, as I said. We felt privileged to attend. But, well, what I really wanted to say was – you know that Meissen plate. Louisa always promised it to me.' She handed Laura her address card, a gold label stuck on a piece of paper, then walked purposefully away.

Bereft of speech, they watched the diminishing back of her red coat. It joined up with the amber coat and the two colours bobbed jauntily off to the exit.

'Can you believe it?' said Allegra. 'What a bitch.'

'What a cow,' agreed Laura.

For the first time they smiled at each other.

'Will she get it?'

'Will she, hell,' and they both burst into laughter.

'What's this?' asked Rosy, feeling left out of some fun.

'Oh, nothing,' Allegra said firmly.

24 ∫

'And don't forget,' said Polly, scooping up a bundle of exercise books and trainers, 'mind you give it its bottles on time.' She went out, banged the door, then shouted through the window, 'I'll be back late from school tonight, OK?'

Tessa made shooing signs of exasperation.

'What on earth is It and what's Its bottle?' Laura had just arrived in Tessa's kitchen where she had joined an eclectic accretion of wormer, coffee mugs and calligraphy pens. An air of chaos possessed the room. Some tell-tale wisps of straw lay on the floor and a rat-a-tat-tat of drumming came from the ceiling.

Laura glanced up. 'What the hell's going on?'

'I'm absolutely furious.' The table reverberated as Tessa slammed down her mug. 'Here I am in the midst of trying to prepare for my first exhibition in years and she's brought home a lamb.'

Laura looked suitably aghast but was actually enchanted. She had sought oblivion from the crises at home and a lamb seemed the perfect diversion.

'Lord, you've nowhere to keep it.'

'Too right. We've had to put it in the sodding bathroom.'

'Listen. Is that it now?'

The two women fell silent and cocked their ears to the ceiling. The tom-tom came again.

'It's its hooves,' explained Tessa. She looked at her watch. 'Oh Christ, it's time for a bottle.'

She turned and fetched a bag from a barrel marked 'Bread'. She spooned out some powder, mixed it with water, then warmed and stirred the brew. All the while she was shaking her head in mystification that she had let herself in for such a palaver. As she poured the liquid into a baby's bottle, the sweet smell of milk substitute mingled with the fumes of turps in the kitchen.

'As though I don't have enough to do,' she muttered in a parody of the harassed housewife. 'Bloody hell, a lamb as well.' She sniffed the bottle delicately, somewhat mollified by the supportive noises her friend was uttering in the background. 'It's orphaned,' she explained more calmly.

'Polly took pity, did she?'

'She did the usual thing. Took pity, but I do the caring. It was rejected by its mother and Poll's pal didn't have another ewe to give it to. It would have died if little Miss Nightingale hadn't stepped in. I've agreed to take it for a week. Maximum.' She snapped the rubber teat firmly on the neck of the bottle. 'Come on,' she said.

The pair of them climbed the rickety stairs to the little bathroom. A loud bleating came from the other side of the door. Laura opened it warily.

'Good God,' she said.

The floor was covered in newspaper and straw. A tiny black lamb hurled itself at her shins.

'Not her – me, you fool, I'm your mother,' said Tessa, folding down the lavatory seat to sit on it. The lamb rushed over to her, transfixed by the bottle, its muscles stiff with a frenzy for milk. It nibbled dementedly at her trousers in a frantic search for the teats of its dam. Laura balanced on the edge of the bath, watching Tessa feed the nipple into the black mouth. For a second the pink lining flashed like a Negro's, then its lips closed, crushing the teat with ardour. Legs braced, eyes shut in bliss, tail wriggling with passion, the whole of its body was concentrated on the rapturous ecstasy of milk. There was silence in the tiny room apart from the smack of the lamb's rhythmic sucking. Its life force was awesome.

'Amazing, isn't it?' said Laura.

Tessa looked down at it. 'It's a peculiar thing,' she said, shifting the bottle to her left hand to give her right one a rest, 'it's made me quite want to have a child again.'

'But you're over forty and unmarried,' Laura protested.

She felt the gulf between them. Whatever she had just said, it was true that Tessa was still young whereas she was old and a grandmother twice over. It reminded her of the paradox that she who had seemingly all was on a decline whilst Tessa who possessed nothing could still realise potential. The lamb was a reminder of her tiny dark grandchild; it prompted the realisation that Tessa had more in common with Allegra than with herself.

She pushed the thought to one side. She was here to avoid matters of substance.

'Forty and unmarried,' repeated Tessa crossly, 'ancient and unwanted. Don't forget to remind me.'

She increasingly wondered why she was fond of Laura. History and old loyalty, she supposed. Habit was a great reinforcer.

'I didn't mean—'

'I know you didn't. I simply feel touchy at being told my age when my pot's been given a stir. There's the new exhibition. Then Miles trying to come back. Things seem to be on the move again after years of treading water. Everything seems possible. Even marriage in theory.'

'Would you really remarry? Someone else, I mean. You always said never again.'

'Hmm,' said Tessa reflectively.

The lamb's sucking had slowed. She put her hand on the tight curls of its flank. Its belly was deliciously warm and rounded with milk. Touching it filled her with calm.

'It's called Ebenezer,' she offered.

Laura was undeflected. 'You're not put off by an unlucky experience?' She felt driven to draw parallels with Ranson. 'You don't feel like running away from it?'

Did he? She had rung him twice since that February night. On both occasions his secretary had said he was abroad. Was it true or was he hiding? Last week she had sent him a newspaper advertisement for a house. Silence.

Tessa looked out of the window. 'Even that old misogynist Strindberg thought that a bad marriage was better than none.'

'That's ridiculous. Perhaps not then, but now, a hundred years later.'

'Of course it's not true,' agreed Tessa. 'I wouldn't take Miles back at any price – but you do get terribly ingrown on your own. Opinionated, compulsive, rigid. I even have a favourite cup and get upset when someone else pinches it. How's that for pettiness?'

There was a gurgling sound as the lamb drained the last bubbles of milk from the bottle. She tried to withdraw the teat but Ebenezer clung on, happy to savour the mixture of rubber and air.

'In any case,' she added slowly, 'however awful one's spouse, he does at least act as a corrective. It's unbalanced being alone. You need someone to tell you you're silly.'

'Oh well,' said Laura, 'lucky old Geoffrey. He'll be pleased to hear that.'

She made a grimace. They had been at each other's throats for ages now, apart from the truce at the funeral.

She had slept with him only once in six weeks. It was an awful occasion: they might have been wearing brown paper bags over their heads. She hated herself for being so foul to him. He had found it difficult to stay stiff.

'Do I infer you're not getting on too well?'

'Rather difficult at the moment.'

'You're definitely moving?'

Tessa felt it was cruel to look at her. She concentrated instead on unsticking Ebenezer from his bottle.

'Keep it to yourself but the house may have to go on the market next month. Some other things too.'

I came here to forget this, thought Laura. She wanted to return the conversation, albeit indirectly, to Ranson, but it was difficult to find a natural way back. Obsession made her plunge on.

'You really would find it sufficient to remarry for negative reasons?' she persisted.

'No, don't be an ass,' said Tessa, feeling Laura was being extraordinarily obtuse. 'You marry for positive reasons but they only come into existence when someone arrives. However, the negative reasons get you into the right frame of mind. And those are quite strong. Make no mistake, independence seems great but it's eventually an illusion. Its charms are finite. You have to be rich and egotistic to make it work. And when you get egotistical, you get crazy. I've quite enjoyed my independence but it's a stage like any other stage and it will pall given time. Besides, there's no doubt that the past hangs round your neck and the future's chilly on your own.'

She was flushed, perhaps from bending over the lamb, perhaps from the analysis of her own thoughts. She stood up and stretched, shaking her straight fawn hair back from her face. Her long legs felt cramped from sitting on the loo. She regarded Laura with suspicion. There must be something behind all this inquisition.

'Look, Laura,' she said carefully, 'I don't know what all this is about, but if you're thinking of leaving Geoffrey at your age, my advice is don't.'

Really, she thought, the first bad patch, and she thinks of a flit. She bent to pick up Ebenezer, who was snuggled into his nest of straw.

'Oh, you darling,' she said, burying her face in his warm, plump, curly folds. 'Here, have a squeeze.' And she handed him over.

'I don't know what you mean,' said Laura, cradling the lamb automatically. 'I was asking about you, not talking about me.'

'Quite so.' Tessa brushed the straw off her jeans to the floor. She managed to convey the impression that the statement of innocence was similarly worthless.

'You don't believe me.'

'If you say so.'

Laura felt like beating her about the head with the excellence of her marriage.

'It may be a bad time but it has never occurred to me to leave Geoffrey.'

'A marriage,' said Tessa slowly, 'can end at the drop of a hat.'

Could it? Laura wondered as she drove home later that day. It seemed, rather, otherwise – a long drawn-out process on the lines of one nail after another in the coffin. The thought reminded her of the funeral and the contents of the will which might yet provide a way out.

She felt plagued by uncertainty. As she drove past the verges of the main road, she noticed the banks of blowsy eggyolk daffodils that the council had planted to prettify the countryside. Vandals, she thought furiously. Everything seemed one more nail in the coffin, and, as for Ranson, he was the hugest nail of the lot. Gone to ground – it was humiliating. She let herself in at the door to find Geoffrey in his wax jacket and boots. He had just deposited a sculptural crust of mud on the hall rug, with smaller off-cuts en route to the kitchen.

'Look,' she said, pointing.

He ignored her finger massively. 'Where have you been? I've been trying to get hold of you.'

'Out.'

'Well, I've been with the police.'

She halted in the middle of unpeeling her coat to stare at him.

'They've found the jewellery. The ring, the necklace, the lot. They needed me to identify it.'

'What? No. How?'

'It was picked up with more recent stuff that's been stolen round here.'

'Who took it?'

'That's just it.' He looked glum.

'Who?'

'It's been traced back to Gary. It seems he lifted it when the garden was open.'

'Oh no. Oh God.' Laura stared at him appalled. 'Oh, poor Beth and Tom. Do they know?'

'No doubt they've been told.'

'Oh God. I was going to let her know this week we'd be moving. Oh, poor Beth, it'll kill her.'

Geoffrey looked at her sourly. He was used to seeing her rivers of sympathy gush straight past him and over someone else. She might have spared some for him this time. It was *his* jewellery, or more to the point, his insurance money which had proved very useful and which he would have to repay. A challenge when a portion was already spent.

25

Ranson sat at his mahogany desk, assessing this year's sales brochure, the largest and glossiest yet. It offered a scenic tour of the world in advertiser's Fujicolor. Atmosphere, that nebulous but potent attribute, was essential to these photographs. His roads were always shown in the few minutes of the purple Kenyan dawn, his bridges during a golden Chinese sunset. He thought of the history behind each of the projects: the bottle-necks of competing companies, the hours spent on squeezing the price, the keen relief at a contract, then the ambivalence of the managers who knew they would only represent a distant pay cheque to their families at home. And where did this end? With a Queen's Award for export and a picture of a bridge in a Shanghai dusk. Was it worth it? I am tied to the wheel, he thought.

From under the stack of brochures, he pulled out an estate agent's clipping from the *Kent and Sussex Courier*. He had received it ten days ago. There was a large arrow in red biro pointing to a mossy, tile-hung farmhouse and a note scribbled in the margin: *I thought you might like to see this. L.* Just L, no with love from L, but Ranson couldn't deceive himself. The note communicated the need to meet again, to continue what had been so abruptly arrested, the desire to remember and to re-ignite.

Ranson felt guilty but resolute. When she had telephoned a month ago, he had told Jenny, his secretary, to say he was out. He had seen a spark of alertness in her blue eyes – this was more interesting than rivets and cubic masses – which was instantly masked. 'Laura,' he now said out loud. He picked out a blank card from the drawer of his partner's desk and wrote in a stiff hand: *How very kind of you to send the cutting.* He looked up, grimaced and carried on. *I hope all is well. I am off on another trip this week but hope* – shit, he thought, noting hope in the previous sentence. He crossed out 'hope' and substituted 'trust' – *but trust that it will be possible to arrange a meeting this summer. All good wishes, L.*

You sod, he said to himself, but he felt at a loss to know what else to do. He thought of throwing the card in the bin and telephoning her, but he would probably get her husband, which he would find utterly castrating. The ruthlessness of Ranson's initial attitude to Geoffrey had evaporated, to be replaced by a certain strange solidarity, sympathy even, after he had been to bed with his wife. And in any case, even if Laura answered the phone, to what avail? It would be a cul-de-sac. No; his card, bare though it was of all normal human empathy, chilling even in its polite platitudes, would have to stand.

Ranson glanced back at his brochure, at his road striding to the horizon of a purple dawn, and ticked his approval. He then turned to the clipping of the farmhouse. It looked promising. Again he thought how artefacts were so much easier to handle than people. He stretched out his hand for the telephone to ring the estate agent for an appointment. He had lied when he wrote that he was about to set forth on a trip. There was nothing booked for months, and in the meanwhile he had every intention of organising his personal life rather more wisely than before.

* * *

Beth had not visited the village shop since the police had informed her about Gary. Indeed she had not gone anywhere and was showing an alarming degree of agoraphobia. She felt acidic with shame, self-contempt and the chips which she was eating blindly in front of the television. She had put the photographs of Gary in a drawer, as well as binned the lace pillow inscribed 'Baby' which she had cherished for nineteen years. She had also thrown out his biker's gear from the wardrobe. With nothing to fill them, they seemed like dead men's clothes.

In the last few days she had resolved on a hysterectomy. It was not the errant flux of her womb that had forced her decision, but rather the fact that it had nurtured an incubus. 'Now is not the best time to decide,' said Dr Collins, who thought she had deserved a better deal in life, but then justice played a minor part in the fate of most of his patients and mercy even less.

The vicar too had shown concern. Beth was no pillar of the church – being a birth, marriage and death prop – but he still arrived on the doorstep, offering to share her pain. It was a formula that he had heard his archbishop pronounce on the *Today* radio programme. It was in deference to this that he had jettisoned his previous formula that it will all come right in the end. However, Beth proved infertile ground for any of his bromides. 'It's nobody's business but mine,' she declared stoutly, closing the door on his presumptuous foot. Private pain might be painful but at least it had dignity; shared pain was better confined to Americans on telly.

It was Laura alone whom she consented to see. It was out of a sense of responsibility, one that Gary alas had singularly failed to inherit. It was the first time Beth had cried. She had struggled to compose her face but parts of it kept breaking out of control when she looked at her employer. Laura had hugged her twelve stones silently.

'Why?' choked Beth.

'I don't know,' said Laura, nor did she.

Deviance, whether minor or major, seemed to be a statistical risk nowadays and you just hoped that the problem would land on someone else rather than you. In a disobedient age, the statistical risk got greater, she supposed. You fortified a child with rules, blinkers and a conscience, but the weaklings rapidly succumbed in a world without piety or rigour.

'I hate him,' said Beth.

'No you don't.'

It was true, of course, she still loved him, and when she had seen him in police custody, her heart had been physically squeezed by maternal agony. Bereft of his gear – no helmet, shoulder pads, black leather jacket, swagger gauntlets, giant boots – he looked frightened and small, a fall-guy for the professionals up the line.

'How could you?' she had asked him.

He was trying to pull off a hang-nail and kept fiddling with the skin of his small finger. He wished they would give him a cigarette.

'Why should you work for them?' he mumbled. 'They're rich. They don't miss the stuff. Why should you do their dirty work?'

'So it's my fault, is it?' said Beth.

He hesitated, trying to choose between keeping her on his side or passing the buck. He opted for the latter.

'Yeah. In a way, innit?' he said sullenly.

The memory flashed upon her suddenly of finding Gary mending his bike last June on the lounge carpet. What was it Tom had told her then? She could hear his rusty voice echoing through her mind. 'You've never been able to control anyone,' he had said. It is my fault, she thought.

*   *   *

My problems are worse than anybody's, thought Geoffrey. He was due to visit the bank tomorrow and felt at his gloomiest for weeks. A forced sale of the house was a public declaration of incompetence, a humiliation in front of his friends. Even the couple of Lloyds names that he knew had managed to stave off a selling. DITW, he said to himself: dead in the water. His chums would be sympathetic and make all the right noises. 'It can happen to any of us' or 'It makes sense to scale back as one gets older.' For a while they would stop bragging about what they were worth, but behind his back they would start calling him 'little Geoffrey Fenton'. The assumption that he was one of the clan would be challenged. Was he part of the pack?

That turd of an estate agent, Patrick Richfield, who had admittedly taken a hard time in recent years, would stick on to him like a burr. Come to think of it, he had already started to click his shoes and flash his teeth. He had a sixth sense about any impending debt, divorce or death – the three Ds that drove the house market. Overtrading, adultery and secondary cancers made him sparkle. I must smell of decay, thought Geoffrey. The predator has sniffed his prey and the parasite waxeth whilst I waneth.

He pushed up the window and looked out. The sunlight on the lawn showed up its first stripes of the season, the mathematical perfection of its dark- and pale-green spacing. Lucky if we'll have a lawn in a wee cott down the road, he thought glumly. They'd get more for their money if they went further afield of course: Wales, Ireland, Scotland, but the pride of the south-east was a deterrent, plus his friends' gag that if all else fails, go to Wales. For a moment, shame at his self-pity corrected his mood. There were worse places after all to live. Earthquake zones and Camden Town, for example. But the thought of the bank manager tomorrow cast him back to despair.

He felt a pain in his stomach, a clench like an agonising vice. Was it his big bowel, little bowel, bladder, spleen, pancreas? – Christ, he didn't know where any of them were. He prodded his tummy gingerly. There was no doubt it was seething with organs like big angry fish in a tank. The pain seemed to be moving around, now one place, then another; it pounced like a piranha. Was it appendicitis, piles or even cancer? Panic seized him. Was this what Patrick Richfield could sense? Was he, Geoffrey, about to bring two of the Ds to the rising house market? He thought of Laura's behaviour over the past two months. All three of the Ds, he corrected himself miserably. Every single sodding one of them – debt, divorce and death.

26

Harris & Goode Solicitors had their brass plate and rooms off the High Street in a red-brick Georgian terrace. It was here on Wednesday that Mary Binny sat smouldering at her desk. She had joined them two years ago on the promise of a partnership that was yet to be fulfilled. Other hopes had been equally disappointed. Litigation cases had been redirected to the senior partner and even the best divorces went to Emma Janes, who had joined the office six months later. It was only the everyday fare of wills and conveyancing that floated to Mary Binny's desk.

She had not dared to complain. Warned on arrival that she must bring in three times her salary to justify her post, she had accepted the tedium of her load meekly at first. It was necessary. Conveyancing might be cyclical, but wills after all were perennial. They were the rip-off part of the trade: fruitful, compulsory and possessed of a sting in their tail. It was the practice to draw up a will for a token fee so long as the solicitor was one of the executors. When in consequence of his client's death he processed the will, he inflated his price to its beneficiaries. They were in no mood or position to argue. It was this rear-end loading that paid for a new office roof, Goode's alimony and Harris's three sons at Sherborne.

A factory cog, thought Mary resentfully. She shuffled

her in-tray, scratching her finger for the millionth time on one of the metal toggles that bound the sheaves together. She looked at her watch. One Laura Fenton was due in five minutes. It was ten o'clock. Mark, her husband, her house-husband to be scrupulously precise, was doubtless sitting at home postponing the moment to start the English translation of some egg-head's novel. French of course. It had been awarded one of those Prix which the Gauls chucked around like confetti.

She had left Mark at half past eight, still in bed, still basically jobless as freelance work counted for nothing in her eyes. How long must she prop him up? For ever, it would seem. I am Mary Binny, lawyer, she had once said with pride, metaphorically tweaking her braces at the sound of her status. Now, at thirty-six, her career was beginning to pall, and so too was her house-husband.

She put her hand on the telephone to tell Mark to organise a replacement ring for the cooker when the internal phone buzzed.

'Mrs Fenton is here,' said Billie, the sixteen-year-old typist who spelt solicitor with an 'e' instead of an 'o'.

'Show her in,' said Mary.

She automatically arranged her face to express the mix of sympathy and competence with which she greeted the newly-bereaved. Prepared for the usual menopausal housewife who had just lost her mother, she was surprised by the apparition of this elegant client. She's never worked, thought Mary grimly, holding out her hand.

'Good morning,' said Laura.

Mary smiled and showed her the one leather chair, which she had fought to secure. She did a ticker-tape of her clothes. Loose camel coat: £800, though might have been less in a sale. Cream cashmere jumper with slight pilling: £200. Skirt, fawn, panelled: the same again. *You* haven't got a house-husband, thought Mary.

'The will seems straightforward enough but I expect as an executrix you know the arrangements already.' She sat down at her desk.

It was not true. Laura fished for a pen in her handbag to hide her embarrassment. Her mother had been averse to discussing the will, secretive even.

'There's a trust,' continued Mary, 'whereby you receive the income and the capital goes to the children on your death.' She studied the summary of the text. 'A few more beneficiaries but there are no important bequests.'

Laura absorbed this in silent shock. She had assumed the capital would be hers.

Mary peered at Clause 3a. 'Your mother must have had a soft spot for the National Trust, however.'

Laura winced but could not sink to asking how soft.

There was a knock and Billie put her head sideways round the door without waiting for permission to enter. Her three-inch ear-rings, a pair of endangered whales, fell at right angles to her face.

'Mr Harris says he wants to see you at half past ten. Right?'

I must groom her out of saying 'Right?' thought Mary, but why bother? – she'll be off in a couple of months anyway, pregnant most likely.

Laura stretched out her hand for the will. 'May I see it? I think there's something wrong here.'

Oh-o, thought Mary, passing it across the leatherette surface.

'I was given to understand that the capital comes to me with some small legacies to the grandchildren.' She felt the onset of palpitations.

'The will has been through various incarnations,' explained Mary. 'This is the latest. All previous forms revoked.' It was always the same, she thought. Those who didn't need the money fought harder to keep it than those who did. 'We'll do everything possible to speed up probate,' she added encouragingly.

It might take eight months, she calculated. Spring was a busy probate season. The old usually lasted the winter but found spring a hurdle too far. She normally handed the work over to a junior but charged it at senior rates. They had to put in quarter-of-an-hour time-charts since Alan Harris's third son had started boarding.

Laura tried to take in the key features of the will. It was impossible. Neither speed-reading nor osmosis helped. Caught in a thicket of obfuscating language, one could progress neither backwards nor forwards. Weighed down by archaic ballast, she came to a halt. The Apportionment Act of 1834 proved the last straw.

'No codicils?' she asked weakly, beginning to submit to fate.

'None,' said Mary in triumph. 'It is the perfect will.'

All previous codicils had been swept up last month into a pure synthesis at senior partner's rates.

'Are there any problems?' She leant forward sympathetically. Any of this client's problems would be imaginary.

'None at all,' said Laura with some dignity. 'It's perfectly clear.'

You don't understand, she thought, you self-sufficient cow. You belong to the career generation. You're trained, independent and in control. You don't know what it's like to have no money to call your very own. This income will be the first I've ever had and the capital's not even my own but my children's.

'Good,' said Mary. 'Here's a copy of your will, then. We'll get cracking at once.'

'I'll study it in detail.'

'If there's a query, just let me know. I'll ring soon anyway about the arrangements for probate.'

She looked down at her client profile chart.

'Of course, we're your mother's solicitor.' She paused tactfully. 'But if there's anything we can do for you personally or your husband, we'd be very happy to help. We are proud of our high reputation, though it sounds immodest to say so.'

It does indeed, thought Laura: word of mouth comes better from others. The two women exchanged looks with perfectly concealed dislike. Mary escorted her client to the door, then returned to ring Mark at home.

'Have you started?' she asked.

'Kind of.'

'What's that meant to mean?'

'Just drinking a coffee before doing so.'

'It's half past ten, for God's sake. I left you two hours ago.'

'I've been thinking.'

'Try doing instead.'

She put the phone down. She wondered about a quickie divorce. It shimmered alluringly on the edge of her vision. It was awful being an unhappily married solicitor. It was like being a doctor with drugs in his dispensary. With such an abundance of neat exits, the temptations were irresistible.

Geoffrey moved his chair closer so that he was leaning over the desk. Paul Watson could see the hairs in his nostrils and smell the meat of his breath.

'We've got big sales pending. We must have an extension of the loan.' Geoffrey brought his right fist down with a controlled thump. It was emphasis he was after rather than a show of temper.

'I can't,' said Watson. He had a receding hair-line in his late thirties and looked harassed. It was no fun being a bank manager these days. No job security and hated like the tax collector.

'You buggers can't pull the rug from under a thriving future business.' Geoffrey forgot about temper.

'It's not my choice.' Watson got ready to press his buzzer in case this client proved troublesome. 'Head office are breathing down my neck. These things are judged by computers. The money shouldn't have been lent in the first place and wouldn't if the computer had been functioning then. Believe me, there's no option.' His rimless spectacles slid forward a little. The bridge of his nose always became sweaty in this kind of encounter. He was nervous of conflict and clients hated their lives to be judged by machines.

'You will not sell my house,' Geoffrey shouted. 'I will put every obstacle in your way.'

The door was supposed to be muffled for sound, but in the next room Watson's secretary looked up from her word-processor at the volcano of noise seeping through the wall. She rose and tip-toed nearer the door.

'You can't take that line,' Watson said doggedly. 'You'll only incur legal costs and the outcome will be the same. The computer says—'

Geoffrey stood up mountainously. The will to burn his boats was unstoppable.

'Fuck your computers,' he said. 'All you are is a small, desk-bound, paper-pushing, ignorant, power-mad, four-eyed, early balding little functionary in the grip of your robots. Just wait. Your computers will dump you too.'

Watson stared down at his hands and hoped his secretary hadn't heard. The rule was never shout back, but Fenton had hit a raw spot. A branch had shut in the neighbouring town and sackings were reaching a crescendo. He had started to carry a note in his breast pocket to ease his equilibrium: 'Take therefore no thought for the morrow; for the morrow shall take thought for the things of itself.' He kept it well hidden. Such an attitude was close to sedition in a bank.

*   *   *

Now that, thought Ranson, is nice. He stared at the oil painting in the window. He had stopped in Westerham to buy a newspaper and had his attention drawn to an art gallery on the green.

The picture showed a small boy in a red-and-white striped T-shirt, sitting in a green and scarlet field of poppies, the flowers and grass tips reaching to his chest. For the first time in adult life, Ranson was transported back to being three years old. Drowned in the long grass of the orchard at home, he could hear his mother's voice calling him to lunch. But he had closed his ears and put his head down to the level of the emerald grass roots. A bee, its fur dusted with golden pollen, hovered an inch from his nose, an iridescent beetle lumbered amongst the blades and the buttercups gleamed like Chinese silk with the sunlight above them. Even now, over the years, he could recall the intensity of discovering that bright intricate world that lay about his ankles.

He peered through the window into the dark recesses of the shop. There was a girl at the desk talking to a woman in blue jeans with her back to him, shoulder-length fawn hair. Several of the paintings on the walls were obviously worked by the same hand. He hesitated. He was on his way to visit a colleague and was already late for the appointment. He had arranged to follow it by a call at the estate agent's house, for which he would be later still. But the lyrical picture of the child in the tall grass bewitched him, its capture of a moment that could not possibly recur. He paused but, impelled, pushed open the door.

Geoffrey was sitting at the kitchen table when Laura walked in, his head in his hands. The biggest spaniel crouched consolingly on his feet.

'Well?' she asked.

'No. He refused to give an extension.'

She looked at him and for the first time in months felt a stir of pity. A fool, certainly, but never an ill-meaning one.

'And you?' As he spoke, he did not meet her eyes. He was afraid that she would have inherited a capital sum which would prove a springboard for departure.

'I have a small income from a trust in the girls' names.' He nodded. He still did not look at her. He hoped it was insufficient to give her the chance of independence.

Laura went to sit by the swans' pool. She would have little time left to enjoy it. The cob ran towards her, beating his huge black wings like a pterodactyl. He snaked his head in menace.

'Osmund,' she cried. 'Darling Osmund, it's me, don't you recognise me?'

He had never attacked her before.

She backed away warily and walked to the other side of the pool. There was a greenish-white stone shining beside the swan's mate. She peered, narrowing her eyes, fearing to approach. Large, oval and contoured, its appearance was as sudden and mysterious as a meteorite. Laura crept closer, but the swan began to hiss. She gasped aloud as she realised the pen had laid her first egg and then closed her eyes at the poignancy of its timing. They would be rearing their brood of cygnets just when she was moving house. What new owner could they possibly trust to look after them now?

27

'Of course,' said Patrick Richfield, pushing away his dinner plate, 'I knew it was coming on the market before he said anything. They leak like crazy when a fire sale is about to take place.'

'How do you mean?' asked his wife, Sophie.

They had married two years ago.

'They try to avoid me for a start or shut up in my presence. They need me and hate me at the same time. I get these mixed messages blasting out at me from their eyes.'

'Oh lovely. What it is to have a popular husband.'

Sophie picked up a large Imari bowl of fruit and carried it ceremoniously to the table.

'In fact, he won't have much option about coming to me. I'm the only class act in the neighbourhood, and the only discreet one, which is more important.'

'Don't be so smug,' said Sophie. 'He can take it to a London firm. I would if I were him. I'd think it would be more discreet.'

'No one is more silent as the tomb than me.' Patrick put a finger to his lips in demonstration. 'Besides, it'd cost him more.'

'I thought the percentage was negotiable.'

She started to unpeel an orange. The zing of its smell made her pretty nostrils flare.

'It is and it isn't.'

He ruminated. Normally he took a cut in inverse proportion to the price of the house. Sharper clients, however, struck a deal in the opposite direction. They promised him a larger percentage if he succeeded in flogging the house for a higher price. It was surprising how often it worked. Since the housing market had picked up, valuations had tended to become more arbitrary. A fire sale, however, was different and could scupper a rising price. The hyenas always moved in on a forced sale.

'Shall we buy it?' Sophie's husky but penetrating voice interrupted his reflections.

'Isn't it a bit grand?'

'No,' said Sophie who fancied ratcheting upwards.

She was blonde, young and a former actress. She was also a second wife, for whom Patrick had discarded her middle-aged predecessor, and Sophie hadn't married an older man for nothing. One had to have compensation for the fact that he would die sooner than the usual run.

'I don't see we can buy it. We can't pay as much as it's worth. It would be unethical to underprice it.'

His voice had become a shade pompous.

He turned the peppermill over and over in his hands whilst thinking. Ethics aside, there was no doubt that Geoffrey would seek a second price as a comparison, so there was no putting one over on him and certainly not on his wife who had assessed him the previous day with an evaluative gaze. Besides, thought Patrick, I just can't afford it. The payments to his first wife were an awful squeeze on his freedom, though here was a topic that was better left dormant at mealtimes. At all times, he corrected himself.

He glanced up at his wife. Her fair, pixie face had turned mulish.

'You're always so downbeat,' she said, frowning. 'Do try and buy it.'

It's the usual thing, she thought crossly, struggling not to let her exasperation reach her face. It's his ghastly alimony. That wife's like a blood-sucking leech, ruining my life. It's her own fault he left her anyway. If she'd fucked him more often, he wouldn't be sitting here now.

She drew in her breath and counted to five.

'What's it like anyway?'

'What?'

'The house. Inside.'

She rather resented the fact that Laura had never asked her to dinner, but then Laura always pretended to have her head down in the garden.

'They've got some nice pieces but the house itself is quite shabby in parts. It would need a lot spending on it. People like them are so mean on upkeep. They take it for granted that what they have always had will always keep going.'

'Romantic decay is what it's called, darling.'

Sophie had just started a course on interior design and was into classification.

'Decay, certainly.'

'And the garden?'

Sophie fancied a spot of serious gardening. It was just like interior decoration in Latin. Roofs, walls, floors were made up of trees, hedges and ground-cover plants. Good borders were the same as rugs.

'The garden is terrific but heaps of upkeep too. A pond with swans and ducks and there are some other animals too.'

'Like what?'

'Bantams with fluffy legs, a few pet sheep.'

Sophie gave a squeal of pleasure. She had once played a non-speaking shepherdess in a Shakespearean comedy.

'Geoffrey says his wife insists the animals, the gardener and the lady who does are kept on.'

'In that order?'

Patrick raised his eyebrows to show he had noted his wife's little perception.

'Who are the gardener and the cleaner?'

'Trouble there, I fear. Rumour has it that they are the parents of the boy who nicked the family jewels.'

'Oh no.' Sophie went round-eyed. 'Really, one would just have to dump them.'

'I doubt if you'll get much cooperation from Laura if she thinks that.'

'If it's a fire sale, she won't have a choice.'

It would be nice, she thought, to put her in her place. It would pay her back for being aloof.

Patrick thought it time to change the subject. This fantasy had run far enough and was nosing towards the point at which it could submerge all reality.

He leant back in his chair and scanned the table and wooden surfaces for the signs of some pudding.

'Nothing to eat?' He spoke with some expectation.

'Here.' Sophie pushed the fruit bowl over to him.

His face fell. 'Fruit doesn't count.'

'Good for you. Inner cleanliness. And we don't want to let the paunch get any paunchier, do we?'

Not for the first time, he felt the penalties of a young wife.

'You don't need to pretend.' Beth spoke stiffly but with the dignity of squaring up to the truth. 'You're getting rid of us because of Gary, aren't you?'

'No,' said Laura firmly. 'That has nothing to do with it. Nothing.'

She wondered whether to repeat 'nothing', but feared it would invoke a law of diminishing returns. In this situation, facts were starting to sound like falsehoods.

Beth stared back without flinching and with total disbelief.

Laura decided to plough on.

'Geoffrey and I can't stay here, you see. The business is closing down.'

Beth did not reply. She could not yield to this new truth. It did not match her understanding, which had set rock solid around a previous one.

Laura began again, thinking it was awful, every bit as bad as anticipated.

'Beth, you must believe me. The business about the necklace and so on is entirely coincidental.'

'Why do you call it "business about the necklace"? I call it robbery, don't I?'

Laura groaned.

'Let's go over this again. We have to sell this place and move to a smaller one, perhaps miles away. We would love to ask you to come with us, but we just can't afford it.'

She was trying to speak very plainly because she was afraid that tiredness and repetition would make her incoherent. Communication was so terribly important. She could pulverise Beth if she sent the wrong message.

'Please look at me,' she said to Beth, unnecessarily since Beth had not blinked since the explanation began.

'I am insisting that the buyers of this place retain both you and Tom.'

This suddenly struck her as a potential insult; Beth was not a chattel to be conveyed forward like the animals.

'Only if you want this,' she added humbly.

As always, Beth was blessedly free from umbrage, but she looked despairing.

'I might want it but they won't, will they? Not when they know about Gary.'

'I'll write you wonderful references. That you're sterling and punctilious and a dear and utterly, utterly, utterly honest.'

Tears began to run down Beth's face at the praise. Laura noted how she had aged in the past month.

'I am, yes,' said Beth, 'but he isn't, is he, and that's that. So whatever you write it won't make any difference, see?'

One is ruined in life, thought Laura, by being totally at the mercy of events. It's Beth who is most destroyed by all this. Not us. People like us will always bob onwards.

'Who was it?' asked Geoffrey.

'Patrick Richfield is sending someone over who wants to view the house.'

'He can't. Ring him back.'

'I agreed. He's on his way.'

'It's impossible.'

'Why?'

Because I won't sell it, Geoffrey wanted to say.

'Because I haven't had a second valuation,' he said instead.

'There's no harm in looking. Anyway, he's Dutch. I can't be rude.'

'*Not foreign.*'

'Geoffrey, for Christ's sake, there's no room for xenophobia. Besides, the Dutch aren't really foreign. They're an absolutely sweet people and we haven't fought them for three hundred years.'

He made a gurgling sound, like an animal protest. Until this moment the sale of the house had little reality. Now, like an image conjured from a void, a rival had suddenly materialised and not just any old outsider but *ein* foreign rival.

He could not cope.

'I'm going out,' he said abruptly.

Fight or flight, thought Laura. He had at least chosen the lesser of two evils.

Geoffrey stomped out to the hall lobby to pull on his wax coat. He was walking deliberately like an elephant to make the floor judder. His feet, lightning conductors for the storm in his head, threatened to bring down the fabric of the house.

Laura shook her head watching him stride out to the garage. Revving the car unnecessarily high, Geoffrey nearly ran into a large, dark-green Mercedes that was pulling into the gravel drive. Tugging the wheel over, he just avoided a scrape. He wanted to scratch him, thought Laura, who had witnessed the scene from the kitchen window. The spaniels, who had lined up at the invisible barrier of a wide-open gate, scattered, reconverging around the appetising tyres of a new car. Laura advanced on the Mercedes with hope. I do hope they're nice, she thought. The Dutch were supposed to be very enthusiastic gardeners with the best topiary in Europe. She longed for them to be perfect.

A tall, trenchcoated man in his late thirties climbed out and helped a younger blonde woman in a loose white linen suit from the passenger seat.

'Jaco Hillemans and Mrs Hillemans.' He indicated his wife and held out his hand which Laura touched limply. She regarded them closely. The signs were not good. Still, it was so easy to misread foreigners. The Dutch were especially confusing: images of gables, gardening and Rembrandt fought with drugs, abortion and euthanasia in her mind. She pushed her prejudices aside. Codes of speech, walk and clothes, so manifest and voluble on home ground, could easily get scrambled by mid-Channel.

'I expect you are used to the country,' she said.

'Oh yes. I am music publisher. Very informal.' Mr Hillemans gave a dazzling grin and adjusted his rimless spectacles and ponytail.

'Please follow,' said Laura and resolved to shut up. Patrick Richfield had warned her against conversation.

A buyer needed space to form an impression. A vendor too, she thought, with a small grimace.

For the first half hour they padded in silence round the house.

'Very nice,' said Mrs Hillemans about the kitchen.

Laura noticed she was staring at the dog hairs.

'I hope you like animals.' She added, 'The outside ones come with the house.'

'My wife has—' Mr Hillemans blew his nose in the air and made a rasping demonstration. 'How do you call it?'

'Allergies, Mr Hillemans,' provided Laura glumly. She decided against showing them the dove barn, which was a bit fusty.

'Do please call me Jaco. We are very INFORMEEL,' he added emphatically.

'The garden is special and is opened every June to hundreds of people,' said Laura, leading them out of the back door.

She paused on the terrace to let them take in the scene. It looked wonderful, she thought with a pang. A clear spring afternoon. The fringed pink and purple tulips glowed in the big wooden tubs and the waxy-white globes of the magnolia had started to unfold like huge waterlilies. New life stirred everywhere and a haze of lime-green leaf-buds spangled the trees. She closed her eyes momentarily to sniff the scented wafts of sweet violets. It was heart-wrenching to give all this up. Were these new people worthy of such bliss? Would they appreciate it? Would they, oh God, look after it?

'The garden has developed over many years.' She spoke warningly, hoping they didn't take it for granted.

'Oh,' said Jaco. He translated this to his wife.

'*Een maximaal effect in een minimale tijd,*' she replied, flicking her blonde hair back.

'What does she say?' asked Laura.

'She says she likes gardens to give the maximum effect in the minimum time.'

'Pop-up gardens,' said Laura scathingly.

The Hillemans exchanged glances behind her back. Jaco's wife did not understand each word but the tone of voice carried an international meaning.

Laura increased her stride. She had written them off.

'Not so fast, please, Mrs Fenton,' said Jaco, whose wife had caught her white jacket tail on some rose thorns.

Laura swept on.

'*Welke boom is dat?*' Mrs Hillemans was pointing at a gingko which was just emerging into its new pleated fans of leaves.

'*Boom*? Does that mean tree?' asked Laura.

'Yes, what tree? she says.'

'The *Gingko biloba* is a deciduous conifer and the only survivor of a family that lived around a hundred and sixty million years ago.' I'll sock it to them, thought Laura. 'In the East, it is considered sacred and is often found by Buddhist temples.'

'Wow,' said Jaco.

'Quite a boom, indeed,' agreed Laura.

'Ha, *een boog*,' said his wife, pointing to the arch leading into the rose garden. In summer it would be smothered in sprays of white flowers.

'*Een maximaal effect in een minimale tijd,*' smiled Mrs Hillemans.

Laura thought of the ages it had taken to coax and prune the rose into the right shape.

'You see, we are real country boys,' said Jaco.

We'll find out, thought Laura.

'The most interesting part of the garden is the pond,' she said, leading them with determination towards the poolside. She could hear little squelching noises from Mrs Hillemans' shoe heels which were sinking in the mud.

Jaco clapped his hands. His trenchcoat blew open and the bottom of his white flared trousers flapped in the breeze. The noise and the sight sent the black swan, Osmund, berserk. He feared for his unhatched cygnet curled up in his egg. Clambering on to the bank, he gave a mighty trumpet. The bugle call to arms, once, twice and again, rang out across the garden. Snaking his black neck close to the ground and beating his huge black wings as he ran, he dived for the trouser leg. There was a tearing sound. A small patch of white cloth fluttered from Osmund's red beak. Jaco screeched. He kicked at the swan. His wife screamed shrilly.

'Don't you dare touch my swan,' shouted Laura. 'Anyway, they come with the house,' she added inconsistently.

'You English are crazy,' he shouted, hopping on one leg. 'No wonder you cause such trouble in the EU. Bad citizens.'

'Appalling,' agreed Laura.

Geoffrey did not return until six o'clock. He nosed the car cautiously through the gateway, making quite certain the coast was clear, then swept imperiously up the drive. He was still the owner.

'Oh,' said Laura, looking at her watch when he walked into the kitchen, 'you've at last dared to come back.'

Geoffrey went straight for the drinks and poured himself a double whisky. He swirled it about at the bottom of his glass.

'Where have you been?' she asked.

'In the office,' he answered abruptly. 'Well?'

'Well what?' She grudged giving him the immediate consolation of knowing that the house was not yet sold.

'You know what "well" means. Did they offer?'

'No. Exit pursued by a swan.'

'You mean that old black devil saw them off.' Geoffrey chuckled and took a large swig of drink. 'Well, well,' he kept muttering and chortling.

'Hillemans tried to kick him.' Laura put the carrot peelings in the pigbin. She was still angry.

'I'll sue him,' said Geoffrey, draining his tumbler. 'These Dutch can be bloody aggressive. Their fleet sailed up the Thames and burnt our ships in 1667. Pepys says—'

'Oh, shut up.' Laura stopped pretending to carry on as normal. Who cared if they ate tonight or not? 'You just make things much worse.'

She subsided on a chair by the table and cradled her head in her hands which were still wet from the kitchen sink. Her anger yielded to an overwhelming depression.

The telephone rang.

'You answer it,' Laura told Geoffrey.

He went over to the sofa end of the room and lifted the receiver from its wall socket. The white cat in its usual position on the cushion stretched lasciviously in expectation of a stroke, but it was not forthcoming.

'Hello,' he said tersely.

Laura watched him grow tense and excited.

'He kicked him. Your chap actually kicked him. Any more of that kind and we'll put the RSPCA on to them.'

He banged down the receiver. He had been longing for an excuse to snub the estate agent.

'Patrick says he complained. It wasn't just the swan, either. Jaco says you were hoity-toity.'

'Hoity-toity,' repeated Laura in a Dutch accent, but her bravado had petered out. It was true and unforgivable. This afternoon she had seen off a buyer, she had turned down a rich but ineligible suitor. But she wasn't arranging a marriage for the garden and its animals. She was just finding a new owner. And no buyer was the worst possible outcome of all.

28

In the next couple of weeks, more people came to view. This time the boot was on the other foot: they loved the house but it was too big, too small, too expensive, too cheap, they didn't want a garden, they did but a different one. One wife even had a bird phobia. From the perspective of a fortnight, Mr and Mrs Hillemans had turned into angels. Laura's confidence, so recently overweening, now fathomed her boots. Only days ago she had been in the frame of mind to bestow her favours on a grovelling buyer; now she was a forlorn supplicant.

In the meanwhile she sought a house to move into. Every so often Rosy rang in the evenings.

'Have you found anywhere?' she asked.

'Not yet,' replied Laura, sensitive to the fact that her daughter did not suggest she moved nearer.

The loss of the portfolio was never mentioned but hung in the air like an invisible spider's web between them. They chattered through its gaps, whilst delicately negotiating the trickier bits. It was painful to both. Laura yearned to remove it but Rosy would have to concede its presence in the first place. For Laura there was nothing to forgive but for Rosy there was a lingering feeling of guilt to deny. It was not eased by the knowledge that she had half her grandmother's money in trust. In the emotion of the moment, she had suggested to William that she should release her share to her parents but William had pointed out her responsibilities were to her child now. Rosy's conscience was largely pacified but had a horrible habit of rearousal when she spoke to her mother.

Relations with Rosy were not Laura's only problem. Quite often she thought of Ranson too. He must be house-hunting also if he was not abroad. Once the idea occurred that it was a waste to have two separate homes but she buried the notion, sensing its shape in her mind but not acknowledging its presence. That would infer erasing Geoffrey from her life, a decision too momentous at this stage to contemplate. 'I shall see Leo in the summer,' she told herself, waiting patiently, all feeling in abeyance until then. In any case, there was little time to think. A fresco of houses passed before her eyes. She scanned them mechanically. She combed stucco cottages, high street caverns and barn conversions. She walked along potholed roads and council tarmac. Zigzagging from Kent to Surrey to Sussex, she toured houses on village greens and in forest clearings, but nothing was right.

On the first Friday in May she set out to inspect the latest offering from an agent, leaving Geoffrey at home. It was a bright, windy morning, tossing the confection of icing-sugar-pink cherry trees and lilacs in the front gardens as she drove past. Summer would soon be here. It would be the first June that the garden had been shut in eleven years. Already the house seemed to have moved into a no man's land, in orbit between one owner and the next. To outward appearances this morning had been like every other for the past month: feeding the doves, dead-heading the daffodils, checking the swans' eggs – now four in all – to see if there was any sign of hatching. But she was feeling increasingly like a caretaker rather than the chatelaine.

With Geoffrey too she was a housekeeper instead of

a wife. Talking had become an exchange of information, punctuated by the occasional row and never by sex. By now his offices had closed and he was spending the greater part of his day at home. She had noticed that the golf course had lost all former allure as he shrank from letting his friends see his downward spiral. Whilst he stayed in the house, she went out, the pattern of mutual avoidance broken only by moments of united loathing for Patrick Richfield. Geoffrey had reported he had said, 'You never know, I might buy your home myself.' An ulterior motive, thought Laura, would explain the recent succession of unsuitable buyers.

She was turning this over in her mind as she arrived in the pretty village where she had arranged to see the latest house. She stopped the Volvo up a side street. A long line of tile-hung, white-clapboarded terraced cottages confronted her. A curtain twitched. They would know every atom of one's existence, thought Laura. Full-blooded, from nowhere, the shape in her mind that was Ranson reared up. Just suppose, it suggested, you were separated from Geoffrey and here on your own; when I visited you, 'they' would know everything. She averted her eyes from his presence and it sank back below the waterlevel of her mind.

Number Eight was detached and set slightly back from the road. Tile-hung and with leaded windows like the rest, it looked smaller than its agency photograph. In theory, there was plenty of room: two large bedrooms upstairs and a long single drawing-room downstairs. A small Indian file of a garden at the rear. I suppose I could fill it with formal plant bobbles, as we're told to, she thought sadly. Lots of pots. A pot garden. She recalled the huge ancient bushes of rhododendrons in her garden, the camellias like trees, the seven-foot striped French roses, the white doves wheeling freely above.

'A pot garden,' she said to herself. 'Think positively.'

She stepped out of the car and walked slowly over the road, her senses on full alert. She noted the tiny front garden was eloquent of a gardener. Ferns fanned like lace around hostas and generations of violas formed a velvet carpet under white candelabra primulas. Lovely, she thought, as she pressed the bell, feeling a greater sense of expectation. Early approval was unusual.

A woman opened the door immediately.

'Mrs Hoskins?' asked Laura.

'Come in,' she said, nodding and smiling. 'You've been sitting for ages outside. I'm just the same. I need the feel of a place before going in.'

'Houses have auras,' agreed Laura.

'Houses are people,' corrected Mrs Hoskins.

Laura followed her through the hall, mesmerised by the doughnut of white hair at the back of her head. Buns were out of fashion and it occurred to her it was time they returned.

'I'll show you round,' said Mrs Hoskins, 'but the agent has told me to shut up. You're my first viewer so I may not be very used to speaking only when I'm spoken to.'

Laura began to laugh.

'Me too. It's awfully inhibiting, isn't it?'

Mrs Hoskins seemed inclined to agree.

Laura scanned the room, wary of being scrutinised for a reaction. She fixed a bland face on her thoughts, but honest admiration began to take charge. Two old rust and blue Saruk rugs lay on the floor, needlework cushions tumbled over the sofa and thick curtains of clotted cream linen framed the windows, looped back with soft plaits. I could be at home here, thought Laura, when one of the cushions came to life with a snuffling noise.

'It's Daphne,' explained the woman as a dachshund unlooped itself and sprang on to the floor. 'As I'm old,

I got a legless dog in case I couldn't take her for walks when I got even older.'

'Not legless at all,' said Laura, as the dog followed them gamely upstairs.

It was tricky as always, she thought, to keep one's mind on the job. One needed X-ray eyes for this task. Forget the rose-scented soap in the bathroom, the patchwork quilts on the beds; it was pipes, sockets and neighbours that mattered. She wandered slowly around. In Mrs Hoskins's prolonged silence, she strove to imagine her furniture throughout the house. The lowboy would fit and the walnut desk and even the blue velvet settee, but the bed was too big and so, sadly, was Geoffrey. Of that there was no doubt. He was indeed the most awkward bit of soft furniture she possessed: large, bulging and mobile. Which room could one stick him into? she wondered. This was a woman's house, and she realised with a shock that this made poor Geoffrey superfluous to requirements.

'I'll leave you in peace,' said Mrs Hoskins, sensitive to some inner turmoil.

'Don't go,' said Laura. 'Can I see the garden, then come back to the house?'

She trailed Mrs Hoskins down the rush-matted stairs, through the kitchen and out of its wide French doors.

Expect nothing, thought Laura, and gasped.

'I so love tulips,' apologised Mrs Hoskins.

The two women regarded the scene. A path of cobbled diamonds ran down the centre of the narrow yard with clipped green box puddings to either side. Swaying between stood great sheaves of lily-flowered tulips. Their elegant, waisted petals glittered in the light: ruby, bengal rose and white.

'It took me ten years to clip those evergreens properly,' said her companion, disappearing to make a coffee. The

Hillemans, it occurred to Laura, would think the stage set had been rushed together yesterday.

Despite the breeze, the sun was warm on her back and she wandered over to a white scrolled iron seat beside the brick wall. The heat was soothing and she felt her mind slowing to the tick of her grandfather clock. She watched the petals of the tulips unfurl voluptuously in the light. I could be happy alone here, she mused; no Geoffrey but Leo could visit me, and the neighbours can go to hell. For the first time she did not turn away but relaxed into the thought.

'I came here ten years ago,' said Mrs Hoskins, advancing on her with two coffee cups. 'My husband died young, my children were grown up and I felt terribly alone. But I've been very happy here. You can feel that, I think,' she added.

'Why are you leaving?'

'I'm getting married again.'

'No.' The word emerged rudely before Laura suppressed it.

'Growing old disgracefully, isn't it, when you're seventy. I'm moving to Fife to marry a Scot, which sounds purse-lipped and flinty with shades of the manse, but it's not like that at all.'

'A new beginning?'

'Oh, I discovered years ago that life couldn't keep on ending.'

A new beginning, repeated Laura to herself: it seemed a signal to leave Geoffrey and start afresh here.

'The unexpected,' said Mrs Hoskins, 'is a normal part of life.'

Mostly bills and forms, thought Geoffrey, drinking his coffee. He sifted through the morning post, leaving anything nasty unopened. Brown envelopes were sinister, but white carried less threat. He shivered suddenly. The warmth outside would take ages to penetrate the house. Normally, the interior lagged outside temperatures by a good week. He opened a plain envelope franked with the name of the estate agent summoned to provide a second valuation. Scanning the letter for figures, he promptly cheered up. The estimate exceeded Patrick Richfield's by ten per cent. He would map out an acceptance.

He scrabbled in one of the kitchen drawers for a pen and rough paper, but it yielded only string, half a Bonio, a wax crayon and some Dulux paint charts. He worked out some back-of-the-paint chart calculations and, writing fatly with the bulky crayon, roughed out a letter on a brown envelope. Having refined it to his satisfaction, he then went in search of headed writing-paper. Where did she keep it? He groaned at being abandoned to thrash around in Laura's absence these days. Life without office or secretary was impossible and an absentee wife made no substitute.

He walked out of the kitchen, crossed the flagstoned hall and entered her small sitting-room. Her personal desk would be the likeliest source of paper. She was forever scribbling plant orders here. He pulled open the top drawer but it jammed on some flower catalogues. He tried the second drawer and found it crammed with complaints: *Please note that the tree peony you supplied is the wrong colour and form. It has clearly been misidentified but it has taken eighteen months for this to become apparent. I would be grateful if* . . . He recognised 'I would be grateful if', oh God, oh yes, how well he knew that phrase. The clipped and porcelain 'I would be grateful, Geoffrey, if you would not . . .' oh yes, women were complainers of quite matchless quality.

He tried a third drawer, which looked promising. Pens in a neat tray in front, calculator, good old-fashioned blotting-paper – ah, headed paper. He heaved out a sheaf from the back of the drawer, dropping a rubber, a torn piece of paper and a pen tip in his impatience. He would normally have left them where they fell, but she would fuss if she found evidence that he had ferreted round her personal desk – a pretty, kneehole piece that she cherished. Better, all things considered, to keep rows to a minimum. The rubber had rolled beyond reach under the chair, but Geoffrey stooped with difficulty to pick up the pen tip and the scrap of paper. As he did so, he noticed the word '*Darl—*' on the fold under his thumb. He smoothed the crumple out. *Darling Laura, I wasn't going to wake you.* He stared at it numbly, the words reverberating in a groove of his brain. *Darling Laura, I wasn't going to wake you.* He raised his head and stared round. The room seemed bleached of colour. It had been robbed of life by the words. Feeling faint, he sat down in her chair. The self-preserving part of his system recognised that it had forgotten to keep him breathing. He was jolted into shallow inhalation. *Darling Laura, I wasn't going to wake you, Darling Laura, I wasn't going to—* Was there no switch to turn it off?

Do I jump or am I pushed? thought Laura. She felt light-headed. The visit to Mrs Hoskins's house had imbued her with freedom. She drove up to the junction of lanes which led to home and Geoffrey on the left, to escape on the right. On automatic reflex, she flicked the indicator to the left, then, uncertain, to the right. She cancelled both and paused in the middle of the road, leaning her arms on the wheel. A burst of hooting sounded from the rear.

'Make up your bloody mind,' shouted a man from a red Ford estate wagon.

'Sorry,' she called into the wind and beckoned him round. What a metaphor, she thought. Home and the past to the left, escape and the future to the right. Make up your bloody mind. Freedom was infectious, though

Tessa had called it illusory. Do I jump or am I pushed? thought Laura again. She felt herself teetering on the brink. The light-headedness returned: the air seemed rich with oxygen.

She turned the wheel to the right. She would pour out everything to Tessa. Setting out in her direction, she passed the little station, then the log-merchant. On to the main road, then, finally, along the lane where a mist of bluebells hazed the copse to either side. Right, left and right again, where a finger-sign had been torn off the post. Into Tessa's road, lowering her eyes to the track to avoid the stones and potholes unmended since winter. She turned the engine off and gathered her handbag from the floor. Would Tessa be in? She glanced up and noted a large car outside her house, with some surprise. She looked again, and harder. She started the engine, backed, halted, took a headscarf from the handbag and knotted it closely over her chin. Keeping her head rigid, she drove slowly past, pouring the whole force of her energy into the car.

Unmistakable, the same navy Jaguar, his car, his coat inside that she had parted in the January wind at Wakehurst gardens.

She glanced beyond to the house: the upstairs curtains were drawn. She began to tremble but kept going. She heard the lightning echo of the night she had spent in London. 'Lie still, lie still, thou little Musgrave, And huggle me from the cold.'

He is mine, she thought, not Tessa's. He could not possibly be Tessa's. She had a second's doubt – a simple explanation, perhaps? – but the truth, so perfect and primal, prevailed.

She was driving very slowly, tense, trembling so much that she knew she would have to stop the car as soon as she had reached safe territory. She saw her white face in the mirror, ethereal, a fantasy. I have been living a fantasy, she thought. Such a fool, no different from Geoffrey. Each in our own worlds, blind to reality when it was thrusting its fist in our face. She recalled the light-headedness of a short while ago. She had been inebriated with a future which never existed, an escape she had neither earned nor deserved.

She passed a small stone church on her left, an oddity she had always noticed because it lacked the company of a village. In search of comfort, she turned the car off the road and stopped beside the open gate. She walked up the path between four funereal yews and pushed at the latch, expecting the door to be locked against vandals. It creaked stiffly open. The smell of old churches met her nose: musty, fungoid and persistent. A pool of crimson and cobalt-blue lay on the floor near the font, thrown from the sunlit saints in the small stained glass window. She walked round the pews, her footsteps echoing in the acoustics of empty ancient space. A plaque on the wall named the young men who had fallen in the mud of the First World War. There were more than forty. It had wiped out the youth of the district.

She sat down at the end seat of the front pew. The hymn list was on the wall ahead: 4, 128 and 312 had been on the menu for last Sunday. How many people had attended? Ten? Twelve if they were lucky. She stared around her. Each pew had one needleworked hassock, the toil of an army of devoted widows, happy to exchange solitude for servitude. She closed her eyes. She felt a huge appetite for some spiritual nourishment, the depth charge of plangent liturgical music rather than the plod of 4, 128 and 312. Restless and unsatisfied, she rose from the pew and walked back towards the door, picking up one of the left-over parish newsletters at the back. She flicked over its five pages. 'It is not too late to sow marrows,' she read, 'always two on edge in a pot because one will surely fail.' On the opposite page there was a photocopy of a starving African child. Overleaf, a recipe for Brown Betty Pudding: 'mix 3 oz of breadcrumbs, suet, flour, brown sugar and sultanas in a bowl with an ounce of ground almonds . . .'

Not much spiritual comfort here, but she felt oddly calmed by the mix of ideals and ordinariness, the brute strength of the eternal and the thin distraction of daily life. She put the newsletter down and slipped a pound in the postbox in the wall for the church fund. The roof was crumbling. So is ours, she thought, wish we could put the hat round too.

By the time she arrived home Laura had recovered some equilibrium, but her spirits shivered a little as she turned into the drive and saw Geoffrey's car in the barn. She had hoped for a little longer to compose herself. One of the dogs barked, triggering the others into their usual set-piece.

'Shut up,' she called out, 'it's me.'

She walked through the hall en route to the kitchen, when she saw that the door to the little sitting-room was ajar. Closing it so that it would retain its warmth, she noticed one of Geoffrey's feet was visible from the entrance. She peered round the door and looked from his leg to his face. She had started to say, 'What are you doing here?' but her voice faded out. He was slumped in her chair.

'Geoffrey?' she said, bewildered.

He looked pale and grim.

'What's the matter? Geoffrey?' She was frightened by the sight of his face.

He motioned to the desk.

'I found this.' He passed her a scrap of paper.

She recognised it instantly without pausing to glance at the words. Her head felt full of blood. The room was silent apart from the surfing inside her ear-drums. Her panic at

Geoffrey's discovery was twisted by her sense of bathos at its timing. An hour seemed to pass. Her mouth felt bitter as though she had eaten a sloe. The mix of farce and tragedy left her breathless.

'You bitch,' he said quietly. 'All this while you've been fucking another man like a stoat.'

'It's not true,' she said, shaking. 'It was just one occasion. Once only, an accident when I was unhappy. I was a fool, Geoffrey, you must believe me.'

He stared at her whitely. Numbed until now, he had not realised the pure violence within him. Rage foamed over his wish to believe her. He heard himself shout.

'You treat *me* like a fool. You expect me to accept that.'

His voice was hoarse and two veins in his forehead were horribly distended.

'Geoffrey, please, you must believe me. It's the truth.'

He lunged towards her, raising his hand to strike her. At that moment he understood how a man could take an axe to his wife. In sudden physical terror, she cowered, awaiting the instantaneous blow. But when she peered upwards, terrified, she saw he had forced himself to stop.

'You deserve to be hit,' he said huskily, lowering his arm, 'but I lack the guts to do it.'

He covered his face in his hands. He felt demented by turmoil. He yearned to beat her to pulp, but that part of him composed of love, friendship, habit, was reducing him to impotence. He uttered a small noise of desperation. Ancient codes demanded vengeance but modern marriage made them void.

He looked at her in despair. He felt he was drowning in a complex whirlpool of miseries. For the first time in his life he knew real terror. He recognised suddenly the difference between the force of mere anger and of dread. Momentarily blotted out by rage, but vast and permanent was his terror that Laura would leave him. It struck him too late that he should never have given her the note. Better to have pretended nothing had happened, but that was impossible: *Darling Laura, I wasn't going to wake you.* How could he ever live in silence with that? In the distance, in another world, they could hear the dogs barking in alarm at the raised voices.

Laura looked down again at the note – such wasted, inert words. *Darling Laura, I wasn't going to wake you.* She almost smiled: better if he hadn't. She shook her head, screwed the tarnished scrap of paper into a little ball and tossed it without ceremony into the wastepaper basket. Geoffrey watched the trajectory but derived no comfort.

'He called you "darling",' he said, and shielded his eyes with his hands. He found it agony to utter the endearment of another man's lips. It was the 'darling' that was such torment, the lie to a quick fuck, ghastly to imagine but perhaps more possible to forget. 'How can I believe you?' he added brokenly.

'It is the truth,' she said with immense sadness. 'It was just once.'

'But "darling" – after one night.'

'It only ever happened once,' she repeated.

'When?'

'When you were away in January. Someone I met. I was terribly unhappy.'

'Have you seen him again?'

'Never.'

'But why "darling"?' he persisted. It was so implausible. He felt a fresh surge of rage as an explanation hit him. 'It's someone I know, isn't it? One of my friends? You bitch, who was it?' He felt his body flood with the notion of a double disloyalty.

'No one you know. No one you've ever met.'

He looked at her wryly. 'A ghost?'

'Funnily enough, yes, in a way.'

They regarded each other, temporarily exhausted before starting again.

'You deceived me.'

'Yes, you deceived me too.'

He hesitated, weighing up the truth of the accusation. 'It was in a different way.'

'As important. It has affected my life.'

'Not as important. You rejected me. I trusted you and you betrayed me.' Stating it made him realise the enormity of her offence. He glimpsed the word 'cuckold' lurking in his brain; till now he had thought it medieval.

'Only because you ignored me. You went behind my back and over my head in mortgaging the house and in giving everything to William. It's lost us our home and broken our family.' She stared at him furiously. How could she feel sympathy for his evident anguish when he didn't even try to understand?

'I was trying to sort out a problem,' he shouted.

'It wasn't your problem but ours. I didn't exist for you. It was only after then that I betrayed you, as you so grandly put it.'

'Betrayal isn't half of what you've done. A wife is exclusive to her husband. Nowadays they pretend it's not true. Everyone's always in and out of each other's beds – on telly, in the papers. They pretend it doesn't matter but it's the very worst thing a wife can do. A wife belongs to her husband.'

'She does, does she? His property? And what if her husband has done the worst thing a man can do? A husband should hunt and gather but what if he squanders and scatters behind her back instead? What's a wife supposed to do then? Is she still his property?'

He hated her afresh. Somehow she had put him in the wrong when he had been well-intentioned but merely unlucky.

'What's this hunting and gathering? You are quite crazy. Neanderthal,' he muttered.

'What could be more feudal than you?' she exploded, dimly aware that the twentieth century had never happened. It was their primate selves that fought.

'You deceived me,' he reiterated. Couldn't he force it into her brain?

She held her ground doggedly. 'Because you deceived me. You forfeited my loyalty.'

They fell silent, knowing they had argued full circle. Laura sank down on the footstool in depression.

'Duplicity is such a disaster,' she murmured.

He looked down at her. He abhorred her but, though alien, they were somehow still linked.

'What's going to happen?' he asked.

'What do you want to happen?'

I want everything to be just the same as it was, he thought, knowing it wasn't possible.

'Well, we seem to be still married,' he said very slowly. 'You don't want to leave me, do you?' Fool, he thought, to utter the choice. He looked away, concealing the return of his terror that she might go. It was always wives who left their husbands. He had already lost the house. If Laura left him, he would lose a home as well as a house. He felt vertigo as well as shame that he so desperately wanted her to stay after all.

Do I jump or am I pushed? Laura remembered thinking, was it only two hours ago? Quite a little comedy that its inference should have escaped her at the time. 'Pushed back into the nest' had not suggested itself as a possible meaning.

'I rather doubt it,' she replied.

'I can't forgive you,' he said, vastly relieved but not conceding.

'Nor I you.' She was unwilling to be put in the position of disadvantage.

'No.'

It was a truce of sorts. In its interlude he pulled a grubby month-old piece of kitchen paper from his pocket and blew his nose loudly.

'I wish you wouldn't carry those messy rags in your pockets. They shred on everything in the washing-machine,' she said emotionally.

'Messy bits seem to have spread outside the washing-machine.'

She looked down and pressed out a tiny smile. 'I'm sorry,' she said. 'You started it, but I might as well say it first as you won't.'

'Who was it?' He rose as he spoke. It was easier to ask if he was taking some simultaneous action.

'As I said, it was just someone I met.'

Had she said it? He felt too gutted to remember all the words they had hurled at each other. Perhaps he would press the matter on a later occasion. He had a sudden depressing vision of a million future replays in the ages ahead, but for the moment, at least, he had no appetite for anything but food. He felt genuinely ravenous. It had been seven hours since he had eaten.

Laura followed him as he walked out of the sitting-room towards the kitchen. She went over to the fur-filled dog-baskets in the corner beside the dresser. She sat on the tiled floor and put her head close to Baba who growled at the intrusion.

'Was it important?' He didn't really want to know and the episode was over but a coda had just popped out.

She looked up at him. From floor-level he appeared to be gargantuan. He must seem like this to the dogs.

She hesitated. 'A minor fantasy,' she replied.

'You kept the note.'

'A middle-aged folly.'

He stared down at her doubtfully. He didn't entirely believe her and the suspicion remained that she was manipulating him, but they seemed to have moved on and, having established she wasn't going to leave him, the urge for food had become imperative.

'What's for lunch?' he asked hopefully.

29

God knows, thought Ranson, how I got myself into this position; a toe in the water and I'm up to my neck. He recalled his resolution only a short while ago to arrange his life more wisely and was bound to conclude he had not been too deft.

He stood staring at the vacant wall in his office, brushing his forefinger over his upper lip as he thought. Tessa had offered to fill the blank cream space with his portrait, but he shrank from the usual vanity props that festooned the chairman's role. 'No gongs,' he had said, 'especially not paid for by me, but I might put the child in the long grass just there,' and he pointed. It would be a private indulgence that would confirm him unfit to govern. His clients may all have started their lives as babies in rompers, but Thor Johansson and Mr Hatano would be loath to admit it.

He ruminated over the events of the last six weeks. He had known what would happen as soon as he was introduced to Tessa at the art gallery. Ensnared by her green sunlit pictures he was ready to surrender to their maker, for some of their magic had brushed off on her. That morning he bought two of her paintings and took her to lunch, deferring his meetings until later in the day. He was entranced by her gaiety, her long, green eyes and the swing of her fawn hair. He had watched her with the dual covetousness of the patron for the artist, and the older man for the younger woman. He noticed the freckles on the skin at the neck of her shirt collar; her long, rough hands; and the trace of red oil paint on the fourth finger of her left hand. He saw there was no wedding ring. He sensed an availability, that state of relaxed abandon that was sensual in itself.

It was not until later during their meal that she said, 'You don't remember me, do you?'

'We've never met,' he replied. 'I wouldn't have forgotten it if we had.'

'In the garden of Lownden House when the Fentons opened it last summer? You remember nothing?'

He had been spooning some lemon flummery into his mouth and choked on the chopped nuts that accompanied it.

'I was on the plant stall. You asked me for flowers to fill two empty tubs.'

He had looked at her aghast. He recalled the occasion but not her face. Seeking Laura that day, he had found only Laura. He realised, not for the first time, that an obsessed imagination casts as much shadow as light.

'Are you a friend of the Fentons?' he had asked cautiously.

'An old friend.'

He had returned the conversation to her paintings.

When he left her that day he was resolved not to contact her, but the compulsion to see her again would not be balked, and he had rung her the following week; and so it began. A toe in the water and one's up to one's neck, he thought again. A push and I'm under. He tried not to consider the thought of a day of reckoning. All he had dared tell her was that he had met Laura briefly in youth. He had avoided mention of their rekindled meetings. The indiscretion was not his to reveal and, besides, nothing had happened and, besides, he added inconsistently, it was over. However, he was aware of some sleight of mind in this reasoning. He knew that love, or whatever one cared to call it, was a feeling not an action. It was true it was over but something, not nothing, had happened and he could not pretend otherwise.

It is a muddle, he thought. How he hated living with muddles. He kept his desk clear, his plans clean, his mind trim and, judging by the last six months, his life in perpetual confusion. I must sort this one out, he decided, but how? Several times he had stretched out for the telephone to ring Laura but each time had withdrawn his hand. He had a sudden memory of Tessa as she had rolled over in bed the other day. She had been laughing and as she dipped her head, her hair had fallen silkily across his belly. Remembering now, he found he had scratched the tip of his biro over the leather surface of his desk and he absent-mindedly tried to erase the marks. Afterwards they had sat up in bed eating scrambled eggs on toast. He had protested loudly: 'Ridiculous, look, crumbs, they'll get everywhere like sand on the beach, soon there'll be crumbs between our toes.' 'Shush,' she had said, alerted by the sound of a stopping car outside, but it had started again almost immediately and driven on. 'Thank God,' she said. She had taken fright it might be Poll, transported early from school for some mysterious reason.

Tessa, me and Polly, he thought, remembering his one previous introduction to the child who had proffered a shy hello whilst holding her pet rabbit. He felt nervous but happy to be young again. For a second time, he looked at the cream wall and imagined it adorned with the painting of the child in the poppied grass. His office would think he'd gone broody like a hen.

With difficulty he forced his mind back to the application

form on his desk – a twenty-five page questionnaire inviting him to pre-qualify for German tenders. He glanced through the huge, cumbersome queries before passing them to his linguist:

Personengesellschaft: genaue Bezeichnung?
Unternehmenskennzahlen (der letzten 3 Jahre) (bitte
Geschäftsberichte beifügen)?

His German was rusty. What did *beifügen* mean?

I must ring Laura, he thought again, and stretched out his hand for the phone. He dialled the number but found it engaged.

'I've been meaning to ask you about someone for ages,' said Tessa. Laura waited, tensed for inquisition. Thank God it was the telephone and not a face-to-face encounter.

'Do you remember the man at the garden opening last summer?'

'Which man?' said Laura, busy deflecting. 'There were eight hundred people.'

'The one we discussed afterwards.'

'Did we?' Talmudic, she thought, to keep hitting a question with a question.

'It's serious. Laura. Do try and remember. Leo Ranson, he said he met you years ago.'

'Leo? That's right but it was a lifetime ago. I can't remember much.'

She was sweating. The rancid smell rose through her light wool jumper. Who knew what about whom? She feared this submerged triangle, its presence secret and invisible. She pushed her dark hair back from her forehead.

Geoffrey, walking past her, said, 'Hurry up. I've got to ring the bank. Look.' He waved this morning's letter before her and paced loomingly up and down.

'What's going on?' asked Tessa.

'Sorry, that was Geoffrey. It's hard to concentrate with all this business over the house.'

'Wish I could buy it,' sighed Tessa. 'Perhaps Leo would like it.'

Laura flushed scarlet. She could feel an array of vital organs thudding and thumping inside her. The memory of the closed upstairs curtains that day flashed before her. Had Tessa seen her pass? Was she fishing? She must be feigning this airy naïvety.

'What's this about Leo?' she said, tracing an L in the dust on the window-sill.

'I just hoped you might remember him better. I met him by chance. I've been seeing him for some time and don't want to make an ass of myself without reason.'

She does know, thought Laura, and is trying to probe. She saw Geoffrey hovering like a predator for the phone.

'Tessa, I'm so sorry, I've got to go. Geoffrey needs the phone urgently.'

'Laura—'

'I'll ring you back later.'

Laura put the phone down and looked out of the window. She said in a sleep-walking voice, 'I think the roses will be late this year.'

'We have a month,' said Geoffrey, 'a month in which to sell this fucking house before the bank does it over our heads.'

At the other end of the line, Tessa sat holding on to the receiver long after Laura had put it down. A screech of protest came from the dead connection. She replaced it slowly and turned to the table where she squeezed out a small tongue of viridian oil paint on her palette. Odd, she thought, how remote. Neither Leo nor Laura could remember anything about each other, nor wanted to.

She felt excluded, uneasy and alone, prey to anxieties. It was true that he was in love with her now, but men conformed to a pattern: out of gear at the beginning; cautious mid-term; and elusive at the end. How could he be any different? He might be Miles all over again: a born runner. She added some brassy chrome yellow to the green paint and mashed the two colours around with the pliant knife. I'll give him up now, she decided, better that than a slow and awful erosion. I'll tell him it's pointless. Just me and Poll, as it has been for years. No fantasies, no rejections, just choose what you know in life and keep on doing it, in the safety of walls and routines.

To release the paint smell, she undid the aluminium catch and pushed open the window for some air. The insistent sound of a distant twittering came into the room from the neighbouring field. She walked outside and lifted her head to find if a lark was its source. Powdery clouds drowsed quietly across, melting and reforming on the milky blue of the sky. She scanned their pattern for the bird. It was invisible, a ventriloquist, throwing its loud voice far from its small body. Just me and Poll, she thought again, safe, the two of us, here, perhaps for always. The clouds thickened a little and floated steadily across the huge larkless sky, then as a patch dissolved, she suddenly saw the bird, tiny and passionate, caught in the sunlight high in the heaven. The telephone rang and she rushed inside to answer it.

'It's you,' she said. 'I hoped it would be. How wonderful to hear from you.'

Laura passed the telephone to Geoffrey and walked out of the house. She crossed the terrace and descended the lichened semi-circular steps to the lawn. Under the pines, where the ground was dry and spongy with dead needles, and past the border with the first of its single Chinese peonies opening their simple silky globes to the light. Pausing for a moment to smell the huge perfumed trusses of the Canadian lilacs, she took care to gather the opulent scent deep within her. She was aware she was starting to store sights and smells for the future.

She opened the tall, spear-tipped iron gate to the wilder garden and walked through a dizzyingly scented swatch of mauve sweet rockets. To either side the thin-leafed bamboos swayed and rustled in the breeze, their plumy fronds dipping down to the ground. The sound of a surging current swirled above her head and she looked up to see the flock of glistening white doves wheel and swoop over the sun. In the distance she could hear the trumpet calls of the swans which had been more frequent of late. Recently she had noticed them crying in the small hours of the morning quite near the house; they often moved about freely on moonlit nights when once or twice she had got up to see their dark shadows on the silvery grass.

She walked slowly towards the pool. There was the sound of splashing and, at the far side of the water, she saw Osmund, the cob, rolling over and over in a fountain of droplets like a porpoise, the sap of the warm early summer in his veins. Laura stood watching him as though in a dream and then looked round the pool for Guinevere, his pen. She was not immediately visible. Laura walked to the rim of the pond where the pendulous rushes drooped into the water. There almost at her feet, she found her with four cygnets. Black-billed and covered in the softest of pale grey down, they must have hatched early that morning.

Osmund, alerted to an intruder and not immediately recognising it to be her, skimmed over the water from the other side of the pool, his wings raised for balance, his webbed feet striking the surface of the pond in panic. Relieved that it was merely Laura, he slowed to a gentle paddle and joined his new family, nudging them softly into place. Once or twice he hooted. He was terribly proud. Laura sat on the bank watching the tender, unforgettable scene. She thought: I'm glad it has happened before we left. The big male swan clambered over the bank and waddled slowly towards her, swaying his black ruffled bottom like a bustle. Beads of water sparkled in his feathers and the soft short coat on his breast gleamed like otterskin. He sat down beside her, succumbing to the stroke of her hand, then almost immediately rose and slipped back in the water again, anxious not to be separated from his chicks.

Laura watched the little group gliding lazily in the water, cutting swathes through the reflections of sky, clouds and light in its liquid surface. The ripples from the parents fanned out in great Vs and even each tiny cygnet created its own wake. She thought of the old house, the ancient trees, the flowers, the doves, the remaining bantams, the pet sheep and now these, the newest to be born. She remembered Tessa's words: 'Wish I could buy it,' and then, 'perhaps Leo would like it'. Was it possible? If he bought it, could she bear for them to live here? For it would be them, not him, of that she felt quite sure. It would be the only large unselfish act of her life, to leave it in the hands of a pair who had excluded her. I am a spoilt and selfish woman, she thought. Not bad, not nasty, but just ordinarily selfish with never a motive to be better. She thought of her mother: do I want to grow old like her? Then: have my children grown up like me? Her mind alighted restlessly on one deficiency after another as she watched Osmund plucking the grass at the rim of the bank. The swans would easily live for sixty years; they were mated for life, perhaps like her and Geoffrey. She considered again Tessa and Leo, replacing the euphony of Laura and Leo which had so foolishly echoed of late in her mind. It's Tessa's turn, she thought, we must all take our turn, flow backwards and forwards, the tide goes in and the tide goes out.

She sat thinking for a little longer and then, when a cloud covered the sun, rose and meandered back to the house, turning to the left to wander between the long yew hedges that were furred with the khaki shoots of the new season. Entering the rose garden, she noticed she was wrong and that the shrubs would not, after all, be late with their blooms. Some of the rugosas were already in flower and as she picked a few sprays of blossom to take into the house, the petals of a single milky Alba blew into her hand.

'Look,' she said to Geoffrey as she opened the back door and held up the sprigs. 'I was wrong.'

Geoffrey appeared to have forgotten the urgency over the new deadline for a sale.

'Someone rang for you,' he said.

'You don't mean about the house?'

She opened the dresser cupboard and bent to fetch a small china jug for the flowers.

'No. It was someone who wanted to speak to you.'

Geoffrey watched her sharply. Laura was made nervous. Without reason she prepared to dissemble.

'Who?' she asked, letting the tap run until the water was fully cold.

'Don't you know?'

'How should I?' She filled the jug with water and began arranging the flowers on one of the draining-boards. It required intense concentration.

'A man called Ranson. He wanted to speak to you as soon as convenient. Laura, look at me, Laura.'

Laura twisted her head and returned his gaze steadily. 'What does he want?'

'He wouldn't say. You must tell me, Laura—' Geoffrey came closer and removed the distracting jug from her hand. 'Laura, is he that man?' His tone was ill-modulated.

She took charge of her voice and ignored the temptation to ask: what man?

'Don't be silly, Geoffrey, paranoid. He's Tessa's friend. They're very close. That's what she rang about this morning.'

She felt that saying it might make her fully accept it. It did in a funny way.

'Not silly, nor paranoid,' he said testily. 'I have every reason to question—' but he managed to haul himself back from exploding. He returned the jug and stepped backwards, furious at being ticked off about his vulnerability. He watched her; she was altering the position of the luscious crimson-purple roses. He wanted to go away, or rather for the last shreds of his suspicion to go away. It was demeaning to be a fusspot, but he felt an urge for circumstantial evidence. Only then could he feel completely convinced. Though would he ever again enjoy the idyll of true complacency?

'What did he want?' he mumbled.

'Want?' she repeated. 'I think he wants to buy the house,' though he doesn't know it yet, she added to herself.

She looked with satisfaction at the harmonious bowl of flowers and carried it carefully to the centre of the kitchen table. Another of the single rugosas let down its petals with a gentle sigh as they fell on to the waxed wood.

'After all,' she said, 'if he and Tessa stayed together, it would be the perfect answer, would it not?'

'We're not selling the house at a cut rate for friends, I hope you realise.' Geoffrey fidgeted irritably. 'No ten per cent off or anything like that. We have a lot of interest now and there are two definite offers, according to the new agent.'

'But they're both horrible,' said Laura.

'I think,' she said, 'I think you rang me.' She had waited until Geoffrey had gone out to the post.

'I have to talk to you.' He sounded stiff even to himself.

'And I have to talk to you,' said Laura. 'I have a proposition to make.'

'No,' he said. 'Don't say anything yet.' He felt panicky. In his state of anxiety, he confused her proposition with a proposal. It was a few seconds before he disentangled the meanings.

'Calm down,' said Laura. 'It's me who's got some explaining to do. We can't have a drink in a pub near here, can we? Later today?'

It was after six thirty when he arrived at the Spotted Dog. Laura was already outside on a bench, facing the huge blue view in the early evening sunlight. As he caught sight of her, he wondered whether Tessa had told her and, if so, how much? More to the point, what had Laura told Tessa? Nothing, surely, and in any case he was blameless, wasn't he? Though that wouldn't stop two women ganging up against one man: solidarities were so unpredictable nowadays.

Yet Laura looked expectant and as he walked up the path he decided he was probably wrong to imagine she was forewarned. He felt a stab of regret for what he would have to confess and his nervousness melted into compassion. When he came by her side, he took her hand and leaned forward to plant a sympathetic kiss on her cheek. Aching with pity, he held on to her fingers. Laura read his face and felt surprised and a little irritated. It was horrible to be the object of his kindness when she had once aroused his desire. She withdrew her right hand.

'Stop treating me as if I'm bereaved or something,' she said ungraciously. 'You have rather a soppy expression on your face.'

He recoiled slightly and bumped into a man in trainers

and jeans nursing a Guinness to his table. Some foam slurped over Ranson's shirt cuff.

'Sorry,' they said simultaneously.

Ranson sat down gingerly, his sense of direction displaced. He watched her ordering him a spritzer and he added a ham sandwich as an afterthought since he had not had time to take lunch. As he turned back to Laura, he thought she looked lovely but older than before, until he remembered with discomfort that it was Tessa who had given him a false sense of his youth.

'And how is the house and business?' he asked, covering ground that he already knew from Tessa.

'The administration of the business is out of our hands now,' she said slowly, 'and, as for the house, I'll come to that in a moment. That's the second of two reasons why I felt we must talk. As for the first—'

She paused to allow a pretty girl to clear the table of used glasses and an ashtray.

'I didn't do that, did I?' asked the waitress, flirting with Ranson's stained cuff.

He shook his head. 'It's nothing,' he said, glad to be distracted from Laura's purposeful list of reasons.

'Try White Wizard,' she volunteered, scorching him with a smile as she walked away.

'She likes you,' said Laura.

He made a self-deprecating moue. He was still uneasy about which way the wind blew.

Laura ran her finger along the rim of the table. One begins, she told herself, by opening one's mouth. She hoped a perfectly formed paragraph would come out, but not even a word volunteered itself. She felt she would have to take an ice-pick to her brain to dislodge a single syllable.

'Perhaps I ought to say,' she stumbled a little 'that I do know about Tessa and, well—' She came to a halt and rested there. It would have been wiser, she reflected, to let him grope towards his own declaration. As it was, the sentence hung between them, demanding the suffix of her blessing. The formulaic 'I am very happy for you both' came into her mind but it was neither scrupulously true nor appropriate to a couple who had met only recently and over her dead body, as it were. She offered a funny little nod and a smile instead, though even this was not an outright success as at least a dozen of the muscles required for a smile seemed to be out of working order.

Ranson could not judge this. He was looking down.

'Tessa told you, of course,' he said.

'This morning. Not much. She implied some involvement.'

'I feel bad about this. Laura, you must understand, I had no idea she was your friend when I saw her at her exhibition and got her paintings.'

So that was when it started, Laura realised. This brought some relief. She leaned forward. 'It wasn't a first meeting, you know. You saw her a year ago in my garden.'

'So she said. I didn't remember. I was looking for you.'

Laura had the sensation of a landslip inside her. She felt afresh the shock that the road which led to her should have proved so wasted a diversion.

'Well,' she said, swallowing hard, 'that's history.'

'The point is – you were married.'

'I *am* married,' she said. She sounded even to herself as though she was facing up to it. 'How much does she know about us?' she added. She remembered again the closed upstairs curtains. Had they seen her drive by?

'Nothing. I simply said we had met briefly in youth.' He picked at a knob on the bench. 'I know that seems like self-preservation, but I had to protect you too.' He raised his dark eyebrows briefly with exasperation. It sounded as if he were trying to salvage points from behaving badly. Laura did not notice this. She remarked instead for the first time that one eyebrow was slightly more cocked than the other. She realised it was too late to notice intimate details of this kind: it was sad but they were superfluous.

'How much did *you* tell her?' he asked.

'The same.'

He looked up with relief, and they both began to laugh at the expression on each other's face.

'She must never know,' said Laura.

'No. Better not.'

Laura felt a dishonourable twinge of pleasure that at least she shared one secret with Leo to which Tessa had no access. For a moment they sat in silence, reviewing the same mental scene from their different perspectives. The girl brought the sandwich and the drinks. She prepared to bestow her smile again, but it was obvious that the pair had coupled and were no longer interested in their fellow human beings.

Ranson picked up the food as soon as it arrived on the table. He was ravenous and bit deeply into the triangle of bread.

Laura took a breath and said, 'I suppose it is serious this time, isn't it?'

'Yes,' he said simply. He brushed a crumb from his mouth and decided against elaborating; it could only be hurtful. Why did one man's happiness always poison another man's life?

'I ask,' said Laura, 'because your answer affects my proposition.'

'Ah, yes,' said Ranson, tensing again. He took another large bite to sustain himself.

'Are you ready to learn what it is?'

'Don't tease, Laura.' He guessed she used this technique on her grandchild.

'I wondered if you would like to buy our house.'

He stared at her amazed, his whole alarm system jangling. He had never anticipated this thought and his first reaction was: no.

'It is too big,' he protested.

'For you alone, yes. But it's been wonderful for Geoffrey, me and the two girls.'

The obvious implication embarrassed and therefore appalled him. She had floated a mirage of him, Tessa, Polly and, perhaps, a second child they would have together. Intimate and intrusive, the bubble hung there in the air between them, a fantasy that could so easily become real.

He stared at her suspiciously. He feared a witches' brew of motives: rum, devious, female and complicated.

Laura leaned forward. She spoke with urgency. 'I know what you're thinking. It seems I'm trying to manipulate you. It's not like that. There are no funny hidden motives. Throw that old windbag, Freud, out of the window and everyone else who followed him. Some things are straightforward and we foul them up by our fancy thoughts. We turn plain truths into curly ones – utter madness. As far as I'm concerned, we've got to sell. I love the place and everything in it and want the gardener and his wife to stay on. I want someone who buys it to look after it. You'd cherish it. I know you and trust you. You're looking for a home. If Tessa, one day, perhaps, God knows, ends there also, she deserves it and you too.'

Doesn't he see? she thought. Doesn't he realise that there is no time? Life is so short, there is always very little time in which to put things right.

He felt hunted and bewildered. It all sounded so simple but relationships had a habit of tainting decisions and events. A fresh start was what was required, not a re-entry into muddied waters. But even as he thought that, he realised that fresh starts were illusory for men of his age. Everywhere was muddy.

He watched her closely. She was leaning towards him, her dark hair falling free from her chin. Those brown eyes, gold-flecked, her best feature, so large and almond-shaped, lit with fervour. She was hard to resist, a fact which kept a solid core inside him still stubborn.

'Where would you live?' He tried to make the question sound idling and neutral, but it wasn't. He could never even contemplate buying the house if she lived nearby, lowering and broody over her lost possessions.

'Far away. I've decided Geoffrey and I must begin again and we can't do so near here.'

'I'll think about it,' he said, not wishing to be cornered.

'There's no time. Go and see it now. I won't come with you but Geoffrey can show you round. You have to decide yes or no immediately. We now have two offers on the table and must make our minds up in the next few days.'

She refrained from disparaging the possible buyers. He would use it as a lever. Years of business had doubtless given Leo a barter mentality when it came to negotiating a sale.

'You're hustling me,' he said. He drummed his fingers on the table.

'Oh no,' said Laura, 'it's your choice, your life.'

'Thank you,' he replied with dignified irony.

He hesitated and rubbed his shirt cuff. The alcohol had evaporated and it was now dry. He sighed, thinking. It was deeply tempting. She had spelt out the future. She had taken him up to a mountain top and shown him a wonderful home, a wife, a family, a shiny new life in middle age, a happy-ever-after vision until death. All it involved was a leap into the light.

'All right. I'll look at it,' he said suddenly, 'but I don't promise anything.'

'Go and ring Geoffrey now.'

After he had left, Laura sat watching the late western light dwindle quickly over the top of the hills until only one tip was gilded. An evening breeze fluttered a piece of cigarette wrapping on the grass and she conscientiously rose to pick it up and put it in the litter bin. It was already drenched with dew. The sign of the Spotted Dog, a shapely, well-marked Dalmatian, creaked back and forth. At a nearby table a foursome – reps from Allied Dunbar by the sound of them – were sipping their no-alcohol drinks before setting off to sell their evening's quota of pensions.

It had become very cold. If the wind died down there would be a frost tonight, blighting the blossom and the future apple crop in the orchards nearby. A frost in May, thought Laura. May, almost a year since she had met him in the garden. 'I was looking for you,' he had told her artlessly this evening. But I proved the shadow, she thought, and Tessa the substance. I shall be nothing to him, and Tessa everything.

It was late when she arrived home. Determined to give Leo's visit to the house a wide berth, she had stayed at the pub until after eight thirty and then dawdled on the journey back, stopping to pick up a few unscheduled groceries from a little shop-around-the-clock. She drove slowly as she neared her entrance, peering through the screen of loosely coppiced hazels to see whether his car was still parked on the drive. Assuring herself he had left, she turned on to the gravel.

'Did Tessa's man come?' she asked Geoffrey, pushing open the kitchen door and unloading a packet of washing soda and a fluorescent mauve nailbrush.

He nodded, his mouth full of the last portion of a Marks & Spencer lasagne which she had earmarked for the end of the week.

She rattled on, 'I'm sorry I couldn't come myself but I got held up clearing everything out for the sale of my mother's flat.' She had actually finished that job several weeks ago.

Geoffrey finished eating and pushed his plate away.

'Well? Did he like it?' She prodded him into replying.

'He'll get in touch with the agent tomorrow.'

'He really thinks it's suitable?'

'He didn't say much. Bit tight-lipped, actually. Just so long as he's not tight-pursed.'

She felt like wincing but didn't. After all, Geoffrey could not be expected to know that the comment was less than fastidious in the circumstances.

'Geoffrey, really. We'd be lucky if he took it. He would be perfect.' She put on a kettle to make some peppermint tea. She had a touch of indigestion.

'Perfect for the house perhaps, but a bit old for Tessa, surely. Still, she's the right age for him. Nice to get a younger woman.'

He did not exactly expect agreement but was surprised by the frigidity of her response.

30 ∫

By early June all the arrangements had been settled. Contracts were due to be exchanged in a few weeks, when Leo, who had not returned since his first visit, would become the new owner of Lownden House. The ripples of relief spread widely, from Watson, the bank manager, to, so Laura claimed, the cygnets who were growing quickly and would soon assume their first mousy-grey plumage. Beth had even abandoned her anti-depressants. These had in any case erred so grossly on the side of success that they had proved a failure, stimulating her to clean the house at three in the morning.

On a noble early summer afternoon, Laura ran into Tessa at the counter of Boots. She did not recognise her at first. There was an elegance about her former friend which she had not registered before. She realised it was several months since they had met, momentous months which had not only changed their fortunes but reversed their places.

'Not ill, I hope,' said Laura, noticing that Tessa seemed to be taking charge of some remedy.

'Not at all. In fact, never weller. This is not for me anyway.' She held up a small bottle of tincture in explanation. 'We have been trying to find a cure for Leo's verruca for weeks,' she went on. 'This will do the trick, I hope.'

He has, thought Laura, not only feet of clay but warts and

all. 'You sound very much married already,' she said.

'Oh.' Tessa flushed slightly. 'Goodness knows what will happen.'

In fact, only the previous night she had discussed with Leo whether she and Poll should move into Lownden House after it was bought. They agreed neither would mention it to Laura. 'The house and garden must be the most terribly sensitive issue for her,' said Tessa, 'especially the latter.' She was prepared to explore this at greater length but Leo had fallen into one of his silences.

Tessa now pushed the little carton into her shoulder bag and the two women wandered out of the shop's artificially lit interior into the drenching sunshine outside. It occurred to Laura that the Siberian irises would unfurl their sumptuous velvety flags today. She would inspect them at once on her return home.

'You won't leave the house without saying goodbye to me, will you?' asked Tessa.

'Of course not,' Laura replied.

'Shall we fix a time now?'

'It's difficult,' she said, stonewalling. 'I daren't plan anything at the moment. We still have no home to go to.'

Tessa looked at her imploringly.

She is asking me to assuage her guilt, thought Laura. Poor Tessa, she feels responsible even though she only knows the husk of what's happened. If she realised the truth . . . She must never guess, sighed Laura, nor Geoffrey. It reminded her of one untied knot that was still a hostage to fortune.

'By the way,' Laura started and then stopped to move out of the way of a woman in an electric wheelchair which was determined to mow her down.

'Mind where you're going,' barked the old trout, who was handling her machine as aggressively as a land tank.

'Sorry,' said Laura.

'Oh dear,' said Tessa. 'Misfortune rarely makes one nicer.'

Laura raised her eyebrows briefly.

'I didn't mean—' stumbled Tessa. 'I only meant my own experience.' How the hell do you talk when there's a sub-text in every word, she wondered.

'By the way,' Laura started again, 'better not mention to Geoffrey that I met Leo when I was a girl. He's got a bit sensitive and touchy lately about the most peculiar things. Poor darling, it must be this house business.'

'No,' said Tessa, looking at her hard. 'Of course not.'

'Well,' said Laura, 'I'd better go.' She leaned forward and kissed the air by her friend's cheek. 'I'll get in touch before leaving,' she said, though she had every confidence that she wouldn't.

Tessa watched her disappear. She had the feeling it was the last time she would see her. She turned round and walked away, checking the swing of her bag in case it disrupted the precious verruca tincture inside it. She remembered sitting in the field by the stream with Laura only a year ago. She remembered wishing for a little something to disrupt her life. Just a small jolt, she had thought, a minor judder to her settled existence. Envy, she thought now. Oh God, envy rewarded. How ghastly that it should become so horribly true.

'Don't know why you're so pleased the house is sold,' said Geoffrey. 'We've nowhere to go.'

'We've got everywhere,' replied Laura.

They were standing in the dining-room. Surrounded by elegant clutter, they were writing a list of chattels for the auction.

'Out,' said Laura, ticking the Coalport service.

'No. It's mine.'

'What's yours is mine. Remember? You seemed to forget it when you loaned the house.'

'Oh yes,' said Geoffrey unabashed. 'I know your version off by heart: "what's yours is mine and what's mine is mine". Recognise it?'

Laura gave a grin.

'Don't quarrel,' she said. 'We've got a lot of sorting out to do. We can't keep much anyway. We'll be moving to a little place.'

'But nothing's come up round here.'

'Here? Forget here.' She felt exalted at the thought of the exotics she could grow in the south, the rhododendrons in the north. 'There's Devon, Northumbria, Scotland. We can rent before we buy.'

'Outer Siberia.' He walked away in disgust.

'We've got to start afresh.' She remembered Mrs Hoskins: 'I discovered years ago that life couldn't keep on ending.'

'But the girls. We'll never see them.'

'Rosy's got her own life and we've lost her anyway. Allegra may move nearer us. She approves. She likes downward moves. Her karma will like us better when we're dispossessed.'

Laura leaned forward to open the flamboyant Jacobean walnut dresser. 'Ugly thing,' she said, 'I never liked it.'

Geoffrey pulled out the silver candelabra, which were tarnished.

'Out,' said Laura, kneeling for a closer inspection.

'And us?' asked Geoffrey. 'Out too?'

'Not yet,' she replied. 'Not just yet.'

She rocked back on her heels and surveyed the next twenty or more years ahead.

She remembered sitting in the dark interior of the little church. It seemed a lifetime ago. Sow two marrow seeds in a pot, the parish newsletter had advised: 'always two, because one will surely fail'. Which meant that one would as surely survive. It is Geoffrey, she thought, who has survived. But then, she thought, so, too, have I.